THE
THIRD SON

a novel

Julie Wu

ALGONQUIN BOOKS OF CHAPEL HILL   2013

Published by
ALGONQUIN BOOKS OF CHAPEL HILL
Post Office Box 2225
Chapel Hill, North Carolina 27515-2225

a division of
Workman Publishing
225 Varick Street
New York, New York 10014

This is a work of fiction. While, as in all fiction, the literary
perceptions and insights are based on experience, all names, characters,
places, and incidents either are products of the author's imagination
or are used fictitiously.

Library of Congress Cataloging-in-Publication Data
Wu, Julie, [date]
　　The third son : a novel / by Julie Wu. — 1st ed.
　　　　p. cm.
　　ISBN 978-1-61620-079-4
　　1. Self-realization—Fiction.　2. Taiwan—History—1985 – 1945 —
Fiction.　I. Title.
　　PS3623.U28T49 2013
　　813'.6 — dc23　　　　　　　　　　　　　　　　2012023446

10 9 8 7 6 5 4 3 2 1
First Edition

To my family,
far and near

 THE THIRD SON

Part I

1943–1957

I

M Y JOURNEY BEGAN WHEN the Americans bombed us, in
1943, because it was during the bombings that I met the girl.

I was eight years old. In the weeks before Taiwan was bombed,
I sat on the floor while my father sat in his armchair by the radio in
our great room. A cigarette burned between the massive fingers of
his hand as he translated the Japanese imperial broadcasts for us.

I placed myself as far out of his reach as I could, just apart from
my six brothers and sisters. We were all afraid of him; just the
sound of his heavy steps on the front walk in the evening would
scatter us like birds, flying off to disappear into the far corners
of the house. Here, in forced proximity, we were silent, as un-
obtrusive as we could be, only our slippers making nervous scuffling sounds on the floor.

We all understood Japanese. Taiwan had been a Japanese colony
since 1895. Japanese was our official language, and even our family
name, Togo, was Japanese. But in our heads and in our home we
spoke and were Taiwanese, descendants of the Mainland Chinese,
and only my father understood the subtle nuances of Japanese language and culture that gave meaning to the official broadcasts.

My father's eyes, set deep in his fleshy face, squinted in con-
centration. He had, at all times, well-regarded local figures at his

side — the magistrate, a wealthy merchant, local village representatives — who nodded or gently disagreed, often to be chided into
silence by my father.

"Valiant," he said, scornfully shifting in his armchair. "That means
they lost."

My oldest brother, Kazuo, his appearance and intellect so fortu-
nately for him like my father's, smirked from the floor at my father's
side, where he knelt and neatly copied columns of kanji onto sheets
of rice paper. Kazuo's handwriting was much better than mine and
had been even when he was younger than me, a fact that my mother
was at all times eager to impress upon me.

. . . *brave sacrifice at Guadalcanal* . . .

"Hm!" my father exclaimed, taking his cigarette out of his
mouth. "Getting slaughtered. The Americans shall attack us next."

By the time we were advised to evacuate Taoyuan, my parents
had already made inquiries into a house north of Taipei, near the
farm where my mother was raised. It was in the same region where
the actual Japanese were being sent, and my father therefore felt
that it would be the safest. The house was large enough to accom-
modate my siblings and me, and all our preparations seemed to be
in order. Then the owner of the country house changed his mind,
saying that it was insulting to be offered such a low rent by such a
wealthy family; he had made inquiries of his own about my parents
and was not about to be taken for a fool.

The negotiations continued long after many of my classmates'
families had left Taoyuan for country houses of their own or to
share. And so it was that I was still at school in Taoyuan the day of
the air raid.

I was, as usual, looking out the window, ignoring the teacher's
lecture and the slow, constant burn of hunger in my belly. I wasn't
a top student like Kazuo, nor did I have a mind only for sports,
like my second brother, Jiro. I was Saburo, the third son, and I
recognized that I was different, somehow, from my brothers. I was

different from these children all around me in their neat rows, filing their kanji into little boxes, contentedly reciting their arithmetic facts by rote. It was far more interesting to me, despite the real and ever-present threat of being struck by my teacher, to study the sky outside. I loved the sky, its boundless, lovely blue, the translucent ruffled pattern of clouds stretching across it. I watched the clouds drift ever so slowly north. And then I saw three tiny spots moving toward us beyond.

I jumped up. "Look!" I cried.

My teacher reached for her stick to strike me, but at the same time the air-raid siren went off. The class erupted in cries of alarm and we hurried to our places in line. It wasn't the first air raid, and we all knew what to do. Some Japanese bureaucrat had decided that the best thing for a schoolchild to do when the town was being strafed was to run home.

The siren wailed overhead, and my schoolmates ran out into the street, holding their writing boards over their heads. In previous air raids I had done the same, but today I had seen the planes myself and could hear the bombs and machine-gun fire quite close by. The last thing I wanted to do was leave the shelter of the school. Heart thumping, I hung back in the doorway, but after all the children had left, the principal followed and locked the door behind her, shouting at me to leave.

I ran to the woods at the back of the school and made my way along a path through them. My heart hammered, but I was in no rush either to leave the cover of the trees or to get home. As shells exploded on our railroad tracks and bullets sprayed the roofs of our houses and schools, I made my way from tree to tree, calming myself with the smell of the damp earth and the moss, and the occasional scent of blossoms from peach trees, now scarce but once so pervasive that they had given the county its name, Taoyuan — "peach garden."

And then I heard the distinct cry of a young girl.

I ran toward the sound and found one girl helping another one up. They both looked about eight, like me, with matching school uniforms and the short, severe haircuts required by the Japanese school system. The one who had fallen — the one who had cried out — looked down at her bleeding knee. The other one bent over her, looking at her friend's wound. They both held their writing boards over their heads, as we had been taught to do during air raids.

"Are you okay?" I shouted.

They jumped and looked up at me in surprise. They were both very pretty and sweet looking in the dappled light, with wide, sparkling eyes, and they instinctively leaned their heads together.

"Are you okay?" I repeated more quietly as I drew near. "I heard someone cry."

"I'm all right," the girl with the bleeding knee said quietly. She blinked and looked down at her knee, her lower lip stuck out just a little. "I tripped over a tree root."

A plane roared overhead and fresh rounds of machine-gun fire burst out, so that the girls clung to each other.

"See you tomorrow!" the bleeding girl said. She took off into the woods.

"Aren't you going home with your sister?" I said to the other girl, who stood, watching the bleeding girl run away.

She shook her head and pointed, still holding her writing board on her head. "She's not my sister. She's my cousin. I'm going this way."

She began to run, and I ran with her, even though she was headed away from my parents' house. The planes were not directly over our heads, but we could hear them and their fire very well.

She glanced at me past her elbow, sections of her hair swinging over her pale face. "Why don't you hold your board over your head?" she said. Then she tripped over a rock and almost fell.

I jumped to catch her arm. "Because it doesn't make any sense," I said. "See? You can't even run that way."

She straightened up, board in place. "But that's what my teacher says we should do in an air raid."

"I've seen bullets go through ceilings and walls," I said. "What good is a writing board going to do?"

"Maybe it would slow the bullet down." She continued on, walking this time, switching to hold her board with her other hand. "My teacher's really nice. She brings me *moachi*. You see how hard the board is? It will protect me."

"She brings you *moachi*?" The very thought that a teacher could be called "nice," much less be a source of sweet treats, was completely alien to me.

"Yes, because I'm number one in the class!" She spoke proudly. "My father brings me *moachi,* too, when I study. He brings the ones from Japan because they're better."

"I don't think they're better," I said, hungry at the thought of the gooey rice cakes. "I like the peanut ones the best."

"Well, that's true," she said. "Those *are* the best."

We reached the edge of the forest. There was a store-lined road a few hundred yards away across a clearing, and we stopped.

"Let's wait," I said. "The all-clear siren hasn't gone off."

"But I'm supposed to go home."

"It's safer to stay here."

"My parents will worry about me."

I listened for a moment, hearing only the leaves rustling overhead and the rushing of my pulse.

"They've gone away," the girl said.

"*Hou,*" I said. "Quickly."

We ran into the open field. Just as we reached the middle, a plane zoomed in from behind us. I jumped in terror, and the girl screamed, holding her writing board over her head with both hands. We had all heard of Americans shooting farmers in the field, of mowing down women carrying babies and market goods on their bicycles.

But when I looked up, I saw the Japanese flag painted on the fuselage. "It's all right," I shouted with relief. "He's defending us."

We stopped in the middle of the field at the awesome sight of the two planes dueling, swooping and firing and curving away over the heart of our town.

"Did you see that?"

"He got him, I think!"

And then one of the planes was trailing smoke out its side, and it swooped too low. We felt the crash through the ground with our feet.

When the other plane rose, we saw, on its side, the American flag.

"Oh no!" the girl cried as she broke into a run.

Terrified, I ran after her and then looked back. I stopped, seeing the plane head away toward the forest.

But then the plane banked, straightened out, and pointed its nose toward us, the pilot aiming his gun at my chest.

My breath stopped. The plane's nose drew near, larger and larger. Everything became clear at once: This man would shoot us down like game. I would die in this field with this strange girl whose name I did not even know. My parents, who had never celebrated my birthday, would mourn my death with a procession, flowers, and incense. I would die hungry.

From a distance I heard the girl's voice. She was screaming.

"Run!" she screamed. "What are you doing?"

I woke from my trance and ran after her. She was smaller and slower than me, even more so holding her board over her head, and in my terror at hearing the plane's engine roaring at our backs, I overtook her easily.

I reached the street and heard her fall behind me. I turned to see her scrambling to get up, still holding the writing board over her head, her eyes large with panic. Bullets started to hit the field. I ran back and grabbed her arm, soft under my grip. I saw the dust rise from the grass behind her as I pulled her, all my muscles straining, and the sound of bullets exploded in my ears and in my chest. I yelled, barely hearing my own voice over the gunfire, not sure whether I was being shot. I pulled her across the last bit of field and through the broken door of a hardware shop. We clung together, shaking, in the corner of the shop while bullets hit the ceiling of the store.

Finally the shooting stopped and the plane buzzed away.

We jumped apart. I looked down. My whole body trembled and my heart pounded furiously. I was dirty, but there was no blood on me.

The girl held up her writing board. Its handle had been shot off. "You see? It did protect me!"

I looked at the frayed rope and said nothing.

WE SAT ON a tool bench in the shop. She was the one, this time, who wanted to wait for the all clear. She took a handkerchief from her pocket and started rubbing at the streaks of dirt on her shoes from the woods.

"My papa says it's important to take care of your clothes because they show what's inside."

She never stopped talking, which I didn't mind, because it passed the time and calmed me. While I listened, I picked up bits of wire and scrap metal from the floor and attached them to a tin pipe I had in my pocket. She told me her Japanese name was Yoshiko and she liked being called that at school because it sounded pretty, though it wasn't officially her name, as her father didn't believe in changing their names to please the Japanese.

"But you would get better rations," I said.

She shrugged. "My mother says that, too. But my papa is very proud, and he says no one can pay him to take a Japanese name. He's going to take us to see the world," she continued. "He has a whole plan."

"What does he do?"

"He's a businessman. He doesn't have any business right now, but he has big plans for when the war ends."

"The whole world?"

She nodded. "Japan *and* China. He says all he needs is a boat."

I paused at this, imagining Yoshiko on a boat to Japan. "What's in Japan and China that isn't here?" I said.

"I don't know," Yoshiko said. "But Papa says we wouldn't be poor there." She glanced at me.

I looked at her from head to toe. She didn't look poor to me. Her clothes were, if anything, in finer condition than mine, though her white canvas shoes looked homemade.

"My papa goes to that movie theater near our old house on Chungcheng Road and it shows movies from all over the world. So he knows."

"Japan and China?"

She nodded. "And Hong Kong. America, too."

"I don't like Americans," I said.

"Me, neither," she said, glancing at her writing board. She caught sight of my scrap-metal creation. "What's that? A plane?"

I nodded and held it up. "The wings are hinged, see?"

"*Oua!* You're so clever." She touched a wing, bending it back a little.

I looked at her in surprise. I had many such creations at home, and to my family they were nothing but junk.

The all clear sounded and we walked out into the street. Her family had evacuated from the town's main street to a house across the river, by the base of Turtle Head Mountain, and I walked with her down toward the bridge, the tin-pipe plane in my pocket. All around us the land thrilled with life, with the white of a heron's wing as it rose from a paddy into the sky's limitless blue, with the central mountains in the distance, lush and green. I wished we could keep walking together forever, just the two of us, with no one else but a distant farmer in a conical straw hat crossing toward us over the bridge on his bicycle.

"It's going to rain," I said. "Probably tomorrow."

"Really? It's so nice today."

I pointed at the clouds overhead. "See those?"

"The ruffly ones?"

"It always rains when you see those," I said. "You'll see. If it was just puffy ones like those up there, I'd say it would be dry."

She walked with her face turned up to the sky. "You have a good teacher."

"No," I said. "I just like being outside."

Still looking up at the sky, she turned around and took a few steps backward. She stumbled and our shoulders brushed together.

"It's a long walk," I said. "Why don't you go to a school by your house?"

"I did," she said, facing forward again. "But I missed my teacher and my cousin, so I came back."

"You're lucky," I said.

"Why?"

"You wanted to come back. And then you got to."

"Hey!" She started running.

"Where are you going?" I ran after her. She was waving at the farmer, her white shoes flashing in the sun. But as he drew near, it appeared he was not a farmer at all. He was, in fact, not even a man, but a boy somewhere in his teen years, and he wore a school uniform. As he pulled up, he threw off his hat and laughed, his face handsome and brilliant as he smiled, his eyes sparkling.

"*A-hianh!*" Yoshiko cried out, laughing. "Why were you wearing that hat?"

Her brother laughed. "Thought it would help me blend in with the landscape, you know." He skidded to a stop and patted Yoshiko on the shoulder. "You're all right! We were so worried!"

"You came to find me?"

"Of course! Hop on. I caught a fish for you. We can fry it up when we get home."

Yoshiko climbed onto the bicycle in front of him. He put his hands on the handlebars, his arms cradling her protectively, so that she looked up at him and smiled. Their gestures of intimacy came so naturally to them but were so wildly foreign to me that I stared.

"Who's this boy?" Yoshiko's brother asked, looking at me with a kind smile. "Do you need a ride?"

"Yes, you get on, too," Yoshiko said. "He ran with me."

"Maybe in the back . . . ," her brother said.

But I couldn't get onto the bike without disturbing their happy balance. And it was so far from my house. "I live way over on the other side of the railroad tracks," I said. "I'll walk."

"But that's where the rich people live." Yoshiko looked surprised.

"That's too far," Yoshiko's brother exclaimed. "You may not get home by sunset."

"Here, in front of me. Your parents will worry——" As Yoshiko shifted, she dropped her writing board.

I picked up the board and handed it to her. "They don't worry about me," I said.

I looked down and waited for her to take the writing board. I closed my eyes, fighting down the ache of being left behind, of being alone and forgotten and uncared for.

I felt a hand on my head. I looked up into Yoshiko's face, feeling my close-cropped hair brushing the softness of her palm.

"You helped me," she said. "You're a good boy." She smiled, and I saw, even in her brother's shadow, that the brown of her eyes was flecked with gold.

As her brother started pedaling away, she cried out, "See you at school, or maybe the movies!"

I watched them ride back over the bridge. I stood watching them until the bicycle receded and disappeared through a bend in the fields beyond.

She had given me the first tender moment of my life.

2

I WALKED HOME, MY feet crunching on the gravel in rhythm with the cicadas screeching in the banyan trees. I wasn't alarmed to be alone in the countryside. I was used to it.

It had not always been this way. I had once roamed the fields with my little brother Aki, one year younger than me. I had played with Aki every day and prevented the others from taking his meager share of food at the table. I had taken care of him as well as a little boy could. But when Aki was four, he woke one morning with his eyes glassy, his skin burning under my hand. *Pneumonia,* I heard the surgeon tell my parents. *You'll need to take him to the hospital.*

How did he get it, Doctor?

The cold weather, the rain. He's very thin.

Ai! You see, Saburo. I told you not to keep him outside so late!

A couple of weeks later, Aki died. I was hiding behind a rice barrel in the kitchen when I heard.

The colors of the countryside deepened in the yellowing light as I reached the railroad tracks. The last train to Taipei hurtled by, blue passenger cars roaring, curving away north, side rods pumping up and down, windows glinting orange in the setting sun.

Brainchild of the Japanese, the train was always on time, and it meant that I was late. For a moment I stood still, thinking of the gray walls of my house and what awaited me there: the front door, so massive it would dam the Tamsui River, my mother behind the door, my father in his armchair, his political cronies by his side.

The train receded, leaving in its wake the smell of coal and the calls of frogs hidden in the light-tipped grass. An egret glided over rice paddies lit like so many molten pools, its wings on fire.

I walked again, my muscles now tense with fear, and crossed the tracks to take the long road toward my house. My stomach clenched at the rich smells of buffalo dung and the marsh grass that swished quietly in the wind, the long blades bending now and again to reveal the far-off semicircle of granite that was the tomb of my first Taiwanese ancestor.

I took out my tin-pipe plane and dragged it behind me, its hinged wings folding and unfolding as I walked. One of the wires broke, and I twisted grass around it instead, thinking that Yoshiko would have thought me clever. I pulled the plane past the tomb of my second Taiwanese ancestor, a rice farmer, and then my third, a doctor. But now I was so close to the house that not even the plane could bring me pleasure. I tucked it back into my pocket and I turned the corner, stomach contracting, mouth dry at the sight of our heavy front door with its old-fashioned wooden lock.

When I opened the door, my mother stood behind it in her worn cheongsam, her face long and tired — square-jawed like mine, one eye double lidded and the other not — with her arm raised, holding a bamboo switch to beat me.

The pain of the first blow knocked me to my knees — the blunt force of the main branch against my side, the sharpness of the little twigs cutting into the skin between my shirt and the waistband of my shorts. And then as she drew her arm back again I scrambled to get facedown on the floor in my habitual pose, arms over my head, nose to the musty floorboards, and braced for the next blow.

"Always late! Do you know what *time* it is?"

My flesh was tender, my skin thin and easily bruised. A child's body is not designed to withstand the kind of blows that an adult can wield with the better part of a tree. Or rather, the child can withstand in the sense of survival, but the nerve endings will never be completely restored. They will remain raw and painful for the rest of the child's life.

THIS HAPPENED MOST days—that I was late for dinner, and that I was beaten. Each day I left school with every intention of going straight home to avoid punishment. But fear alone was not enough to keep me hurrying toward the dreariness of our great room, filled at all times with my father's many important guests, the hallways piled with newspapers and broken knickknacks my mother could not decide what to do with. Even our courtyard was to be tread carefully, with its woven trays of drying daikon and *pei tsai* on their way to being pickled for the winter. We had few toys except for the tools left overnight by workers fixing our roof, and after I was caught planing the corner of our dining table, we no longer had even those.

I found every day that the riches of my life were outside, in the fields and roads. I could not believe that being under the beautiful sky had killed Aki. He had fallen ill at home. It was much more plausible to me that the joylessness of our home life had done him in, and so I could not stop myself from pausing to play a game of marbles or to fashion scrap metal into some kind of vehicle. I became so absorbed outside that I forgot my fear, and so my mother's punishment was the daily price I paid for an afternoon of freedom. I did not ever regret my adventures outside, and I did not regret having walked with Yoshiko at all.

THOUGH MY MOTHER beat me every day, I never once saw her beat any of my sisters and brothers, even if they came home late. I came to understand that this was my punishment for Aki and for the rebellious core within me that refused to take the blame for my brother's death.

I spoke, my lips brushing against the fraying edges of my sleeve: "No."

The bamboo wavered over my head. "What's that, stupid?"

My shirt had ridden up, and the floorboards were cool against my belly, which churned inside, seething and resentful. I spoke again, my voice dead between my arm and the floor. "I don't know what time it is."

The bamboo landed on my head, my chest, making me gasp with pain. Her voice rose with frustration. "Imbecile! Talking back to your mother! What do you want? A gold watch? How come all the others come home on time? How many times must I punish you for you to come home on time?"

I was quiet then, drawing into myself, hardly more than nerve endings on fire. I thought of Yoshiko's brother cradling her in his arms. And inside me grew the seeds of my self-righteousness. Because I knew that my mother was wrong.

3

I DREAMED THAT I was at Yoshiko's house. I was in a bright, small kitchen with banana trees outside the window. Yoshiko's brother fried fish on the stove while Yoshiko watched, perched on a stool. She beckoned, smiling, and I woke up to the delectable smell of hot lard. For a moment I thought perhaps the dream had been real, but when I sat up I felt my bruises from the bamboo switch, and then I smelled the egg.

Stomach growling painfully, I jumped out of bed and dressed quickly in the same handed-down shorts and shirt I had worn the day before. I ran into the kitchen.

I arrived just in time to see Kazuo get up from the table, licking the oil off his girlish lips. My mother was taking his bowl and the frying pan to the sink. She studiously looked away, her asymmetrical eyes weary and cast down. Her jaw was set.

"What's for breakfast?" I asked.

"Steamed bread, as always," she replied. "Why do you ask?"

I understood that this was a question I should not answer. In our home, ancestors were worshipped, elders respected and never questioned. But still dazzled by the happy picture of Yoshiko and her brother, I was feeling particularly resentful of my mother's coldness.

"I smelled the egg," I said.

"Stupid," she said. "It's wartime."

"I saw the rations come yesterday morning," I said. "We got eight eggs." We got more provisions than other Taiwanese families; our Japanese names ensured that we received the same rations as the Japanese, and my parents bought even more food on the black market.

"We have five now and guests coming for lunch." She worked with her back toward me, scrubbing traces of the precious egg off her pan, her shoulder muscles tensing and relaxing against the shapeless fabric of her dress.

She glanced over her shoulder, not quite at me. "Always talking back and disrespectful." She gestured at the kitchen with her chin. "Look at all I have to do."

On the stove, a pot of baby bottles boiled for my youngest brother, who sat on the floor sucking his thumb and pulling his hair. A wet stain showed through his diaper. On the kitchen table were piles of tofu for preserving, a bowl of beans soaking in water, and half-chopped bamboo shoots. I heard my sisters arguing from the great room and the maid scolding them. There were seven of us children, all under the age of ten. I knew that was a lot of work, even with a maid. Most families had grandmothers to help, but my mother's family lived in the North and my father's parents were dead.

I sat down at the table and tore at my white lump of bread, thinking of the girl, Yoshiko, and her *moachi*. I finished the bread in seconds and my stomach still ached, but my mother started slicing the tofu with her sharpest knife and I was not stupid enough to continue asking for more food.

"They canceled school because of the air raids," she said.

"Then I'll go out to play."

"*Hou,*" she said.

I walked east, across the railroad tracks, through the deserted town, passing the low office building where my cousin, Toru, had recently started practice as a physician, and then the hardware store where Yoshiko and I had taken shelter. The buildings ended, and I headed toward the river and Turtle Head Mountain, where Yoshiko and her brother lived. I wished now that I had gotten on that bicycle with them. At least then they would have known where to find me. Now I had to find them, and I had no idea where to go once I got to the bridge.

I walked past several rice paddies that looked abandoned. The house amid them was boarded up and I saw no signs of people or water buffalo. But the herons stalked the paddies, and as I drew closer I saw telltale ripples on the surface of the water and knew that there were fish within.

Why not bring them another fish? Perhaps they would fry it right up. My stomach gurgled at the thought, and in a second I had slipped off my shoes and stepped into the cool water.

I waded through the paddy and then crouched, dipping my fingertips through the reflection of the rippled clouds and of my eyes, alert and unblinking, their slight asymmetry evoking my mother's face. A mosquito bit the back of my neck. The water was dark with buffalo dung, with fish droppings and algae. I could sense it resting in the warm water by the bank — the fish, mistaking my light almost-touch for the swaying grass.

Let Kazuo have his egg. I could do better on my own.

My fingers closed ever so slowly over the fish. Its smooth body rocked back and forth in the water between my hands.

But hunger had made me careless, and I realized the body was too smooth to be a fish. I had my hands around a snake! My heart pounded, sending a surge of warm blood through my chest and arms. My second cousin had been bitten three years ago by a water krait and had died within two hours.

If I backed away, the snake would realize I was there. If I continued to close slowly on it, the snake would bite me. I took a breath and hurled the snake into the air. It writhed, zigzagging, black and white against the pale blue sky. And then I saw to my horror that I had accidentally thrown it almost straight up, and it fell back into the paddy at my feet.

I jumped back and fell into the water on my bottom. As I scrambled to my feet, I felt a quick bite on my calf.

I got out of the water and looked at my muddy leg. Try as I could, I couldn't find the bite. I had felt it, though, I was sure. How stupid I was! And so far from home . . . It would take me at least an hour to get back.

Another child might have run home for his mother, no matter what the distance. But I had no illusions that getting to my mother would be worth the time.

Cousin Toru! Maybe he was at his clinic in town.

I ran. I panted, and by the time I reached the nearest buildings I felt a cramping in my belly, different from my usual hunger pangs. I stopped, out of breath, my forehead dripping with sweat.

The air-raid siren went off.

My heart stopped. I saw the image of the American plane bearing down on me, the pilot aiming his gun, Yoshiko screaming. I found my legs running of their own accord through the empty streets, past the shuttered windows and the padlocked doors of corrugated steel.

Toru, Toru. Please be there.

His door was locked, and I stood in front of it in a panic as the sirens wailed. I pounded on the door, yelling.

"Toru!"

The window to the side of the door was locked, too, and I hit it with a rock. But I was not strong enough and the window only cracked slightly.

I picked up the rock to smash at the window again. But then suddenly the door opened and Toru's head poked out. He stared at me for a moment. He was a young man, but his eyes were gray and serious like his father's — my father's oldest brother.

"Toru!" I dropped the rock. My fingers were tingling.

His eyes flicked to the sky at the sound of distant planes. "Get in," he said.

I went in, and he hurried me down a set of very steep stairs into a tiny area in the basement that had been outfitted as an air-raid shelter, with water, dried foods, and piles of books. At the bottom of the stairs I crumpled as the cramping in my belly intensified.

He bent toward me, his eyes intent.

"I'm sorry about the window — " I began.

"Never mind. Why did you come?"

"I've been bitten by a krait."

"You're sure it was a krait?"

I nodded. "Black-and-white rings. I saw it."

He took a rag and wiped the mud off my leg. The faintest traces of a bite appeared on the full of my calf. He looked me in the eyes again. "Seeing okay?"

"Yes."

"Breathing okay?"

I nodded.

"Well, we'll have to treat you in the clinic upstairs. *Lai.*"

He helped me up the stairs again and into his examining room, which was cluttered with large boxes. He pulled down the shades, set me on his examining table, and started rummaging through a box, his movements quick and fluid. There was the distant sound of machine-gun fire.

"You're lucky." He unwrapped a long metal needle. "I was just getting ready to evacuate." He glanced at me. "Now, lie down."

"I can't. My stomach hurts . . ."

"Slowly. Breathe."

I lay back shakily, puffing my cheeks, squinting at the lamp overhead. "You're not supposed to have your light on during an air raid."

"Well, we need it, and it's daylight. It won't matter."

I felt a jab of pain in my belly and winced. "I want to stay alive," I said.

Toru straightened up. He had an armful of equipment and a small brown vial in his hand. As he spoke, he dumped the armful of equipment onto a chair and placed the vial carefully on the counter. "Well, hopefully you will. You were smart to come find me right away." He dragged a metal pole to my side and hung a glass bottle of clear fluid on it. "I have a little antivenom. It's new, but I think we should try it."

"You haven't tried it before?"

"No," he said. "But it's your only chance. Abdominal cramping is the first manifestation of envenoming. After that it attacks your nervous system . . . Well, no time to waste talking."

He unrolled what I thought had been a label on the little brown vial and unfolded it into a sheet of paper. He read it, then attached tubing to the bottle of fluid. He worked methodically, without any appearance of haste, extracting a small amount of fluid from the vial and injecting it into the bottle.

He began tying my arm tightly onto a wooden splint. I winced.

"Shouldn't you hurry?" I said.

"I have to make this secure. It's to keep the needle in place. If it moves, you'll be in big trouble." He tied my arm, splint and all, to the bed and inserted the needle into my arm.

He put his hand on my shoulder. "Now we just wait for it to infuse." He bent toward me and looked into my eyes again. "Your eyelids were always asymmetrical?"

"Yes." I hesitated, then said, "Toru?"

"What is it?"

"The nervous system. That's my brain, right? And the nerves going down my back? It makes your hands move."

He straightened up. "How do you know that?"

"Kazuo was talking about it. He wants to be a doctor."

"That's right. The nervous system controls all your body's functions, including breathing. That's why krait bites are so lethal.

Though you should be fine." He fell silent and began to examine me, telling me to look this way and that, open my mouth. He lifted up my shirt. "What are all these scratches and bruises from?" he said.

I pulled my shirt back down and said nothing. They were from my mother.

He sat down on a box beside me so his face was level with mine. He watched me closely. "What were you doing outside, so far away from home? It's not safe outside these days."

As if to prove his point, the sound of a shell thundered in the distance.

"I was hungry, and I was looking for some friends."

"Hungry? But your family gets plenty of rations."

"Kazuo gets all the eggs," I said. "And my little sister gets the meatballs. I have to chop them for her on Saturdays and I never get to eat any."

"Why?"

"I don't know." I hesitated. "Maybe because of Aki. And I'm not the firstborn."

"Aki?"

"I kept him out too late. That's what she says. It's why he died."

"But you were what — six?"

"Five."

He was silent for a moment, looking down at the needle in my arm. The lamplight flickered and he absentmindedly checked the ties on the splint. "Your poor mother," he said.

I looked up at him in surprise.

"I don't think she ever wanted the life she has," he said. He looked back down and his eyes slid toward my midriff. Without speaking, he dug a small jar of ointment from a box and smoothed it onto my skin. "Sometimes people are unhappy, Saburo, and they make others suffer to feel better. Do you understand?"

"No," I said. I closed my eyes, feeling the sting of the ointment on my wounds. I thought of Yoshiko chattering so happily about her father and his plans to see Japan and China. I wished I could have been like her.

"It wasn't your fault, Saburo," Toru said.

He finished applying the ointment and washed his hands. It began to rain, the raindrops pattering against the windows.

"Finally," I said.

"What?" Toru looked over at me as he dried his hands on a towel.

"It's finally raining. I knew it would."

"Why? Because the air strike's ending?"

"No. The clouds. When they look like fish scales, it always rains. Only this time it took a whole day." I imagined Yoshiko hearing the rain, too, and remembering me.

Toru laughed in surprise, the absent look leaving his face. "There's a lot going on in that head of yours, isn't there? What else do you think about?"

"Toru," I said, "have you seen the world?"

He smiled. "The world? I have seen Tokyo. I studied there for a year. I wanted to go to America, but I didn't have enough money and my English isn't good enough for me to take classes there."

"America? Why? They're destroying Taoyuan. They tried to shoot me yesterday."

"Ah, well," he said, sighing. "That's war. These young men with guns think it's all a game. But America itself—it's a country founded on principles, on personal freedom."

"I'd like to see America, too," I said. "And Japan."

He patted my arm. "Then we will get you better. And when you get better, stay inside and study and be a good boy. You're very smart, very capable, and if you study hard you'll go anywhere you want to go."

"But I'm not smart," I said. "The teachers punish me every day."

"They do?" He folded his arms and watched me for a moment, then leaned back to stuff the vial of antivenom into his box. He turned to face me again. "There's a certain kind of mind that most teachers do not appreciate," he said. "Teachers like rules. And they like the children who follow the rules, not the ones who question them. Mothers, too, I should say. Some mothers, anyway, are like this, too."

He got off the box he had been sitting on and foraged around inside it.

He pulled out a book and handed it to me.

"Keep your questions inside. Direct them toward your studies and you'll be a great inventor or scientist, a famous artist. My old math teacher gave me this. The best teacher I ever had. Something to read until you're feeling better."

I drew my finger over the book's rough blue fabric cover. Gold kanji spelled out the title, *The Earth*.

4

AFTER TWO WEEKS IN the hospital, I was placed in an oxcart and sent north. My father had finally agreed on a price for the country house and evacuated our family.

Toru had saved my life, and the antivenom had saved me from any neurological damage. But I did not feel as lucky as I was. As I sweated in bed, first in the hospital, then on a musty futon with a view of Guanyin Mountain, the scene in the rice paddy played over and over in my dreams. The snake writhing, black and white against the blue sky, its fangs dripping with venom. I willed it sideways, away from me, behind me. I tried to run away, scramble out of the paddy. But my legs were stuck in the mud, and every time, the snake fell straight down, ruining everything. I would never find Yoshiko and her brother and their happy home.

Periodically I awoke to find on the floor beside me a cup of tea and a bowl of rice with a speck of egg on top. I guessed it was about a quarter of one scrambled egg, my mother's concession to my illness. I ate, the rice sticking to the sides of my mouth, and then fell back into my terrified dreams.

I opened my eyes one day feeling suddenly clearheaded. I threw off the damp covers, stood up, and nearly fainted. I held the wall for a minute to keep from falling. But then I kept walking, feeling very odd as I left the rancid bedroom and found my way outside. My mother was sitting on a bench by the back door, trimming beans. My littlest brother and sister were poking at an army of ants with a stick a few feet away.

My mother looked up. "Ah, you're up," she said, and she bent back to her work.

I had seen Yoshiko's brother enfold Yoshiko in his arms. I had heard the worry in his voice. And now I knew how a child should be greeted after escaping death.

I was starting to wish I had never met Yoshiko. Before meeting her I had not known how very much I was missing at home. I felt again that rising ache inside and turned my face from my mother. I closed my eyes and breathed in deeply, soothing myself with the scent of sun-warmed grass. The wind blew gently on my face, and bamboo leaves rustled beyond the house, calling me to explore their shady, hidden-away places.

I felt light headed again and sat down on the stairs. "Where are Kazuo and Jiro?" I asked after a moment. "Are they at school?"

"There's no school here," she said. "I told you many times that I had no access to school when I grew up here. They're with their tutor."

I remembered Toru's admonishment to study. "Do I have a tutor?"

"No."

"I'll sit in with Kazuo and Jiro, then," I said.

She looked up at me, eyebrow raised. "With Kazuo and Jiro? You're still sick."

"I'll be better in a couple of days," I said.

She snapped the ends off a few more beans, eyes flickering as she calculated the extra costs, which were probably close to zero. *"Hou,"* she said. "But you're not to slow them down. I will not allow her to change her lessons to suit you."

TWO DAYS LATER I sat in the kitchen with Kazuo, Jiro, and a curly-haired Japanese tutor named Keiko Sato, who was reciting arithmetic drills. Kazuo was in his element, eyes focused on Sato Sensei, his plump hands calmly folded over the neat rows of writing on the papers in front of him. He answered with great speed and just enough scorn to let everyone know he knew the sums cold, but not enough so as to be punished for being disrespectful. Jiro sat beside him, stumbling over his responses, his eyes wide with panic and doubt. Before him was a pile of his own work, each of his strokes neat enough, but just a bit too short and uneven to be considered beautiful.

Sato Sensei glanced at me, her round, freckled face smiling kindly. "Sorry, I know you've only just finished second grade."

"It's all right," I said. Though I took a bit longer, I did the problems as well as Jiro, who was two years older than me.

Sato Sensei cocked her head. "How did you figure out that sum?"

"Well," I said, "you count up by twenty to one hundred sixty, and eight threes is the same as two twelves, so I subtracted two tens and a four."

Jiro looked at me, mouth open.

Kazuo snorted. "That's not how you multiply!" His voice was scornful, but I could see him looking off, trying to figure out what I had just said.

After our session ended, I overheard Sato Sensei talking with my mother in the entryway.

"He's exceedingly bright. He figures these things out intuitively, and his fund of knowledge is extraordinary —"

"I don't know what you're talking about. His school reports are mediocre at best."

"Perhaps he's bored at school —"

"Bored! He's just lazy. Not like my Kazuo! He's already said he wants to be a doctor. Have you seen his calligraphy?"

The following day, Sato Sensei quizzed us about the water cycle and laughed in amazement at my answers. I had never had a teacher who paid so much attention to me. I grew bolder with her praise, enjoying Kazuo's crestfallen looks, and I thought that perhaps Toru was right, that if I studied I might go places.

But on the third day, I overheard my mother and Sato Sensei again.

" . . . the boy is distracting him and Jiro from their work—"

"On the contrary, he enlivens the discussion—"

"That's not what Kazuo tells me. I will not allow him to be slowed down any longer—"

"And how will Saburo's education be achieved? With all due respect, Mrs. Togo, not all firstborn sons get such preferential treatment."

"Some sons are more deserving than others."

The next day, the door to the room was locked, and I had no more tutoring sessions with Keiko Sato.

WE STAYED IN the country house for three years. While Kazuo and Jiro were tutored, I roamed the fields and forests until well past the time my mother considered to be late; on rainy days and evenings I sat by the courtyard, carefully turning the damp pages of *The Earth*.

Sometimes Keiko Sato came to the house early on rainy days, shaking the water off her umbrella and resting it against the courtyard steps, and I wondered whether she came to the courtyard on purpose to find me.

"I've learned the names of the clouds," I said, whispering so my mother would not hear me. I was ten and it was March. It always rained in March. "I've learned how they're formed."

She leaned in close, also whispering, her curly hair streaked with gray. "Tell me."

But more often than not, when I returned from my outside adventures, Sato Sensei was gone and I was left by myself in the evenings to read and reread *The Earth*.

The years passed, and I grew taller, thinner, fed as much from my growing knowledge of the stratosphere, the ionosphere, and the aurora borealis as from the berries and mushrooms and silvery fish that I gathered from the countryside. And as I did, those two days in Taoyuan — the day I had met Yoshiko, and the day the snake had bitten me — crystallized in my mind like two glittering windows into worlds I had never considered it possible for me to see. They created such longing in me that my dreary existence became almost too painful to endure. I had only this blue book, which proved that other worlds — other planets, even, and other galaxies — did exist, that our lives were infinitesimal in the face of the universe. That there might be no limit to what I could learn or where I might go some day.

The Japanese surrendered. The war was over, and we could now return to Taoyuan. Sato Sensei came by to give Kazuo and Jiro her last lesson, and I waited in the courtyard for her to finish. My mother packed boxes in the entryway, pausing every few minutes to sigh or complain.

Sato Sensei stepped into the courtyard. She put her finger to her lips and bowed hastily. Glancing toward my mother, she tapped my book, pointed mysteriously toward the sky, and, picking up her umbrella, disappeared forever.

As we returned to our house in Taoyuan, I looked up from my seat in the rickshaw into the night sky. The rickshaw bumped and swayed beneath me while the stars shone down, their light piercing through the outer reaches of their own galaxies and through all the orbits of our solar system, through all the layers of oxygen and ni-trogen, dust and heat, ire and disappointment, to reach me. I knew what Keiko Sato had been trying to tell me, and it was something I'd always felt — that the stars, the sky, the earth, would save me from this life. I just didn't know how.

5

As for Yoshiko, I did see her again, on the day the Mainland Chinese soldiers—Chiang Kai-shek's Nationalist army—arrived.

I had been reading *The Earth* and was as usual the last member of my family to get ready. I hadn't heard them calling me or noticed them getting ready.

"Saburo!" my mother called. "You'll make us all late for the parade!"

A parade, to welcome the Chinese Nationalist takeover.

The jubilation over the departure of the Japanese and the imminent arrival of Chinese Nationalists confused me. We had been taught in school to identify with the Japanese and revere their culture. Hadn't we bowed low before our classroom portrait of Emperor Hirohito and whooped when our principal announced the attacks at Pearl Harbor? Hadn't we just finished cheering on the Japanese fighter pilots, the ones who didn't shoot us down?

My teachers had taught us all the good things the Japanese had done for Taiwan. They had built our schools, our airfields, the rail lines stretching north to Keelung and south all the way to Kaohsiung. They had even let the Taiwanese people elect local representatives. Representatives like my father.

My father grunted and shifted in his armchair when we asked him these questions after a particularly breathless radio commentary about Chiang Kai-shek. "Only at the end did the Japanese let us do these things. At the beginning they squashed us down like bugs. Tens of thousands of Taiwanese. Like this." He drew his finger across his throat and pointed to our family altar, where incense smoldered in a small pot before a scroll of our family tree. "Our ancestors are from China. Never forget it. Japan and China have been warring for many years. In 1895, Japan defeated China and got Taiwan. Now, with this American bomb, Japan has lost the war and lost Taiwan. We are going back to the Chinese, and people will always be glad to be ruled by their own kind. This is why everyone celebrates." He paused, frowning into the distance.

"But the situation is more complicated than many people realize. It is not just any Chinese who come to rule us, but the Nationalists, and they are not coming here because they want to," he said. "They are coming in defeat."

"I thought you said they beat Japan," I said. Kazuo snickered behind me.

"China is split," my father said impatiently. "The Nationalists have ruled for a short time and the Communists are rising and decimating the Nationalist power base. The Communists and the Nationalists fought off the Japanese together but were also fighting each other, and the Communists are winning. Chiang Kai-shek is almost done for. But the Americans support him. They dislike Communism, and that is why, though the Nationalists are losing control of China, they get us as a booby prize."

He took a couple of puffs on his cigarette. "And so the losers get the sweet potato," he said, referring, as we all did, to Taiwan's tuber-like shape, "and we welcome them with open arms."

I STUFFED MY book into my rucksack and hurried outside, where the whole family except for my father was piled into the bed of a delivery truck.

I climbed in and squeezed between Jiro and my younger sister Mariko on the metal bed. I felt a pull on my rucksack. "What are you doing with that?" Kazuo said from behind me. "It's dirtying my trousers."

I yanked it back and curled my arm around it. Jiro moved over to make room. He looked at me. He had grown bigger, like me, nearly as tall as our mother, but his eyes were still fearful as a little boy's. "Why are we going to see the soldiers? They're so loud."

Their march, he meant. The only army we knew was the Japanese imperial army, whose synchronized march was so loud and terrifying that the streets would empty long before any soldier was visible. We naturally assumed the Chinese army would be the same.

"A parade!" my father scoffed. "We fought the Japanese when they came. People weren't stupid then." I looked to the side of the truck, where my father approached the cab with the Taoyuan magistrate, a thin man who wore black glasses and a friendly smile. He had been a leader of the Home Rule Association under the Japanese.

"Come, old man," the magistrate said. "For so many years we have dreamed of this moment. Celebrate."

"We have dreamed of the Japanese leaving, not of the Chinese Nationalists coming. Don't you wonder why they were so unpopular in China?"

The magistrate laughed, his thin face creased deeply around his mouth as he opened the cab door and clapped my father on the back. "Such a man! Don't worry. The Chinese are our brethren. Even the Japanese were beginning to concede to our demands."

"Yes." My father's face was dark and mirthless as he shrugged off the magistrate's hand. "But Chiang Kai-shek is a general, not a monk. He won the whole of China before he lost it to the Communists. And he did not win it by asking politely."

My father slammed the door shut, and the magistrate, smiling and shaking his head, walked around to climb into the driver's seat. The windows were open and my father's voice carried through the air.

"Think," he said. "Chiang's Nationalists have been brutalized not only by the Communists but also by the Japanese, and here we drink sake and sleep on tatami. The West has given Taiwan to the Nationalists to punish Japan, not because Chiang Kai-shek loves us."

The truck started up, and my father's words rose over the roaring of the engine.

"Only a child believes his rulers have his best interest at heart," he said. "We would be wise to disabuse ourselves of such illusions."

WE WERE UNLOADED onto a set of tiered platforms in the downtown section of Chungcheng Road, with my father joining the magistrate and members of the town assembly at the top. There were three chairs sitting on the lower platform where my brothers and sisters had been deposited, and they quickly busied themselves squabbling over whether the oldest or the youngest should get to sit. Only Jiro stood looking down the street, a fearful expression on his face.

I looked down over the crowd standing on the sidewalk around us. The populace of Taoyuan lined either side of the street, waving red-and-blue Nationalist flags and scarlet banners saying WELCOME, GENERALISSIMO CHIANG! Though in fact only Governor Chen Yi and his troops were coming today.

And then I saw Yoshiko.

She was standing on the other side of Chungcheng Road at the front of a crowd, all of whom were peering down the street for their first glimpse of the Nationalist Chinese soldiers. Her face was obscured by the wide brim of a hat trimmed with blue ribbons, but I could tell it was her by the way she stood—feet together, inclining her head with a polite, expectant air—and the way she held, on one side, her brother's hand, and on the other side what I took to be her father's. The three of them were easily among the handsomest and most finely dressed of the crowd. Her father was slim and dapper in an elegant, well-tailored suit with a silk handkerchief in the breast pocket. His teeth flashed with a smile as he bent to talk to Yoshiko. Her brother was a young man now, as tall and handsome as his father, laughing and patting Yoshiko on the head as she pointed down the road. Yoshiko's white dress, trimmed with blue ribbons to match her hat, billowed out into her brother's fine dress pants in the light breeze.

"Oh, look!" I heard a man near me say to his friend. "There's Frog Face with his daughter."

"The guy who owns the Tiger Café? With that girl in the white?"

"I don't see his wife —"

They chuckled together.

I wanted so much to talk to Yoshiko. Had she seen the world? Was she no longer poor? I jumped down from the platform onto the sidewalk.

Gasps and quiet cries of surprise arose around me, and I caught my breath. Had I done something wrong? I looked around in alarm, but no one was paying attention to me. They were straining to look at something in the street, and in the general commotion I squeezed through the dress suits, the lace-trimmed sleeves, the embroidered silk cheongsams from Shanghai, and the traditional Chinese dress robes released from decades of storage and emerged at the front of the crowd.

There was no question of crossing the street to get to Yoshiko; groups of bedraggled men now strolled down the road, pots and pans dangling from yokes around their necks. Cooks or servants for the soldiers, I thought. The men were gaunt, their clothes faded, with sloppy white stitches meandering across holes they had clearly tried to mend themselves. Seeing loose chickens in the street, they lunged after them, pots and pans clanging together.

A chicken scampered between my legs, and I leaped back, falling onto the dusty road. A man stepped on my toes with his boot and nearly hit me in the face with a frying pan.

I scrambled to get up, but when I did, I held an upside-down, empty rucksack, and the man who had given chase to the chicken was holding *The Earth*.

"My book!" I yelled at the ragged man.

"Be quiet, young man!" someone whispered behind me. "He's a soldier."

"A soldier?" I stared at the man's rotten teeth, his hollow cheeks. This could not possibly be a soldier. Soldiers were terrifying men who wore crisp uniforms and marched in formation. They might demand a chicken, but they would never stoop so low as to chase one in the street.

The man did not hear me, and if he had, he most certainly would not have understood me, as he was shouting and pointing at my book in a language I had never heard. His words swooped and chopped, his face grew red, and he waved my precious book in the air, marking the cover with his dirty thumb.

"It's mine," I said, reaching for the book.

He struck my hand back and grabbed me by the arm. He smelled like the goats on the farm near my parents' country house. I heard him say something that sounded like "*Fujian ren,*" and he dragged me into the street where the rest of the men still ambled by.

"Ow!" I struggled to loosen his grip on my arm.

The man waved down another man who wore no yoke around his neck and appeared of higher rank. I felt a shock as I realized that this actually was an army and that this second man was an officer.

This officer bent down to me, his hollow-cheeked mouth forming words that were comprehensibly Taiwanese, though with a very odd accent. I would understand later that he must have been from the province of our ancestors, Fujian.

"What is your name? Why do you have a Japanese book?"

I began to shake. I had never been face-to-face with a soldier. I had always run from the Japanese soldiers, like everyone else. Any kind of contact with a soldier was sure to bring dire consequences.

"My name," I said, my mouth sticking together, "is Sa——"

"His name is Tong Chia-lin." My father pulled up at my side, his jacket unbuttoned to reveal his ever-present bow tie and the expanse of shirt over his belly. His eyes were cold and fearless. I had never heard the name he had just called me, ever. I looked up at him in amazement.

The soldier straightened up, chastised by my father's aura of authority. "You're his father?"

"I am," my father said, and he glanced at me in a way that made it clear he was not entirely happy about that fact.

"Excuse me, Mr. Tong, but a soldier in my troop found your boy hiding this book." He held up *The Earth*.

"Sir," my father said. There was just the faintest trace of derisiveness in his tone that only those who knew him well would recognize. "That is a textbook. We have been occupied by Japan for fifty years and all our textbooks are in Japanese."

The officer looked down at the book. He opened it and looked down with disgust at the mixture of kanji and hiragana. "What if I don't believe you?" he said. He turned the page, and there was an illustration of the solar system.

"You see?" My father pointed at the picture and, at the same time, deftly dropped a small red envelope — the kind people used for New Year's money — on top of it. "The solar system."

The officer quickly pocketed the envelope and closed the book with a snap. "I see that it is a textbook. You may keep it. Forgive my mistake."

As my father's hand closed around the book, relief and gratitude flooded through me. I reached for the book. "*Otosan!*"

In the same instant that I cried out, the soldier was called away, hurrying after the last of the soldiers. The crowd, silent and shocked by the parade of bedraggled soldiers, began dispersing, their welcome banners slack.

My father whirled to face me, bending so his face was close to mine, his eyes menacing. "Fool!" he whispered. "Don't you ever talk to me in Japanese in public again. In front of a Nationalist soldier!" He tucked the book under his arm and grabbed my elbow. "I will burn this stupid book when we get home!"

"No!"

He dragged me back to the truck, his fingertips digging so hard into my arm that my eyes watered and I knew there would be marks for days.

Why my one book? Our house was filled with Japanese books. They were on every shelf, in every book bag. That book was the one thing I owned that mattered at all. My throat swelled, but I took a deep breath. I was twelve years old and I didn't want to give my father and my brothers the satisfaction of seeing me beg and bawl like a baby.

I climbed onto the truck bed and squeezed again between Jiro and Mariko, who complained that I was wrinkling her skirt. Jiro turned to me, eyebrows lightly furrowed. "What happened?"

I wanted to answer, but my throat was still swollen.

Kazuo was standing by the truck with my father. "Nice job, rice-for-brains," he said to me. And then, to my father: "How did you know what to do?"

My father grunted. "These people are obviously desperate and corrupt. There's only one way to deal with people like that."

Kazuo chuckled, shaking his head. He put out his hand. "I'd like to have that book," he said.

My father handed it to him. "It interests you?"

Kazuo leafed through it. "It does."

"Keep it, then."

"Hey!" I jumped to my feet and nearly fell over the side of the truck. "That's my —"

"Shut up!" my father barked up at me. "You've caused enough trouble today."

I sat down.

Kazuo climbed up onto the truck bed and smirked, brandishing the book and then sitting on top of it, right in front of me. "That's better. And now you'll have no more advantage, little boy."

"That's not fair," Jiro whispered to me, his eyes wide. "That was yours."

I was breathing so hard I had a stitch in my side. I would sooner have burned the book than give it to Kazuo. "I'll get even with him someday," I said under my breath. "Someday I'll —"

I stopped, remembering to look back at the street.

Yoshiko and her family were gone.

6

I WAS FOR A time consumed by feelings of helplessness and rage. Walking by Kazuo's room, I could see *The Earth,* shelved between his geometry and physical science textbooks. Kazuo never read the book, to my knowledge. For him it was a trophy, an assurance that he retained his superiority.

I could simply have taken it back. But since my mishandling of it had caused so much trouble, and since my father had in fact taken a great risk in retrieving the book from that Nationalist officer, I did not feel justified in taking it back. I was lucky enough that my father had punished me only in this way. At least *The Earth* was safe in our house. I tried to be satisfied with stealing into Kazuo's room when he was not there and flipping the book open, its pages fluttering in the breeze that passed through the large screened windows of his room.

Reading the book was a balm for me through all the changes in the world outside. The Taiwanese textbooks we had studied between the Japanese departure and the Chinese takeover had been swept aside, and I was now called by that strange name, Tong Chia-lin. Outside, we were once again forbidden to speak our own language and forced instead to speak a foreign language. This time it was Mandarin Chinese, the four tones of which—as opposed to the eight of Taiwanese, the atonality of Japanese—we were still training our ears to recognize. We chanted, "*Bo po mo fo,*" and recited Chinese nursery tales in our cracking preadolescent voices. Between classes, I stole off to clamber up piles of hacked-up desks and peer through the windows at soldiers who lived in a blocked-off section of our school. Some sat on beds of rags, smoking. Others stripped our classrooms of shelving, lighting, the very outlets from the walls. They sold these things, I heard. They sold everything they could remove except for our Japanese textbooks. These they set fire to in the courtyard, along with our desks, cooking over them in huge blackened woks and squatting to eat on the ground, like the poorest of beggars.

In the streets, sirens wailed, signaling bank robberies and the looting of stores and factories. Toru's own clinic was looted for stomach powders and antibiotics.

Once, I passed a grocery store where sacks of rice, barley, and sweet potatoes were piled outside the door. A small crowd had gathered and a small, wild-looking woman fended them off.

"I paid good money for these! They cost one hundred of those new dollars. My son's upstairs, but he'll be right down to carry these inside, so don't get any ideas."

"He's too sick, Ma!" A girl's voice called from inside the house.

"What are you talking about!" The woman wrung her hands, standing in front of the sacks. Her cheekbones were sharp and there were hollows beneath. "Well, my other son will be back any minute now."

Why didn't anyone help her?

"I'll carry them in," I said. Then, as I went to pick up a sack of rice, I saw that three men in the front of the crowd wore Nationalist uniforms. My heart flip-flopped, but I couldn't fathom how helping this woman with her own rice could be wrong, so I kept my head down and carried the heavy sacks in, one by one.

"*Chit pieng.* Here." The woman pointed me toward the dusty, empty shelves. Inside, she whispered, "You see those pigs think they can just take what they want."

The crowd broke apart and I left the store as quickly as I could. I heard a voice call out from the second-floor window, but I was too scared to look back.

THROUGH THE MONTHS that Taiwan sank into chaos, I continued to steal into Kazuo's room. He had a tutor to help him prepare for his high school entrance examinations, and as their voices sounded in the kitchen, I stood by his bookshelf flipping through *The Earth*. I didn't dare sit, for fear of leaving traces of my presence on his chair or futon. It was in Kazuo's room one day, as I carefully pushed *The Earth* back onto its shelf so the spine lined up with the others, that I saw a sheet of paper on his desk. It was set in the middle, as though it were especially important.

> Examinations to Determine Eligibility to Pursue Graduate Study in the United States take place yearly in October. The top twelve scorers in the country will be allowed to apply for a United States student visa. Subjects to include English, mathematics, physics, history, biology, chemistry . . .

Scrawled across the top of the announcement was a handwritten note:

No one's passed from Taoyuan County. Let's be the first! — *Li-wen*

And at that moment, looking down at Kazuo's fine, neat desk, surrounded by the handsome screened windows facing the court-yard and the stacks of new, folded clothes I would someday get thirdhand, I knew what I had to do. I would take that examination. I would beat Kazuo to America.

TORU HAD BEEN right: academic success could be my ticket to see the world. And I needed to make up for lost time. The Taiwanese education system was rigidly tiered. All the students who had passed the American entrance exam had graduated from one school—Taiwan University, unequivocally the best school on the island. If I wanted to get into Taiwan University, I had to go to the top high school, and if I wanted to go to the top high school, I had to go to the top middle school. There was no dodging this tracking system. One misstep now would send me down a lesser path, and I would never get the education I needed to pass the most difficult exam in Taiwan.

And so when the time neared for my middle school entrance exams, for the first time in my life I was nervous about them. Even so, I was unable to study systematically. I was distracted by too many things — the fields, the sky, a neighborhood dog who loved to roam and splash in the paddies when I threw sticks. Only after the dog bit me on the calf did I sit down for one or two days with my Chinese schoolbooks. This was more than I had ever done for an exam, and strangely, the pain focused my mind. I sat in the examining room, blood seeping into the iodine-soaked rags my mother had wrapped around my leg, and sorted through logic problems that I would normally have found too tedious to undertake: *There are thirty legs in a roomful of turtles and storks, and twice as many turtles as storks. How many of each animal?*

In the end I passed my first hurdle: getting into the premier middle school in Taipei — Chien Kuo. Chien Kuo's high school was likewise considered the top high school on the island, and going through the middle school was considered the inside route to Taiwan University.

The fact that I passed Chien Kuo's entrance examination had caused much surprise and celebration — even announcements in the newspaper and on the radio. I was the first from my elementary school ever to have passed, and I had not been one of its top students. My family considered my success a fluke; one of my uncles asked frankly whether my father had interceded on my behalf. But my mother, in a fit of appreciation, made a pair of navy-blue shorts just for me — the first brand-new clothes I had ever had. I stroked the seams, marveling at how many times my mother had poked her needle through the cotton. Of course I knew that she had made pants for Kazuo out of the same fabric. But even so — so much labor! For me! I strolled around in those shorts like a king.

IF I WANTED to be one of the top twelve students on the island, however — the best student Taoyuan County had ever seen — I would need to actually study. I was not at all one of the top students in my class at Chien Kuo, though according to my teacher, who said so in a rather peeved way, I could be if I paid as much attention to his lectures as I did to the workmen outside who built the concrete walls of our school's new wing.

I resolved to turn a corner, to take my studies seriously. And so it was that, one February morning in 1947, I hopped off the train at Taipei Station having actually read the books that were in my bag. My brothers Kazuo and Jiro ran off toward their school, and I toward the part of the city by the botanical gardens. I smiled to myself, confident that from now on I would be that stellar student Teacher Lee thought I could be. I imagined myself without my brothers, in a world of movie stars, Cadillacs, and freedom.

But in the streets, there was a sense of disquiet that I had not noticed before today. Since the Nationalist takeover there had been much grumbling in houses and behind closed doors, but now clusters of people stood together at newsstands, talking loudly.

"She was just trying to make a living!"

"They just want the money for their own pockets!"

"Tell them to go try a day of work for a change!"

"I would've given them something to remember — "

A freshly painted banner hanging over the street read, THE DOGS GO AND THE PIGS COME!

I had never seen anything so bold. We all knew that "dogs" referred to the Japanese, and "pigs" to the Nationalist Chinese, but to hang it out there in broad daylight . . . Though I never thought I would have missed the Japanese soldiers, I missed the feeling of safety and order we had had before. As my book bag slapped against my side, I hastened past a bashed-in bank and a grocery store sporting the sign RICE! BUY TODAY BEFORE PRICES RISE TOMORROW! Glass crunched under my feet and I smelled something burning.

When I reached the school gates, I breathed out with relief and only then realized I had been holding my breath for quite some time. Inside, though, we were shuttled from our regular classroom into the newly constructed wing of the school.

It was the first Friday I was actually prepared for our test, and Teacher Lee was late. The principal — a Mainlander, of course, like all our teachers — poked his head in and said in his usual severe way that Teacher Lee was at a special teachers' meeting and that we must wait patiently and cause no trouble or we would be in trouble ourselves. As we waited for him, my classmates talked, louder and louder, our voices deadening in the still-drying walls of cement that surrounded us.

"What can the teachers be talking about all this time?"

"Whatever those Mainland pigs talk about. Who knows?"

"You'd better be quiet!"

"Why? We're all sweet potatoes here — we're all Taiwanese."

"It smells like cow dung in here."

"Did you hear about that woman selling cigarettes?"

"Didn't she die — "

"No, I heard they shot into the crowd and killed people that way."

"Did you see that banner?"

I went to the wall, stuck my finger in it, and dragged my finger through the mixture of mud and rice straw, tracing out a square Mainlander face with a round nose and a single hair growing out of the chin. "Teacher Lee," I said. I curved out my line to make the potbelly.

Everyone burst out laughing behind me, and I smiled, enjoying the feeling of being liked, the center of attention.

Soon others joined me at the wall. "Is it okay to draw here?"

"Sure," I said. "They'll just put plaster over this. Usually they just score the wall with bamboo branches. The drawings will do the same thing and help it stick."

The smooth surface of the wall disappeared under googly-eyed faces and B-29 bombers. I laughed, jubilant at the sensation of being for once in the thick of a group rather than on the fringes. And then suddenly, footsteps sounded on the plywood outside our classroom door.

We tripped over each other, scurrying to our seats.

The door opened, and Teacher Lee appeared — bald, his brow furrowed, his nose bulbous and red. "Rise," he said, walking to his desk, and we all stood.

"Good morning, Teacher Lee," we chanted in Mandarin.

"Sit."

And it was at that point, when we had all sat back down and he turned to the chalkboard, that his eyes widened. He walked slowly around the classroom, looking at the walls. He stopped in front of my drawing of him, and I saw, with a mingling of pride and fear, that my classmates had given it a fairly wide margin in their own doodlings.

But could it be? The nose I had drawn looked just like a pig's snout. How could I possibly have drawn such a thing on a day like today? I hoped desperately that he would think it was something else, a caricature of some other person.

Teacher Lee's ears turned red. For several agonizing moments he said nothing but only stared at my drawing, nostrils flaring, belly heaving.

Then he turned to us. "Who has done this?"

I looked at his face, flushed and twisted. I could not have drawn his nose any other way.

I stood. I was in the front, as we had been seated by exam score, and I knew my classmates would stand up also, because everyone had drawn on the wall and all we had to do was explain.

But then I saw that only one other boy, the one directly behind me, was standing, too. He sniffled, eyes watery and terrified as he wiped them on his sleeve.

My mouth went dry. I felt a rushing sound in my ears. Yet still I felt, if only I could just explain how the wall was constructed. My teacher was an intelligent, educated man, but he was a *gua shing-a* — a Mainlander — and Mainlanders did not seem to understand how things operated. They ran wires across railroad tracks. They ran flat tires into the ground. They gathered in groups to gawk at elevators. "Teacher Lee," I said, facing him, "the walls are not actually ruined. All the pictures will disappear. You see, they put plaster over — "

"Tong Chia-lin," he said sharply, "did you vandalize this property?"

"Well, yes, but — "

"Two black marks! And you?" He pointed his chin at the boy behind me.

"I am s-sorry, Teacher Lee."

"You get one."

"But — "

"Shut up, Tong!" Teacher Lee pointed at me, his finger quivering. "Two black marks means you are on probation. I will notify your parents immediately."

Indignation flashed up inside me. "But Teacher Lee — " I said.

He stepped toward me, glaring, his face scrunched up in fury. I was almost as tall as he was, and he breathed into my face, the capillaries of his skin crisscrossing his nose.

"Tong Chia-lin," he said, "do not say another word. You have the mind, you have the opportunity to get the best education available on this lousy, ungrateful island. If you say one more word, you will lose that opportunity."

My heart pounded on the front of my chest. I opened my mouth.

"You people," he said. His shaking finger jabbed at me, then at the window facing the street, where a siren wailed, its pitch rising, then lowering as it passed. "You people think you can get away with breaking the rules, with insubordination. You think you are better than me, do you? Well, we will see about that, won't we? Because *I* am the one with the upper hand."

My heart hammered. I knew that I should be prudent and swallow my pride, that my future was at stake and I would do well to save my fighting for another day. But my indignation swelled up. It rose on a hot tide brimming with fury over losing *The Earth,* with the headiness of the anti-Nationalist banners and the crescendo of discontent in the streets, and it exploded forth, over the threats and the fear and the prudence. The truth was on my side. "But Teacher Lee," I said, "we did not cause any damage. You're punishing us for being honest!"

Teacher Lee stepped toward me, his face quivering. His finger pointing. "Tong Chia-lin, I told you not to say one more word. You have defied me, and *I expel you from this school.*"

His eyes bored into mine, his face engorged with hatred that extended far beyond my preadult body, into the streets and city squares, the valleys and dormant volcanoes, that were at Taiwan's heart. No one spoke. The silence was broken only by the sound of his quickened breathing and a class letting out for recess down the hall. The chattering and footsteps receded. And then a door slammed shut.

I walked out through the school gates, legs wobbly, arms trembling.

I expel you!

Why hadn't I kept my mouth shut? How could I go home now?

"Sweet potato or pig?" a man shouted at me.

I jumped. A group of young men encircled me on the sidewalk. They were dressed like college students but clutched bricks and empty bottles by the neck.

"*Hun-chi,*" I said. Sweet potato. My voice shook, a half whisper.

They brushed past me, walking toward downtown Taipei. They

broke into a Taiwanese folk song my relatives often sang at parties to celebrate the midnight orchid's annual bloom.

Rainy-night flower
Blown to the ground by the wind and rain
No one takes heed of you
When your petals touch Earth, they will never return to life.

I watched, erupting in shivers. Sirens sounded. Their sound waves overlapped, distorted, as though the air itself no longer conformed to the laws of physics. I no longer recognized the world.

A government car zoomed down the street, and the young men who had challenged me pelted the car with bottles as it passed. A fist emerged from the car window. The sight of this, and the sound of angry shouts, roused me, and I ran toward the train station, ducking into a side entrance.

The train platform overflowed with people — people in business suits, farmers with chickens under their arms, children like me in their school uniforms.

"What's going on?" I asked a boy.

"They've shut down the railways."

I wandered through the restless, anxious crowd. How was I to get home? I climbed onto an empty vendor's cart to look over the sea of black heads to the empty tracks.

"Saburo! Saburo!" Toru's face popped up out of the crowd, and he waved.

I scrambled down, and he pulled me by the arm through the crowd and out of the station. A jeep was waiting at the curb, engine running, and Toru ushered me into the backseat between him and Jiro, who looked out the window with a stick clutched in his hand. His eyes were wide and scared, his other fist clenched so the muscles in his arms bulged. The Taoyuan magistrate sat at the wheel, my father and Kazuo squished beside him.

Toru slammed the door shut.

"What's the stick for?" I whispered to Jiro.

"In case we need to fight. You should get something, too."

I pictured him in the street, all muscle and male instinct. All I had in my bag was a pencil. Even my schoolbooks had been taken away.

"Okay," my father said, glancing around, his eyes fearsome. I had no doubt he could have commanded an army. "Let's go."

The magistrate pulled away from the curb. "Let's try this way."

"What's going on?" I asked.

"Riots," Toru said. "The police beat up a Taiwanese woman for selling foreign cigarettes without a license last night. People saw it and went crazy, attacked the police. And the police fired back."

The jeep swerved and stopped suddenly, jamming me into Jiro. His stick whacked me in the chin. I cried out at the pain.

"*Aiyo!*" In the street in front of us, a truck blazed, flames roaring out of its windows. People ran past us on either side, away from the fire. The acrid smell of burning oil filled the jeep.

"Let's go! Let's go!" my father said.

The magistrate turned the jeep around and drove on, and I leaned into Toru.

"We can get out this way. Look!" The magistrate indicated a crowd gathering to our left in front of a large building. "The governor's mansion! I've heard they've taken the Monopoly Bureau, too. The workers just gave up and left."

"Hm!" my father said. "Went home to get their guns. Let's not be stupid. Come on, this isn't a sightseeing tour."

But the magistrate paused, hands on the steering wheel, head cocked. The crowd was singing.

"Listen!" the magistrate said. "It's 'Repairing the Fisherman's Net.'"

Looking at the net, my eyes redden — such a hole!
I want to repair it but have not a thing . . .

"Let's go!" my father cried out. "*Kianh-kianh!*"

"Taiwan's only happy folk song," Toru said quietly.

The magistrate laughed, obviously stirred as the crowd continued. "Happy?"

Who knows my pain?
If we let it go today, our future is hopeless . . .

"The last stanza," Toru said. "She fixes it."

"*Kianh-kianh!*" My father shouted, reaching for the steering wheel.

"*Bien-la. Bien-la.* We're going." The magistrate wheeled the car around. "I still think you should join the Settlement Committee," the magistrate said to my father, pushing up his glasses. "I think the people have shown their will and we might be able to get Chen Yi to——"

"Enough!" my father said. "A minnow does not negotiate with a shark! Who cares about words when they have Chiang's army across the strait?"

As they argued, Toru whispered to me, "Where were you? We went to your school to pick you up, but you weren't there."

For a couple of moments I had forgotten about being expelled. Now I remembered again, and shame washed over me. What would Toru think of me now? I had failed more completely than I ever thought possible. I looked up at him, but he was now peering out the window.

"Wait!" he said suddenly. "Stop the car! Someone's injured."

The magistrate braked, but my father roared, "No! Drive on! We don't even know who it is!"

"It doesn't matter!" Toru said.

"Of course it does!"

I peered out the window. A small group of people were clustered around someone lying on the ground.

"If it's a Mainlander, they'll lynch us! Go!" my father yelled.

"I've treated Mainlanders before. I treated one just last night and he was very grateful. He was injured by a mob——"

"Exactly! What would you do, anyway? You have no equipment."
The crowd turned to look at our car.

"Go!"

A man raised his arm as though in greeting and then casually lobbed a stone toward our jeep. The stone sailed straight at us through Toru's open window.

Suddenly, Toru's arm was across my face and he was leaning hard on me, pushing me into Jiro. Jiro screamed.

"Ahh!" I cried out. "I can't breathe."

"Saburo! Jiro! Are you all right? Toru!"

The jeep squealed away, pressing us all backward. We pulled out of downtown Taipei, and Toru sat up.

"Are you all right?" he said. As he looked at me, I saw that his cheek was bleeding.

"Toru!" I said. "The rock hit you in the face!"

Toru felt his cheek, then folded up his handkerchief and held it to the wound.

My father looked back, his eyes dark. "We are not the Red Cross," he said.

WHEN WE GOT home, I tried to sneak off unnoticed, hoping that in all the furor over the riots the termination of my academic career would pass without notice. But after a few moments my father called to me, and I found myself facing him in his great-room armchair. I closed my eyes for a moment, knowing what was to come.

He paused, looking into the distance, one massive hand holding a smoldering cigarette, the other on the radio dial as the reports continued.

. . . *It is unclear how many men perished when police fired into the un-armed crowd at the governor's mansion, but the killings only seem to have fueled more outrage in the native populace* . . .

He jumped up, surprisingly nimble for his weight, and smashed his fist onto the table so the ashtray jumped. I flinched.

"I knew Chen Yi was a butcher!" he said. "He killed all those students on the Mainland, I heard it from the Japanese. What would he do here? Hand over his mansion with no fight?"

I said nothing, as I knew this tirade was not for my benefit; my father rarely discussed politics with me. But I realized at that moment that we had gotten out of Taipei just in time, and that he had knowingly risked his life to pick up Kazuo, Jiro, and me.

He straightened up to face me.

"I have received a message from your school," my father said. He crossed his arms so his bow tie tilted. He looked at me, his eyes black and impenetrable.

I looked down. I knew the best thing for me to do now would be to grovel on the floor, pounding my head and crying for forgiveness and mercy. Distracted and distressed as he was about the riots, it might have done the trick. But perhaps because I knew it was what he wanted, I could not bring myself to do it. "It was just the underside of the wall," I said. "They put plaster over it."

My father unfolded his arms and narrowed his eyes. "Stupid! Why are you giving me excuses?" He swung out his arm and struck me across the head.

My head exploded with pain. I hit the floor, gasping. The pain was like a weight on my temple that I couldn't lift, and I moved my legs like a squashed bug, trying to rise off the dark floorboards. When my father spoke, I could hear him only through the ear that was against the floor; the ear he had hit was filled with a loud ringing. The words came to me, pinched and dim:

"Stupid! No school will take you now! You've ruined your life!"

My father clicked the radio back on, and as my breath moistened the floor, I heard the announcer's voice, muffled by the floor and my half deafness.

. . . government has been paralyzed. Native Taiwanese leaders are planning to organize a set of demands to set forth . . .

This was my father's trademark form of punishment. Not a continuous beating like my mother's, but the one blow that lasted for hours.

I LAY ON my futon, head throbbing. My hearing was coming back, and I listened to the wind. Winter was coming, sweeping through the porous walls of the house, rattling the window frames. I was cold all the way through.

My father talked in the next room with the magistrate and the former railroad commissioner.

A burst of wind shook the house so hard that a bottle fell off the windowsill and spilled gentian violet on the floor. It pooled, iridescent, on the blackened pine.

I heard the magistrate's refined voice: "At least the Japanese were not corrupt. If you broke a rule, they tortured you—"

"Killed you, you mean—"

"If you didn't, they left you alone."

"They knew how to govern," the railroad commissioner said. "How to grow industry, how to run the railroad. They wanted a good economy. They weren't just out to strip the land and sell everything to the motherland for profit."

"Yes, while these *gua shing-a* ship all our rice to their troops in China."

"They're saying we hoard it."

"Of course they deny it! But we can tell. The people at the docks can all see the rice being loaded onto ships."

"At least the Japanese knew how to distribute the rice. No one liked the rationing, but—"

"But at least they cared whether we ate."

"Don't forget how many people they killed during the resistance!" my father said suddenly.

"Well, but it was straightforward. It was an armed resistance, like a war. What I'm talking about is—"

"Fool!" my father exclaimed. "Remember that 'amnesty celebration' where they slaughtered their guests of honor? How many were there? Three hundred?"

"We don't need the Japanese or the Mainlanders!"

"The dogs go and the pigs come!"

I pulled my blanket around me and listened to the wind that swept south from Siberia and whistled through the cracks in our walls. I closed my eyes, seeing the burning truck, the legs of the person we had left injured in the street. I saw Teacher Lee's shaking finger, the Nationalist officer waving *The Earth,* Yoshiko holding hands with her father and her brother. She touched her palm to my head. The snake bit me. Keiko Sato pointed to the sky.

7

THE OUTDOORS BECKONED, THE long grass bending in the cool wind with innocent grace, but we were not to leave the house. The streets remained anarchic and my parents could take no risks that we might either get into trouble ourselves or incriminate the family with careless remarks. Lying on my futon, trapped and despairing as I was, I developed stomach pains. Yet I was ravenously hungry. At each meal, Kazuo taunted me, calling me a dropout. My mother, as she always had, apportioned the meat to him first, my youngest sister next, then the other siblings. Since my expulsion, her rations were even harsher, and by the time she got to me, there was no meat left.

"What will you be now? A janitor?"

I was silent, chewing my rice, flavored with soy sauce and invective.

As I lay back onto my futon, I heard snippets of news from the radio. The Settlement Committee, of which the Taoyuan magistrate was a member, had presented the Thirty-Two Demands to Governor Chen Yi and his government, calling for steps toward greater Taiwanese representation — the enactment of a provincial autonomy law, new elections of the People's Political Councils, freedom of speech and freedom of assembly. Governor Chen Yi announced that he would meet with the Settlement Committee to negotiate.

My father snorted. "They hope the Americans will hear," he said. "They could just have knocked off all the Mainlanders, but they think this way they'll be let into the United Nations." He spoke derisively, but as he brought a teacup to his lips he had a wistful expression on his face.

But then, on March 8, my father's cynicism was once again proved correct. Chiang Kai-shek's Twenty-First Division arrived at Keelung and Kaohsiung. These were not like the bedraggled troops we had initially welcomed with a parade; they were the Nationalists' most notorious soldiers. They had been told Taiwan was host to a Communist uprising, and having lost so many lives to the Communists, the new troops were vengeful and unmerciful. They swept through the cities, killing every man, woman, and child they encountered in the streets. Chen Yi's concessions had been a farce, designed to buy time as the division boarded boats on the other side of the Taiwan Strait.

The next morning, the magistrate was dragged out of his house and shot in front of his wife and children. In the days to come, a similar fate befell all other members of the Settlement Committee who had not yet gone into hiding, as well as the members of the Loyal Service Corps, university student activists, prominent doctors, lawyers, politicians, and any person who performed or had ever performed the criminal act of showing leadership or offending a Mainland official.

We stayed inside. My parents would not even answer the door, as they had heard that the Nationalists would shoot whoever opened it. It was a fail-safe way of eliminating heads of households.

During our isolation I dribbled a ball in the courtyard with Jiro or folded airplanes for my youngest brother and sister out of musty old newspapers. But my stomach pains worsened and I began having diarrhea with blood in it. I grew so light headed and weak that I retreated to my futon, seeing, on the way, Kazuo's room with *The Earth* tantalizingly on his shelf as he studied, his broad back hunched over his desk. Just walking the few yards from the courtyard to my

room winded me. My body was dwindling with my dreams; I was
becoming a shadow.

One day my parents summoned Toru to the house to attend to
a painful rash on my mother's shin. As he was already out seeing
patients, they didn't mind asking him to make the trip to our house.
Doctors weren't safe from persecution — a prominent physician
downtown had recently disappeared and was presumed dead — but
Toru was a young doctor who was not yet prominent or politically
active, so he seemed less likely to be targeted.

I heard Toru's calm voice in the great room. "It's a spider bite,"
he was saying. "There's nothing to do."

"I've been putting this cream on it to make it feel better," my
mother said.

"*Ane hou.*"

"I wanted to be a nurse, you know. It was my parents who wanted
me to stop school and help on the farm. Otherwise I was very smart
and I could have gotten into a good nursing school."

"Of course you could have," Toru said.

I stood in the shadows of the hallway. I wanted so much to see Toru,
yet I felt too ashamed. He must have learned of my expulsion by now.

My father asked him for news. Toru, lowering his voice, replied
that he had treated a university professor who had been held for
questioning. For two days the professor had been tightly bound with
sharp wire, so that every movement had caused the wire to cut into
his flesh.

". . . and I saw a ten-year-old boy with stumps for hands because
a soldier wanted his bicycle. The child told me he refused to give up
the bicycle because it was his father's, and the soldier simply sliced
off the boy's hands with a bayonet, took the bike, and left the child
screaming and bleeding on the street. Luckily there were passersby
who stopped his bleeding and brought him to me. They picked his
hands up, too, but I am not a surgeon, nor could I find anyone else
skilled enough to reattach them."

"*Ho!*" my father exclaimed. "What a horror!"

"I dream about that poor boy at night," Toru said. "You are right to keep your children at home."

My mother insisted that Toru stay for dinner.

I sat listlessly at the table, picking at my rice and avoiding Toru's eyes while he talked in low tones with my parents about the government crackdown.

"Boats are having trouble passing through Keelung Harbor," Toru said, "because it's so plugged up."

"Plugged up with what?" Jiro said beside me.

"With fish," Toru said, turning to smile at Jiro.

But I knew that Toru had meant with corpses.

I pictured the harbor filled with blood and floating bodies, the boats knocking against what was someone's father, someone's daughter.

All of a sudden, I realized Toru was staring at me. I stared back at him. What had he said? Had he said something about my expulsion in front of the whole family?

"I—I haven't done . . . ," I stammered.

"He's pale as rice paste!" Toru said.

"Ah," my mother said, waving her hand dismissively. "I keep telling him to get up and move around. All he does is lie on his futon—"

But Toru had risen and come to my side. He kneeled, putting his hands on either side of my head, and finally I realized he was not talking about my expulsion at all. He pulled down my lower eyelids with his thumbs and tilted my head back to look into my mouth. Though I had been avoiding him all day, I felt, at his sure touch, an immense relief, and it was with gratitude that I watched him swiftly turn my hands over to inspect my fingernails.

"My God! It's a wonder you're sitting upright at all," he said. "You're terribly anemic!"

. . .

ONCE AGAIN I lay on the examining table of Toru's clinic. His window was now covered with iron bars, and his front door had been reinforced with a chain and a large dead bolt. My arm lay in a modified version of the immobilizing splint he had used to infuse the antivenom into me four years ago.

He moved about the room, setting a bottle of rubbing alcohol on the counter and unwrapping a needle and a syringe. He opened a steel cabinet and pulled out a large bottle of yellow fluid.

"But where did all my blood go?"

He shut the cabinet and twisted the needle onto the syringe, pulling yellow fluid into it from the bottle. "You're malnourished," he said. "You'll need daily treatments."

As Toru pierced my skin with the needle, I winced. "I thought it was from being sad," I said.

Toru pulled back on the syringe, and my blood swirled up into the fluid. He pushed it back into me. He moved quickly, preoccupied; a baby wailed in the full waiting room next door. He glanced at me, pushing the fluid into my vein. "You have reason to be sad," he said. "Many roads are closed to you now."

I turned my head away from him. I had hoped that he might offer words of comfort or encouragement.

"One thing you need to keep in mind," Toru said, pressing on my arm as he pulled out the needle. "The people who govern us now value only power. If you want to survive, you need to keep your mouth shut. You will have a more limited life, now that you have been expelled, but at least you are alive. Be grateful, lie low, and keep yourself out of trouble."

BE GRATEFUL, LIE LOW. In the time to follow, I would be grateful for many things. The Mainlander whose mob-induced injuries Toru had treated on February 27 turned out to be the son of Chien Kuo's middle school principal. The son's gratitude to Toru was so great that when he returned to the clinic for continuing treatment, he brought gifts, and Toru seized the opportunity to plead my case.

His father agreed that expulsion should really have been his decision as principal, and it was conceivable that Teacher Lee had been unduly influenced by the events of February 28. My punishment was reduced to two black marks, and I was allowed to resume studies at my middle school. This was a great relief to my family, but Teacher Lee was deeply angered and struck me down at every turn. The remainder of my time at Chien Kuo middle school was nothing but misery, and though I won admittance into Chien Kuo's prestigious high school, out of spite I refused to go.

I ENROLLED WITH some elementary school classmates at Provincial Taipei Institute of Technology. This was a junior college, which my classmates convinced me would save me from three miserable years of high school and an additional round of entrance exams. And in fact my life did improve. The teachers at my new school were kind and fair, if not rigorous, and the courses required little study. As I was still weak I did not complain. I was no longer on track to take the American entrance exam, but at least I was in school and I was alive. White banners hung over the train platform every day with the freshly painted names of those who had been executed that day: My classmate's father, a chemistry professor. My cousin's friend, a university student. Hundreds of students at Taiwan Normal University and Taiwan University had been arrested, obliterating entire departments. Mothers with drawn faces made the walk to the station every morning to look up at the banners, scanning them for the names of their sons. Had they been killed? Sent to the prison on Hue Sho To, Fire-Burnt Island?

About twenty thousand people died during that time, the White Terror. Taiwanese, aborigine, and Mainlanders, too. "Communist sympathizers," they were called. I was lucky I had a father savvy enough to keep me alive.

Toru continued my daily infusions. My family's company, Tai-kong, was branching into pharmaceuticals, so my parents got the yellow fluid free of charge. Sixty milliliters of vitamins — B_6, B_{12}, C, glucose, and who knows what else — every day for months without end. My veins shrank from the assault, burrowing deep into my flesh and making each needle stick more excruciating. The very sight of Toru's office made me sick.

8

W HAT DOES 'REFORM' MEAN, *Otosan?*" Jiro asked. "They
keep talking about it on the radio."

We were in our jeep, on our way back from a meeting at my
uncle's house in Taipei. My father and his brothers met every few
months to discuss their finances, which were all joined together. My
father sat in the front seat, between our driver and Kazuo.

" 'Reform,' " my father said, folding his arms, "means that Chiang
Kai-shek wants the United States to send him more money. It means
he is trying to make the world forget about the many thousands of
people he has killed since February twenty-eighth and all the American dollars he wasted when he failed to beat the Communists."

"But things are better now, right?" Jiro said. "Since Chiang
Kai-shek came here? He killed Governor Chen Yi, right?"

"*Tyo,*" my father said. "He killed his friend after he realized it
didn't look good to the West that he was being rewarded. And
once he had a replacement who went to Princeton University, in
America."

The jeep slowed to a stop as we passed through downtown
Taoyuan. American jazz drifted through the jeep's open windows
from a record store.

"Governor Wu Kuo-chen," Kazuo pronounced, adopting our

father's scornful air. The folds of fat on the back of his neck bunched up as he turned his head to address us over his shoulder. "His new cabinet is mostly Taiwanese. But it's just for show——"

"*Shh,* stupid! There are soldiers there!" my father growled under his breath.

Kazuo looked wounded and glanced out the window. Just a few feet away, outside a barbershop, two Nationalist soldiers stood in their familiar uniforms, smoking cigarettes and chatting. The jeep rumbled under our seats, and we all looked forward, silent, pretending we knew nothing of February 28, the White Terror, or any need of reform.

THE MOLECULES FROM the yellow bag swirled through my blood, reinforcing the scaffolding of my bones and the marrow within them. My cells feasted, divided, and grew. I grew tall—taller than my brothers, taller than my father, my legs so long they earned me the new moniker Horse when I joined the school's track team.

Toru gradually decreased the frequency of my injections to once a month, to three times a year, and then discontinued them entirely. I was able to eat more now because my mother gave me money for my train fare to junior college. Most days I did ride the train, stumbling about in a blue cattle car with my classmates, commuters, and farmers carrying goats, chickens, and baskets of eggplant to the market. But when I could, I sat on the back of a friend's motorcycle and used my train fare to buy spare-rib soup or oyster omelettes, slurping the food quickly in front of a stall on Gongyuan Road. It was not much food, not nearly as much as I would have liked, but it was enough to sustain the production of my blood.

IN MY FINAL year at junior college, before my mandatory military service year, I hitched a ride home with my classmate, Yi-yang. I'd rapidly become the school's track star, and suddenly I was surrounded by friends. Yi-yang, with his easy smile and impish attempts to introduce fun into my life, was one of my best ones.

I hadn't been paying attention while we rode, and realized he had stopped his motorcycle on Chungcheng Road. "I thought you were taking me home," I said. It was Friday. Kazuo would be coming home from medical school for the weekend, as he usually did. I had taken to borrowing *Fundamentals of the English Language for Foreigners* from his bookshelf during the week. I had finally discovered certain tricks to help me study. I wrote things down and quizzed myself forward and backward—even upside down, like a game. I listened to Glenn Miller on a radio I'd put together in class. The music, paradoxically, helped me focus on my work and made it so much less dreary that I began thinking I might make a living building and refurbishing radios. And since I finally had a handle on studying, I couldn't resist the temptation to learn English. But Kazuo's book was still in my bag and not where it belonged, on his shelf. I needed to get it back fast.

Yi-yang looked back at me slyly. "There's Wen-shen. Let's see what he's up to."

He waved to our classmate Wen-shen, and we crossed the street, Yi-yang pushing his motorcycle along in neutral. We had just learned about fuel cells at school, and as we walked I listened to the motor-cycle's purring, its controlled, compartmentalized fire. We dodged people walking, riding bicycles, hauling rickshaws. Despite the po-litical oppression, Taoyuan, and Taiwan as a whole, was booming. The buildings along the street shot skyward, fueled by our economy, which had recovered—depending on whom you spoke to—either because of the Nationalist's Land to the Tiller Act, which had given my grandfather's hard-earned hectares to the farmers he had hired to farm them, or because of the restoration of our already robust Japa-nese infrastructure. There was so much scaffolding on the buildings along the street that people could hardly walk down the sidewalk. Each story was different from the one below, with larger windows and squarer construction, like an upside-down mountain terraced with rice paddies. Workers in conical straw hats climbed through the scaffolding, hammering above our heads.

We reached Wen-shen, a stocky young man with a dispropor-
tionately big head, and he smiled.

"Need some medicine?" Yi-yang said.

Wen-shen giggled, smoothing his shirtfront.

Yi-yang laughed, turning red, and glanced at me. "Come on,
Tong, we'll show you the prettiest girl in Taoyuan."

"Oh no," I said. "Another of your schemes." Kazuo's book banged
against my side through my bag. "I have to get home. I've got to"—I
thought quickly— "I've got to practice for the meet tomorrow."

"I know, Saburo," Yi-yang said. "You're in love with that florist girl."

"Oh no." I looked away, embarrassed. Being an athlete had also
attracted attention from girls, and there was one, a very pretty girl
with a delicate chin, that I had been on a few dates with.

"What?" said Wen-shen. "Are you engaged?"

"*Bou-la,*" I said. "I'm not seeing that girl anymore."

"Why not?"

"She was always giggling," I said. Actually, the headiness that I
had felt, watching the pretty girl laugh and flash her eyes at me, had
not survived the excruciatingly painful silences that occurred when
her laughing stopped. I had tried talking, asking her questions, but
every story I told seemed to fall into a bottomless hole, and everything she said was prefaced by "My friend, Bu-chi, says . . . "
I simply couldn't endure it any longer.

"Well, then, come. This one's not giggly at all. And don't give
me that excuse about your meet. You shouldn't tire yourself out
the night before a big race." Yi-yang indicated for me to follow and
blithely pushed his motorcycle up the wrong side of Chungcheng
Road. "You'll like her, you'll see. She goes to a business school in
Taipei. We followed her home on Tuesday."

"You're stalking the girl?"

"Tong Chia-lin," Wen-shen said, "how else can you know where
a girl lives? Will you just walk up to her and ask her address?" He
turned to Yi-yang with mock concern. "You need to teach Saburo

here, or he'll end up arranged to marry some ugly woman with a big bank account." They erupted in laughter.

We crossed Fushing Road. It was a brilliant day, and the winter winds had subsided into a mild breeze. The crowd bustled, women carrying baskets of *nappa* and *ku tsai,* bags of rice noodles, bolts of striped or brightly flowered cotton. We passed a grocery store, the sweet smell of cloves and allspice wafting into the street.

I envied my friends' lightheartedness. Mine had gone long ago, flying out the window of my middle school and splashing into the lotus ponds in the botanical gardens beyond.

We stopped just past Jin-fu Temple in front of a small, glass-fronted pharmacy.

"*Hou,*" Wen-shen said. "Time to get some aspirin. Foreign, you know." He winked at me. "Should take her some time to find it."

They headed for the door. I hesitated. "I'll watch your motor-bike," I said.

As soon as the door closed behind them, I wished I had not offered to watch the motorcycle. Kazuo's train would be coming in anytime now, and I needed to slip his book back on the shelf. Why hadn't I done it last night? I did not normally cut it this close, but I was down to the last chapter of the book and had thought I could finish it on the train.

I stood on the sidewalk, looking up and down the street at the throngs of bicycles. I couldn't help feeling like a fool. I should have either gone in with my friends and had a good time or gone home. I glanced through the glass front of the pharmacy. Behind the counter, a girl with short styled hair, a plain white blouse, and a navy-blue skirt deftly counted out pills and then lifted her head to answer a question. Now I knew why my friends had taken the trouble to follow her home from Taipei. Her eyes sparkled, off-set by skin whiter than ivory. When she smiled, she covered her mouth demurely, not obscuring dimples on either cheek. Though she wasn't tall, she moved about the pharmacy with a proper, swift grace. She paused at times over the abacus, keeping her back straight and inclining her head gently over her flying hands like a Japanese koto player. She was not all sweetness; in moments when she was not directly talking to customers, her face drew quiet and sad. She plunked certain medication bottles down with an air of impatience, and at a word from a sullen young man unpacking boxes behind the counter beside her, she frowned. But her frankness only made it more breathtaking when she did smile. I watched, dazzled by the transparent display of emotions on her face. She dispensed medication to others, but her face alone was a balm for wounds. She was a woman, and any residual thoughts I had about the tiresome florist girl blew away like so many petals in the wind.

"Here to gawk?"

I whipped around at the sound of Kazuo's voice. He stood facing me, his thick lips pressed together in a smirk. His belly swelled over the waistband of his dress pants. At his side, his pompous, plump-faced friend Li-wen caressed the leather collar of his jacket. Li-wen was a member of the Anti-Communist Youth Corps, an instrument of the Nationalists.

"I'm waiting here for my friends," I said.

The pharmacy door opened, and Wen-shen and Yi-yang burst into the street, looking sheepish. Their smiles vanished as Kazuo brushed by them and took hold of the door.

"You're wasting your time," Kazuo said to them. "You think a girl like that wants an electrician from a vocational school? You think she wants to help you sell radios?" He looked at me pointedly.

I felt a surge of anger and helplessness. Because I knew he was right.

"*Hou lai tsao*," Yi-Yang said to me quietly. Let's go.

"Some girls don't care about things like that," I said.

"Smart girls do," Kazuo said. "And I happen to know, that girl is smart. All I had to do was tell her I was a student at the top medical school on Taiwan and the oldest son of the new mayor, and——"

"What's your business here?" The sullen-looking young man who had been behind the counter was now in the doorway. He looked around at us, his eyes sharp and unpleasant.

"Who are you?" Kazuo said.

"I'm 'that girl's' brother. You all are clogging up our store."

"What a pleasure to meet you," Kazuo said, his voice unctuous. "I'm Mayor Tong's son. Li-hsiang answered my letter and asked me to meet her here. And this is my friend Li-wen, a high-ranking member of the Anti-Communist Youth Corps."

The girl's brother looked shrewdly at Kazuo and Li-wen and stepped aside. The door closed after them.

"I can't believe it!" Yi-yang exclaimed. "No offense to you, Saburo, but that girl has poor taste. Your brother's an ass."

"What happened when you went in?"

They giggled. "Great plan!" Yi-yang said. "He asked for aspirin, and she put the bottle on the counter before he could finish his sentence."

"And then," Wen-shen said incredulously, "she charged me a dollar!"

"For one bottle of aspirin?" I said. "That's about four times what it should be!"

"I know," said Wen-shen.

"Look!" Yi-yang said. "Your brother's talking to her."

We pressed in at the window. Kazuo stood at the counter, bumping it nervously with his stomach as he spoke, gesticulating with his hands. The girl watched him, head inclined slightly, looking up at him with a wary expression. Her gaze flickered over to where we watched. In a shaft of sunlight from the window her eyes sparkled, flecked with gold.

It was Yoshiko! A flush of excitement rushed through me. I had wondered what she might look like grown and thought she might be friendly and pretty, but I would never have imagined that she would be like this, a beauty. But it couldn't be. Yoshiko had been so happy, and her brother, laughing and handsome, full of love. This girl seemed angry somehow, and her brother's face quite twisted and ugly as he argued with a customer. With a look of impatience, the girl broke away from Kazuo and reached over her brother's arm to click a few beads on his abacus and hand change to his customer.

Yi-yang and Wen-shen laughed. "She's a feisty one," Wen-shen said.

"Too bad her brother's an imbecile."

"What's her name?"

"Lo Li-hsiang. That lumberyard family, you know, the Chengs and the Los."

The girl had returned to her customers. Kazuo stood to the side, writing something down on a piece of paper.

"Do you know her Japanese name?" I asked.

"Of course not. Why?"

"She looks like someone I met once. Does she have another brother?"

"No, just two sisters," Wen-shen replied immediately, and Yi-yang and I looked at him in surprise.

"They came to my cousin's wedding!" he said. "I haven't been stalking her any more than usual."

Yi-yang slapped him on the back. "Well, if you had been, I'd be very impressed."

"Are you sure it was her?" I asked.

"Of course," Wen-shen said. "Her, her nasty brother, and two sisters—one very dumpy and one very sour looking like this guy. Mom was weird looking, wore an old dress, must have been a hundred years old."

"And her father? Was he dressed well?"

Wen-shen gave me a look. "It was a wedding. All the men were dressed the same—"

The pharmacy door opened, and Kazuo emerged, smirking, with

his friend Li-wen. "Well, children," Kazuo said, "she's coming with me to the meet tomorrow. How do you like that?"

He strutted down the street, slapping Li-wen on the back and laughing.

I looked at the girl through the window. She was frowning as she poured powder into a paper bag and didn't look at all excited about having just arranged a date.

"I'm going to talk to her," I said.

"Forget it," Yi-yang said, grabbing my arm. "She's a gold digger. Come on. You said you had to get home."

I hesitated, looking through the window, seeing not the pharmacy but the girl on the bicycle, smiling contentedly in her brother's arms. The girl standing before me today was not Yoshiko. Yoshiko wouldn't have behaved like this, wouldn't have agreed to go out on a date with a man she didn't like, just because he was going to be a doctor.

"*Hou,*" I said. "*Kianh.*"

And we got on the motorcycle and sped away.

9

ALL NIGHT I LAY awake on my futon, listening to Jiro's snores on the futon next to mine. I twisted and turned, worrying about *Fundamentals of the English Language for Foreigners,* which was still in my bag, as the maid had been tidying up Kazuo's room until he came home.

It must have been Yoshiko. I had seen the gold shimmer in her eyes in that shaft of sunlight. But that wasn't her brother. And Wen-shen's description of her family didn't sound at all like what I remembered seeing. I went over and over the same arguments in my mind. I saw the girl's wary look at Kazuo, and Kazuo's smug face. I should have said something, should have told him I knew she didn't even like him, that I admired her less for saying yes to someone like him.

As soon as the sun rose, I got up and dressed in my track clothes. I took the first train into Taipei for my meet.

Normally I liked to arrive just after the flag-raising ceremony—I generally avoided these as much as possible—but today I had plenty of time to warm up.

"Horse! Last meet of the year! You ready?" our school coach called to me from the field as I lay my jacket down on an aisle seat in our school's section of the bleachers. "Go stretch."

The stadium gradually filled. Kazuo brushed past me, wearing a neat button-down shirt smoothed flat over his belly, and sat in the section behind mine with his classmates. The seat next to his was empty. At last, the red-and-blue flag rose against the clear blue sky, and we all stood, keeping the irony to ourselves. In an autocracy, brainwashing was just one more part of the day.

San Min Chu-i
Our aim shall be
To found a free land
World peace be our stand . . .

I had developed the habit of experimenting with my voice as a way of occupying my mind in all the flag-raising ceremonies we had endured over the years. I sang now, my voice, a clear baritone, ringing out into the spring air, and thought happily that perhaps the girl would stand Kazuo up.

The song ended and we were urged to take our seats. And at that moment, in the general bustle as people sat down and the fifty- and one-hundred-meter runners from my school scooted past me to get to the field, I saw her stepping up the stairs toward me in high heels, her eyes down, her face melancholy.

The sun shone on the sophisticated wave of her hair, and the wind blew the silky fabric of her dress, with its brown stripes making an inverted V at her waist, the fabric sliding against the soft white of her arms. As she drew closer, I noted the delicacy of her upturned nose, the gentle curve of her cheek.

"Yoshiko!" I said.

She turned her face quickly to me, her gold-flecked eyes sparkling with surprise, the early morning light gliding over the luminescent skin of her face.

I felt a jolt as her eyes met mine. "It *is* you!" I said, and I searched her face for traces of the girl I had thought about so many times—the wide eyes, the dimple in her cheek. I had found her at last.

She blinked. "Do I know you from school?"

The announcement came over the megaphone: *One-hundred-meter dash.*

"No! The war. The air raid. Remember? I saved your life! Your brother picked you up on his bicycle . . ."

It was her turn to stare at me, her eyes flickering back and forth across my face, her foot paused midstep, her hand gracefully holding the skirt of her dress. Her expression softened, and then, to my alarm, her eyes filled with tears.

At that moment, Kazuo's buttoned-down belly appeared in my peripheral vision. "Ah, I see you know my little brother."

Yoshiko hastily looked away, blinking, and nodded her head.

"He's sitting with *his* school. We'll sit with mine. They're calling your event, Saburo," Kazuo said to me. "It's time to run in circles."

Yoshiko turned and followed Kazuo up the stairs. I felt a draining sensation in my chest and arms as Kazuo, who had everything — from my mother's love, to the best chunks of meat, to my book — now took from me the one girl I had thought about all these years. He would sap me dry. The blood surged to my face and I began to shake with fury — at Kazuo for taking Yoshiko away, and at Yoshiko for allowing herself to be treated as a trophy.

But then Yoshiko turned back to look down at me. She met my gaze openly, her eyes full of sadness and confusion and longing, and, heart still pounding, I held my breath. The wind rippled her dress and blew her hair across her forehead, and still her eyes, rimmed with the remnants of her tears, looked into mine. I heard the applause of the crowd, and my coach calling my name from the field below, but I could not bear to break Yoshiko's gaze.

Then, to my despair, she turned again and climbed up the stairs after my brother.

I rushed down to the track, my legs trembling. I ran my race in a rage, hardly noticing who ran in the lanes beside me, and won. But even my win brought me no joy, for I knew that Kazuo was right. All I was good at was running in circles on the ground. He was the one with the way out.

ON MY WAY home from the meet, I was more alive than I had ever been; I felt the blood coursing through me, the muscles of my body contracting and relaxing as I walked, their movements smooth and coordinated as an animal's. I felt, as though for the first time, the warmth of the sun on my hair and the back of my neck, the coolness of the wind blowing through the woven cotton of my clothes. And yet, awakened as I was to the physical world, I was so consumed by replaying, over and over in my mind, those moments when Yoshiko had looked into my eyes, that a motorcyclist nearly ran me over in front of the Taoyuan Train Station.

But she was Kazuo's. Kazuo's, I reminded myself bitterly, as I waved to the motorcyclist, who exclaimed and shook his fist at me. Kazuo was the one with the future. And fury so overcame me that once I got home, seeing that Kazuo was in the kitchen having lunch, I boldly stepped right into his room and plunked his book onto his shelf.

"What are you doing?" He appeared in the doorway behind me.

"Putting this book back."

"I never said you could borrow it."

"You never even look at it."

"It's mine nonetheless."

He walked past me, pulled *The Earth* neatly off its shelf, and strode out of the room.

I followed him. "What are you doing with that?"

"I'm going to burn it," he said. "I know you've been looking at it. I should have done this a long time ago."

My stomach dropped. I caught his arm on its backswing and lunged for the book, but he dodged me and then jabbed me in the stomach with his elbow. I grabbed his shirt as he ran away, and it came untucked from his pants, one of its buttons rolling around on the dark floorboards. I felt like a schoolboy scuffling over a marble, but I could not let him destroy the one object I treasured.

"*Otosan!*" he called.

I heard my father's lumbering step, and I released Kazuo.

Kazuo sneered. "Try to get it from me now."

Five minutes later, *The Earth* flamed in a pit behind our house, along with some old Japanese newspapers. The smoke curled up into the sky.

Kazuo watched, arms folded, a smug smile on his face

"Why did you do that?" I said angrily. "It meant nothing to you."

"It's caused us a lot of trouble," he said. "And I don't want you thinking you can take what's mine, pretty boy." He looked at me and cocked his head, eyes narrowed. "Stay away from Li-hsiang."

"Who?" I said.

He glared at me. "The girl!" he said. "She's mine."

10

I SAT DOWN IN a chair facing Toru across his desk as he wrote something in a large notebook. He glanced at my twitching leg and then up at my face. "What's the matter?" he said.

I opened my mouth to speak, but there were so many thoughts swirling in my head that I closed my mouth again and looked at the floor.

He watched me for a moment and then resumed writing. His hair was now shot through with strands of gray, and his face looked worn and tired. He took my military-service form from me. "Let's take a look at you."

I followed him, towering now over his slight figure as he led me to the examining table. I sat, eyeing the cabinet that held the detested vitamin solution from Taikong. Toru peered into my eyes and mouth. "How is your father enjoying being mayor?" he asked.

"He complains," I said. "When he can. There are Nationalist agents crawling all over our house spying on him and telling him what to do. The security general's son is his new best friend."

"I've never seen him."

"Just like his father. Big lips, square glasses, ugly suit."

"But your father didn't run as a Nationalist."

"No."

"But I suppose all the parties are controlled by the Nationalists."

"Of course," I said. "All this 'reform' is just for show."

He stood in front of me, holding his otoscope, blinking. "Your father's not afraid?"

"No. They want to look good for the Americans now. You know, after losing the Mainland and slaughtering—"

Toru glanced toward the door and motioned for me to be quiet.

I lowered my voice. "They need American support. They wouldn't dare do anything overtly bad. It's what my father thinks, anyway."

"He must be right. He's a shrewd man, your father." He picked up my wrist and began taking my pulse. "Your heart's racing."

I felt a flush of resentment at Toru's admiration of my father. Though, of course, he was right.

"He burned the book you gave me," I said.

Toru looked up from his watch. "What?"

"Kazuo." I felt like a schoolboy, tattling on another boy. "With my father's blessing. He burned my book."

Toru looked down at his watch again for a moment and then dropped my wrist, putting his hands on his hips. He fixed his eyes on mine. "Why did he burn it?"

"Because of a girl," I said.

"You want the same girl?"

"Yes," I said. "The same girl I was trying to find when I was bitten by that snake."

"The snake? You were just a boy."

"I was."

He watched me for a moment, then walked over to the counter and absentmindedly stamped my military-service form with his signature. "Well, and now you're a young man. Your service starts next week?"

"Yes."

"And what will you do after that?"

"My uncle's lining me up a job at Taikong, doing the wiring for some new buildings they're planning. It can't take me more than a few months, and then I have no idea what I'll do. I guess that's why girls just want to marry a doctor," I said bitterly, and then I stopped, suddenly wondering why Toru was not married.

He handed me the form and walked to the counter by the sink. He replaced the lid on a canister of cotton balls, then threw a used muslin wrapper into a hamper under the sink. He opened the window shade and closed it again, and I was surprised that he would do something so purposeless. Then he turned to face me, his hands on his hips again. "Saburo," he said, "you only have one life. Fight for it."

I blinked at him in surprise. "You're the one who told me my life would be limited."

"It is," he said. "But limits can be surpassed."

"You mean . . . the girl?"

"I mean"—he waved his hand—"everything."

"Why would a girl want an electrician when she can have a doctor?"

He sighed, looking at me. "Believe in yourself. Let her be the one to decide."

THE NEXT MORNING, I bicycled downtown, my hands gripping the handlebars.

Of course, Toru was right. Had I grown up so soft? As a child I had stood up after all my bamboo whippings and gone out to play again. I had, knowing that it might expel and harm me, told Teacher Lee and my father that they were wrong. Why would I let Kazuo's threats keep me from Yoshiko? He had already burned my book. What else could he possibly do if Yoshiko chose me of her own free will? And if she chose Kazuo over me, then so be it.

I pushed through the glass door of the pharmacy. I watched Yoshiko close a cabinet and then return to the counter, neatly entering figures into a large ledger book. I admired the soft angle of her cheek and the smoothness of her neck. As I drew near, I could even see a thin gold necklace glimmering at her throat as she breathed and frowned a little, murmuring arithmetic calculations in Japanese. What had happened to that happy little girl, so full of love and trust?

"What do you need?" Her eyes were down as she snapped the book closed and put it under the counter.

I plopped a little paper bag on the counter. There were darkened spots of moisture on the sides.

Her eyes shot to the bag and then up to me. I felt a shock as her eyes met mine.

She straightened up in surprise. I drank her in, intoxicated by her proximity, by the transparent mixture of pleasure and uncertainty on her face, until she peeked down at the warm peanut *moachi* nestled in the bag.

"You said it was your favorite," I managed to say. Just as I was going to tell her there was a movie ticket inside the bag, too, her brother stood up from a low stool behind her where he had been opening cartons and glowered at me. I had not even thought of a pretext for coming to the pharmacy. Hurriedly, I turned away.

"Wait!" I heard Yoshiko say. As the door fell closed behind me, I saw her watching me, eyes wide and searching, one hand on the counter, the other clutching the *moachi* bag, her brother at her back.

I SPENT THE next two days in torment. School had ended and I walked the grounds of the family company, Taikong, with my fourth uncle so he could show me the layout of the buildings they planned.

He waved importantly through the air. He looked very much like my father, except that his face, instead of being rounded like an egg, was longer and concave in the middle, indicating, according to tradition, less good fortune. He was a powerful man, equal to my father in his position in Taikong. "Though we've expanded into other pharmaceuticals, injectable glucose still constitutes a large part of our sales . . ."

As he talked and our feet crunched across the gravel grounds of the factory, I berated myself for not being more cunning, more bold. I didn't even know whether Yoshiko had seen the ticket. Perhaps she'd eaten the *moachi* and thrown the bag away without looking. Perhaps her brother had taken the entire bag, and I would find him next to me at the movies instead. If I could just have told Yoshiko or indicated with a look or pointed, then I could be sure she had seen it. If she didn't show up at the movies, I wouldn't know whether she was rejecting me or simply hadn't known I had invited her.

On Saturday I paced in front of the cinema and was the first person to enter.

I sat in my seat, one away from the aisle, and waited. Every time I heard the door open, I turned to look.

The theater began to fill, and the air grew thick with a thousand conversations. Many times I stood to let gangly young men in short-sleeved button-down shirts shuffle past me, their dates' flouncy skirts brushing against my knees.

At two minutes to the hour, I realized she wouldn't show. She hadn't checked the bag. Her brother had taken the *moachi*. Or she had seen the ticket and thrown it away in disgust. Worse, she had thrown it away with regret.

I looked at my watch and again at the door. A single girl walked through in red high heels and a ponytail. Not her.

The lights dimmed, and the national anthem began. We stood at attention, watching the Nationalist army marching across the screen under the benevolent eye of Generalissimo Chiang Kai-shek. How many lives had he snuffed out with that paternal smile? Like the repeated sticks of a needle, the sight of that patriotic sequence made me sick to my stomach every time.

I felt a rustle at my elbow and looked to see a girl put her purse down in the seat beside me—the aisle seat. Her face was shadowed from the screen by the man in front of her. Was it her? I had heard of girls playing tricks, of taking tickets from adoring young men and giving them to their friends.

The anthem ended, and we sat. The countdown began and I turned toward the girl beside me. The light from the screen flickered across her face; her eyes, flashing golden brown, looked straight into mine. I flushed in the dark. She turned to the screen, and so did I, for the moment, only to turn back again and watch the images slide over the soft contours of her face.

The first reel was a travelogue—*Midwest Holiday.* It had a story, in which a jaded journalist followed a beautiful painter and her father through endless plains, across the Missouri River, and through the Rocky Mountains. I had seen images like this before, and mostly I watched Yoshiko. Occasionally she met my gaze, then turned back to watch the screen. Only toward the end of the reel, as the camera panned across the carved granite foreheads and noses of George Washington, Teddy Roosevelt, and Abraham Lincoln, did I sit up in wonder. Later in my life I would realize that these scenes were fleeting and distant, far less grand than the true place. But perhaps it was because of my elation at having Yoshiko here beside me at last, so close that I could hear her gasp and feel the movement of her elbow as she brought her hand to her mouth in surprise, or perhaps it was because we were finally watching an American movie in the cinema that she had spoken of as a child and that I had so often frequented hoping to see her, that I thought there could be no grander place on earth than Rapid City, South Dakota.

I turned to Yoshiko. "I should like to go there," I whispered.

She turned to me and smiled so her dimples showed.

I barely registered the film that followed. I had chosen it merely because of the time and location and waited impatiently for it to end.

Finally the lights came up, and the theater filled with the rustling of people rising and gathering their things.

I stood, leaning aside to let people by, and as I did, I noticed across the aisle the broad back of a leather jacket. The jacket twisted, and my eyes met those of Li-wen — Kazuo's friend who belonged to the Anti-Communist Youth Corps.

I quickly looked away. Yoshiko had stood, too, the top of her neatly coiffed hair reaching only as high as my shoulder, her elbows brushing into me as she buttoned an embroidered cardigan over her yellow silk dress.

"Let's go," I said.

She looked up at the urgency in my voice and saw me glance at Li-wen. He was talking to someone next to him.

Yoshiko looked back to me, her expression anxious. "Where shall we go?"

"The elementary school?"

We hurried out of the cinema, Yoshiko delicately clutching the strap of her imitation-leather purse with the first three fingers of her hand as we passed the cafés and the brightly lit night markets hawking smelly tofu and cheaply made clothing, shaved ice with red bean, and ginger ice cream.

We turned off Mingchu Road toward the school, our footsteps crunching on the gravel as we stepped between a pair of blossoming peach trees. A breeze blew, laden with the delicate fragrance of the trees, whose petals fluttered above us in the cool air. Past the trees, the sky was clear and high, and the stars showered down light from past millennia upon our heads, upon the modest little building and its schoolyard of dirt and grass.

Yoshiko stopped walking and stood in the starlight, a peach petal in her hair, looking at the school.

"This was your school, wasn't it?" I pulled up beside her, my throat constricted with emotion as I indicated the dark silhouettes of trees behind the school. "We met in those woods."

"We did," she said quietly.

I turned to her, and she looked up at me with glittering eyes. "I'm sorry," she said, "but it's a bittersweet memory for me, as my cousin and my brother are both dead."

A motorcycle roared by in the distance, its tail-end growl fading into the screeching of the cicadas, the calling of frogs at the foot of the fence, the rushing rhythm of the blood pulsing through my heart.

The shadow of her eyelashes played along her cheek as she blinked and looked away. "My cousin, Ah-hiang," she said. "You remember she fell and cut her knee?"

"I remember," I said. "She was holding the writing board over her head."

She nodded. "It was a stupid thing to do, as you said. So she fell, and she got tetanus, and I never saw her again."

"Tetanus!" I looked away at the silhouettes of the trees swaying in the darkness. I lost my bearings for a moment and had to step back.

"Your brother, too? But I saw him later, at the welcoming parade for the Nationalists . . ."

"Did you? Well, he died soon after that." She frowned. "It's a long story." She looked up at me. "What about you?"

"Me?" I had so longed to hear what happened to her that I had never even thought of talking of myself. "Well," I said, "I was bitten by a water krait and expelled from my middle school." I said the words without thinking, then quickly regretted it. It was not what a young man was supposed to say to win a girl.

"Expelled? Why?"

"Well . . ." I hesitated, but she looked curious. "I drew a picture of my teacher with a pig's nose, and unfortunately it happened to be February twenty-eighth."

To my surprise, she laughed, and her laugh rang out in a womanly way that reassured me.

"So that's why I went to junior college. I was lucky, actually. They reversed the expulsion."

"Junior college? That's pretty good. College is college."

"Well, it's not Taipei University, or"—I looked at her slyly— "medical school."

She shrugged, looking away. "It doesn't matter what school you went to. Your father didn't go to college at all and he's mayor."

"Well, that's true." Why hadn't I thought of that when he said I'd ruined my life?

She waved toward the fence. "Let's sit. My shoes are killing me."

We sat. She smoothed a lacy handkerchief onto the fence railing first to protect her skirt. She patted the railing. "This wood is from our lumberyard. I remember when they built this."

"Your family owns the lumberyard past the temple?"

"Well, now it's just my uncle's. He kicked us all out after the war. My father had no say. He's number three, like you." She glanced at me.

"How did you know I'm number three?"

"I asked around."

She looked down, and I thought she looked a little embarrassed. "Are you seeing my brother again?"

"I agreed to have dinner with him tomorrow night."

My stomach lurched, but I saw the faintest trace of a frown on her face, which reminded me of her wary look when Kazuo invited her to the meet. "I saw you at the pharmacy," I said. "Before we met at the stadium."

She looked up at me, and I told her about Yi-yang and Wen-shen and their scheme to ask her for aspirin.

She burst out laughing. "I charge all those guys a dollar," she said. "Here I have this whole long line of customers, and these boys are asking for things they don't even need."

I laughed, too, glad I hadn't gone in to gawk with Yi-yang and Wen-shen or made up a story when I had gone myself.

She smiled up at me, eyes shining in the silvery light. "So that *was* you watching in the window when your brother was there?"

"It was." I smiled, too. "I should have gone in."

"Why didn't you? Were you afraid of your brother?"

I changed the subject, telling stories about my classmates. She laughed easily and often, and so I told her more. I found myself telling her stories I'd never told anyone—about fishing with my bare hands in the countryside, and how I'd worked on my running technique at Taikong. I told her how I was teaching myself to repair radios. Everything I said seemed fascinating to her, and it was almost impossible for me to stop talking, as though I'd saved up all these things to tell her for my whole life.

"I think I could make a radio shop work," I said. "It's just a matter of building up the capital first."

She turned her head to the side for a moment, her face in shadow. "You will. I still remember that car you made in the hardware store," she said.

"It's late," I said.

"I should go."

I touched her elbow to help her off the fence, and her hand rested for a moment on my shoulder as she stepped down. A memory roused in me that I could not trace, and as she began to pull away I held her arm. She looked up at me, eyes reflecting the starlight. I could smell the perfume of her hair.

"You're meeting Kazuo for dinner?" I said.

"Yes."

I thought of Kazuo burning my book.

"Then meet me in the morning at the train station," I said. "We'll go to Taipei. Do you know the Sintori Noodle Shop?"

She laughed. "All right."

I left her by the big front windows of the pharmacy and walked home, mind racing, heart bursting, my body flushed with warmth. The cicadas screeched in the dark alleys between the buildings I passed, and the spicy moistness of the night air filled my lungs. Yoshiko, the girl I had looked for all my life. I had been a fool not to look harder. I would be an even bigger fool to stand by and let her go.

I turned south toward my parents' house, and as I walked, with the feel of her hand still on my arm, the memory came, flashing through all the curtained years of solitude and pain. She had touched me that way after the air raid. It had been my first such touch, and my last, until today.

II

WE HURTLED EAST TO Taipei, the train's whistle amplified in the metal interior of our passenger car. I breathed in the smell of burning coal sweetened by the light scent of Yoshiko's perfume.

Her head swayed gently as she looked out the window, her eyes reflecting Guanyin Mountain and the northern countryside where I had wasted three years of my childhood. With the train's rocking movements, the red wool of her jacket shoulder brushed against my upper arm. She was so slight and gentle. I wanted to claim her, make her mine, promise her a world of happiness. But what did I have to offer her? After last night's euphoria I had awoken feeling the burden of my past mistakes, of my limited life.

She looked out the window with sadness in her face.

"I leave for my military-service year tomorrow," I said.

She turned to me, her eyes illuminated with the sunlight slanting in from the window. "Tomorrow! Where will you go?"

"Kaohsiung. I'll be taking that train instead." I pointed ahead to the train approaching on the adjacent tracks.

The train whooshed past, filling our car with its roaring clickety-clack, clouding our window with steam and flecks of black coal.

Yoshiko blinked in the filtered light, shadows of the passing windows sliding across her face as she watched the train, so I could not read her expression. When the train had passed, she was silent for a moment, then absently indicated the direction the train had gone. "My mother is from Hsinchu. Actually, she's from the mountains, but she lived in Hsinchu before she got married."

"The mountains? She's an aborigine?" I said.

"No—well, she says no, but she grew up among them, and she looks so different from other people. She calls herself a hill person. She has white skin like mine, and those high cheekbones. It's possible she's part aboriginal or part Dutch or something."

"Why did she leave the mountains?"

"Her father sold her when she was twelve. They were desperately poor. He made cedar mothballs for a living and they had to haul them down the mountain to the market and all the way back up again every week. She kept complaining about it—she's a terrible complainer—and finally when she was twelve and complained one more time, her father said, 'Fine. We'll sell you.' And he sold her to a rich banker and his wife in Hsinchu."

"Then how did she end up in Taoyuan?" I asked.

The dimple on her cheek reappeared as she smiled. "Well, the vendors at the market all talked about this pretty girl and asked who her parents were, and somehow word got to my father's family."

"I see."

"A pretty good match for an adopted daughter, even with my father's name problem."

"What problem?"

"Perhaps you don't know what my surname is?"

"It's Lo, right? I asked my friend and he said—"

"That's right. And the odd thing is that my father is the only one in his family with that name. His father, brothers, cousins—everyone else is named Cheng."

"Why? Is your father adopted?"

She shook her head. "Only my grandfather knew, and he became senile before he died, so there's no way to know now. We know he's not adopted. But he's been treated the same as his brothers, so for my mother it was a very good match."

"Does she still complain?"

"Of course. But she has a better life than she would have if she'd married someone poor like her father and stayed in the mountains."

She glanced at me sideways and my heart sank.

WE GOT OFF at Taipei Main Station. On the crowded platform, I saw other men glance her way, and I was both proud to be with her and ashamed not to be worthy of her.

She walked on with a confident click of her black patent leather pumps, knowing the exact location of the Sintori Noodle Shop, as her sister, Tsun-moi, worked in a bookstore down the street. I recognized her sister's surname as one of the Hakka minority that were commonly adopted as maids.

"The sister she was supposed to replace works near here, too. My sister Leh-hwa—given away at birth, you know, to save dowry."

"Yes." I knew of poorer families in which a daughter was given away at birth. The family then adopted another girl to take her place and serve as a maid and future daughter-in-law.

"But she didn't like her family, so she ran back home when she was sixteen."

We walked a few paces before she spoke again.

"I was supposed to be given away, too, but I was sleeping. Bad omen. They took my cousin instead."

We turned down Zhongshan Road, busy with signs, banners, bicycles, and motorcycles. We crossed the street to get to Sintori Noodle Shop and passed by a radio shop along the way. I stopped for a moment, looking in the storefront window.

"I thought Hsimenting, but this is a good location, too," I said. "For a radio shop. Lots of foot traffic here."

"True," she said. "But shops are fancier in Hsimenting."

"True."

I saw the reflection of her in the window as she scratched her arm briefly. "Why not keep working at Taikong?" she said. "It's so successful."

A rickshaw whirred past behind us. I wondered which would be more important to her — my success or my happiness.

"I want to be on my own," I said.

I WALKED HER home from Taoyuan Station. In only a couple of hours she would be meeting Kazuo, and then I would leave for my military service. I'd made her laugh many times, but was that enough to counteract my lack of promise as a provider?

Chungcheng Road still bustled, even on a Saturday, and we weaved our way up the sidewalk, dodging the bartering crowd, the crates of mangoes, and the dank puddles draining into the sewer. I pulled her out of the way of a series of drips coming off a red-and-white awning, and she smiled up at me, covering her mouth delicately with her hand to hide her front teeth, which were fake and crudely outlined in gold. Her eyes followed my glance. "I'm embarrassed about my teeth," she said, with charming candor.

"Oh no," I said. "You don't need to be."

"It's because of all the treats my father brought me as a child."

"All the Japanese *moachi*," I said. "I remember."

We made our way through the throngs surrounding the Jin-fu Temple gates and onto a quiet patch of sidewalk.

"My house is just up there."

"It's near the lumberyard," I said.

She cocked her head, looking up at me. "Would you like to see the lumberyard?"

I nodded. I didn't really care about the lumberyard, but I didn't want her to go home.

We crossed the street and walked a block west. The crowds thinned, and our heels scuffed the sidewalk as we walked. We turned up a dirt lane, passing a row of small concrete shacks with corrugated iron roofs. She laughed and shook her head. "That's the first thing my mother saw when she was brought in her palanquin from Hsinchu for her wedding. She nearly told everyone to turn her around."

"What are they for?"

"Some are for storage, some are housing for the workers. Actually, my parents did live in one at first, but they soon moved into that house." She pointed down the lane at a large two-story house. "We lived on the top floor with the number one and number two families. The first floor was all filled with wood shavings." She smiled, forgetting this time to cover her mouth. "I played there with my cousin. And here, too." She pointed to boards propped up into pyramids to dry. "We used to play hide-and-seek in them, though it was dangerous."

She got a pebble in her shoe and sat down on a rock by a pile of logs, emptying out the pebble and rubbing a spot of dirt off the shoe's heel with a lacy handkerchief, as she had when she was a child.

I sat next to her, looking around at the stark landscape. "You're lucky to have so many happy memories," I said. "No rich man can buy you that."

She put the shoe back on her foot and stood, saying nothing.

She was silent all the way back to the pharmacy.

I hesitated in front of the door, despairing at having offended her. There was only an hour until she would meet Kazuo, and then I would be gone. Once again, my frankness would be my downfall.

She looked to the side, fiddling with her purse strap.

"Listen," I said. "I didn't mean——"

She turned to face me, eyes flashing. "You think I'm a gold digger, do you? You think I just want to marry a man for jewelry and fancy clothes?"

"I don't know," I said, taken aback.

She bit her lip and then motioned for me to follow her. "Let's go to the temple."

"The temple?"

I followed her back south, through the crowds. She reached Jin-fu Temple and pushed her way through the outer courtyard, where children threw wooden balls and old men sat talking between rows of flickering candles.

I leaned forward to whisper into her ear. "Watch your purse."

She nodded, clamping her purse under her arm. She led me between the warrior guards, painted in all their twisting fury on either side of the massive gate. In the inner courtyard she stopped, pointing toward the corner of the temple. "There's my mother praying to Matsu. She spends almost every day here since my brother died."

Through the clouds of incense I spotted a slight gray figure bent in prayer. In my mind, a memory stirred.

Yoshiko sat on the edge of the low stone step behind a table where an orange-robed nun sold incense and oil. Yoshiko put her feet together and inclined her knees to the side, her legs tapering gracefully to her black patent leather pumps, so white that they shone in the smoky light. I sat next to her, leaning away from the passersby holding candles, paper money, and bundles of incense, and my shoulder touched hers.

She turned to face me. "You want to know how my brother died?"

"Yes."

"Hou." She folded her arms. "My father always had all these grand plans to go off somewhere and get rich."

"I remember," I said. "You said he was going to take you to Japan and China."

"Did I?" Her eyes turned to me absently. "I trusted him then. That was before the restaurant failed, and the café, and the grocery store . . ."

"So you never went?"

"*I* didn't. But he did. He always wanted to go, and then he met a Mainlander who kept whispering in his ear and convinced him that if he could only get a boat, they could sell sugarcane to Japan and get rich quick."

"When was this?"

"Just after the war."

"But we weren't on good terms with Japan——"

"Of course. So my father and his friend spent all our money to lease a boat from the government. They sailed into Japan with the Nationalist flag flying and got arrested before they even reached Okinawa."

"They went to jail?"

"House arrest. And by the time they were released, the boat's lease had expired and they didn't dare come back to Taiwan because they were afraid of what the government would do about the expired lease. That's what he says, anyway."

"So they stayed in Japan?"

"No. They went to China. For a year."

"A year! And what about you?"

"We starved. We still had the grocery store at the time, but my mother knows nothing about business——she's illiterate. My brothers quit school to help in the store and I did the books. I was twelve, but even I knew the money was going in the wrong direction. We closed down more and more aisles of the store until we were just selling rice.

"Every week my mother would cry, 'Li-hsiang, what will we do? Your father has left us, and now we will eat only sweet potatoes all winter.' And I would get her one of the red envelopes of New Year's money that relatives had given me over the years. Then my mother would nod and say, 'Now we can eat for this week.' But then I ran out of red envelopes, except for one, which I hid in case of emergency. That's when my sisters ran away to Taipei. They couldn't take it. And that's when Kun-tai got pneumonia."

"My little brother died of pneumonia," I said.

"Oh!"

"He was just three. Go on."

She looked up at me, her eyes searching mine. "Kun-tai was so weak. He couldn't lift the sacks of rice anymore. The delivery men would dump them on the sidewalk, and all the soldiers would gather around like vultures. My other brother got tired of doing all the work, and sometimes he took off with his friends. My mother was helpless. One time there was a boy who helped her, a brave boy—"

"But your uncles with the lumberyard—" I said, "didn't they help?"

She laughed bitterly. "My number one uncle would drop by in his rickshaw and give me a little sweet treat and shake his head. My mother treated him so well, warmed up sake for him whenever he came . . . Even at twelve, I couldn't understand why he wouldn't help us.

"The police kept breaking into our house at night because of the ship. Swept through our beds with flashlights, looking for my father. One afternoon there was a knock at the door, and this strange man ran into the house, all in white, with sunglasses and a mustache. My mother and I screamed, thinking it was a policeman, but it was my father in disguise."

She laughed briefly. "He was so excited. 'I have been to Mainland China! I have brought back textile manufacturing equipment that will make us a fortune!' "

Yoshiko looked down at her purse, playing with its strap.

"But by that time, Kun-tai was already dying. I used my last red envelope to send him to a Western doctor, but there was nothing to be done."

Her voice broke. From the adjacent hall came the sound of a nun's chanting, accompanied by the piercing hollow beats of the *muyu*.

"The equipment my father brought back—it was junk. Worthless." She shifted, part of the fabric of her skirt falling onto my knee.

"So after that," she said, "I decided my fate is my own, and my life is going to be different." She turned to look me full in the face, her eyes glistening and fierce. "My family's going to survive. Memories are good," she said, "but living people are better."

I stood up, incensed. "My brother died, too, though we had plenty of money," I said. "Money is not enough for life." She looked up at me in surprise. My heart raced and I felt the heat rise to my face. "Have Kazuo if you think he will make you happier!" I said, my voice shaking. "But I'll have you know I am not your father. I would not leave you to starve. And that boy who brought in the rice for your mother — that was me."

I turned my back to her and made my way out of the temple. At the door I looked back and saw her watching me. She was standing motionless among the flickering candles, the curling ascent of incense smoke, and the people stepping up and down to the different levels of the courtyard. The gray figure of her mother rose from where she had knelt. As she turned, the shadows pooled beneath her cheekbones.

I turned away and went into the street.

12

KAOHSIUNG WAS NOT FAR enough away for me to go. The thought that I had lost Yoshiko, that Kazuo would bring her home as his bride, their bed just steps from mine, so enraged me that I barely registered the endless military exercises in which I was forced to participate. Rousing from my tortured thoughts, I found myself at various times singing the national anthem, polishing my shoes, and running in formation in a field, shouting, "We shall take back the motherland!"

At night my bunkmates laughed and teased one another and dragged me to cafés and dances. One of the other servicemen was a ballroom-dance instructor and taught us to waltz, tango, and fox-trot. In the dance halls, I held the hand of one girl or another and impressed her with my steps, which seemed decisive merely because I made the steps without taking the least notice of what my partner was doing. The breaks between dances were the most awkward. The girls I danced with wanted to talk, and even if they were very pretty, it was all I could do to keep my mind from wandering off, from wondering where Yoshiko was and whether she was with Kazuo. I had never had a chance to dance with her. Had Kazuo, holding her waist, like this? Had he touched her?

"You're not listening to me," one girl said, her perky, round face suddenly falling into a frown.

"Yes, I am," I said. "You teach . . . eh . . ."

"Kindergarten." She turned and walked away.

The next evening I pretended to have a stomachache and stayed in the barracks when my bunkmates went dancing. I reached into my bag and pulled out *Fundamentals of the English Language for Foreigners.* I had taken it from Kazuo's room when I left.

I had been through the book before, but that night and in the weeks that followed I read it with renewed intensity. I forced myself to think about conjunctions, prepositions, and auxiliary verbs—all the strange little connecting words that Mandarin Chinese did not have, or that Japanese used, but quite differently.

As I studied, I thought, Why not try the American entrance exam? The common belief was that only Taiwan University gave adequate preparation for it, but I had access to books. I could read. What did I have to lose except a little pride?

My stomach growled, unsatisfied by our wretched meals—rice with pickled cucumber, soggy yellow daikon, and fried gluten. But my hunger only spurred me on to study more, because I knew what hunger was. Hunger was home, and only by leaving for good could I truly be free of that gnawing in my belly.

I had brought other books, too. Chemistry, physics, engineering. Mostly they were American, bearing the imprint of universities I imagined to be massive, humming with brilliance and intellectual activity.

I studied, and the time, which had seemed so interminably slow, seemed now to fly. The next American entrance exam was in less than a year. In ten months, in eight, in six.

I WENT HOME for spring leave. The rain was just lightening to mist in Kaohsiung when the train pulled away. It had been raining for days, and as we passed the verdant central mountains, the rivers spilled forth, splitting into gurgling branches that infused the land below — the broad valleys and plains encompassing Taipei and Taoyuan — with the possibility of life. I imagined Yoshiko's mother as a child, bumping down the mountain in an oxcart and up along a coast she had probably never seen until that day, hoping that whatever lay ahead would be better than what she had known.

To her right, to my right, farmers toiled on the paddies that checkered the broad Chainan Plain; farmer after straw-hatted farmer, knee-deep in the water, pushing down the plow behind his water buffalo, as he and his fathers had under the Dutch, the Spanish, the Japanese, and now the Mainland Chinese.

IN AN OPPRESSED society, there are three main means of survival. There is the farmer's way, plowing on as he has for centuries, his hat shadowing his face. There is my father's method, of opportunism. And then there are those who cannot or will not accept things as they are. Like Yoshiko's mother, who came down from the mountains, and the Taoyuan magistrate, who was killed, they must either speak up or leave and seek freedom elsewhere. This last option, I was increasingly beginning to feel, would be my way.

I had never felt so sure that I would escape as I did on that bus. Though I was going home to discuss a potential job at Taikong, I had gotten all the way through my English-language textbook. I had mastered that idiosyncratic language. How many people knew the intricacies of tense or the different uses of articles as I did? I wouldn't need a job at Taikong for long. I was going to America.

At my parents' house, I pushed open the heavy oak door, and the smell of an egg fried in lard hit me full across the face. Kazuo was home from medical school.

I went into the kitchen, where Kazuo read the newspaper over his empty, egg-smeared bowl. He looked up at me, his thick lips open in surprise.

I looked around for my mother. "Where's *Kachan?*" I said.

"Getting ready to go to the market."

"I suppose she's out of eggs," I said.

"Yes." Kazuo smiled slightly.

I felt a surge of anger. "I haven't heard anything about you getting engaged, by the way."

"What? Oh, you mean that girl." He waved his hand dismissively and shook out his newspaper. "Superstitious bitch. She said our zodiac signs were incompatible." He glanced at me over the paper. "She's engaged to a friend of mine. Studies poetry at Taiwan University. Got a job lined up in his daddy's bank."

My stomach lurched.

You think I'm a gold digger, do you?

"Don't fret, my boy." Kazuo smoothed down the page of his paper. "She's not worth it. There are plenty of girls prettier than her."

I SPENT THE rest of the day lying on my futon, brooding. But by the next morning I realized that nothing had changed. I had not had Yoshiko before, I did not have her now, and I never would. It was time to get out.

I went downtown and registered for the American entrance exam.

I zoomed home on my father's motorcycle, eyes tearing in the wind, ears filled with the roaring of the engine as the buildings and marketplaces streamed behind me in a blur. As I passed Jin-fu Temple, a small boy leaped from a cart into the chaotic street after his dog. Honks and curses rose up around them and I swerved to a stop behind a rickshaw. I put my foot down and couldn't resist looking to my left at the familiar little two-story building flanked by towers.

But behind the large windows where the pharmacy's counter had been, there were now mannequins in flowered skirts and tailored suits.

I walked the motorcycle onto the sidewalk. Next to the window, red silk was draped over a chair, the folds shimmering in the light of the street. Dress forms stood around the room on tables, wearing inside-out blouses or swathes of lace, and in the back, a woman with curly, gray-streaked hair and glasses spread a bolt of fabric on the counter and sketched a line on it with chalk.

Had Yoshiko's family moved? I sat on the motorcycle, looking at the woman at the counter. Who was she? I toyed with the idea of going in to ask her what had happened to the pharmacy, but I felt foolish at the idea of entering a dress shop.

What would be the point, anyway? Bitter again, I revved the engine and started off.

"Aiiieeeeee —"

A woman screamed and jumped out of my way. I swerved and fell with the bike to the ground. As I tried to get up, a searing pain went down my leg.

"Saburo?"

I looked up. There above me was Yoshiko. She was wearing a deep red long-sleeved dress that made her skin look even whiter and more translucent than I remembered. Against the grimy striped awning overhead, the peeling wall of the building behind her, she was absurdly beautiful.

"Yoshiko!" I flushed. "What are you doing here?"

"I live here."

I stood and righted the motorcycle. Her eyes shone and she smiled as she looked up to meet my gaze, the white of her throat stretching from the rose-trimmed neckline of her dress.

I looked away, unable to bear her loveliness or the warmth in her eyes.

"What's the matter?" she said. "Aren't you glad to see me?"

"Where's the pharmacy?" I tried to be polite, but my tone came out gruff.

"Well, it failed, of course. We're just renting to this seamstress. She's very nice. I'm already good friends with her daughter."

"How could it fail?" I said. "It was always busy with all your boyfriends."

"It's my father's specialty, failing businesses." She spoke smoothly, ignoring my aggressive tone. "What about you? What are you doing here?"

I meant to explain that I was on leave, that I was preparing to meet my uncle at Taikong, but instead I blurted out, "You said no to my brother."

She searched my face. "That was months ago."

"Why?"

"I didn't like him."

"You didn't like him? Or you found someone else who'll make more money?"

She looked taken aback for a moment, and her brow wrinkled. "What do you mean?"

"You're en—" I stopped, seeing the indignation on her face, her unadorned hands. "Kazuo told me—"

"Told you what?"

"That you found someone else."

"He did?" Anger flashed across her face, and then she folded her arms, looking at me. "Well, I suppose he's right. I did."

"Who?"

She put her hands on her hips, frowning, and then laughed so her dimples showed. Her eyes flashed. "Me!"

"What do you mean?"

"I won a job at the national bank! Now I make more than my father and my brother combined."

"Oh!" I said. "*You're* working at the bank!" I looked into the street, where a jeep honked at the boy's dog, which had gotten loose again.

I felt suddenly light. "So you mean, you don't have to marry rich anymore."

"No," she said. "I didn't really want to, anyway." She glanced up at me with hurt in her eyes, and anger. "You believed him!"

"I—I'm sorry," I said.

"It's a good thing you saved me those times." She jabbed her finger toward my chest. "Otherwise I would kill you."

"You saved my life, too, you know," I said.

"What do you mean?"

"You told me to run," I said. "When the plane came at us."

"You mean you wouldn't have?"

"I don't know," I said.

Her eyes searched mine, scanning my face, back and forth, and then she looked down, the back of her neck flushing pink. Her eyelashes quivered over her cheek, and her rose-trimmed collar rose and fell against her collarbone as she breathed. Inside me, any anger or shame at being duped by Kazuo drained away, subsumed in a tide of warmth.

"Well, that's too bad," I said.

She looked up, wide eyed. "What do you mean?"

I laughed. "Too bad you don't need to marry rich. Because I'm going to be a rich American."

She laughed, too. "Oh yes? How?"

"I'm taking the exam in the fall."

"Hm." She looked thoughtful. "Don't tell my mother. She didn't even want me to date anyone from Taipei."

I laughed. "You don't really think I'll pass, do you? The pass rate is one in five thousand."

"Of course you will. Only, I'm sad about the radio shop."

"That's still over ninety-nine percent probable."

"You don't pass an exam by chance."

"I didn't even go to a real college."

"You have books," she said. "The books are the same."

I laughed to hear her speak my own thoughts. "Just don't throw away your broken radios."

"I'll hang on to one, just in case."

I took her hand, utterly surprising in its softness, as though she lacked the rough exterior everyone else had. My heart pumped, and she smiled up at me, her face open and radiant. It was like looking upon the sun.

THOUGH THEY GRUMBLED about the speed of our court-ship and impropriety of the third son marrying first, my parents had no good reason to prevent our engagement. For our part, we pushed to get married as soon as possible. Once we had made up our minds, every day that stood between us and our wedding night was excruciating. Plans began for the engagement ceremony, the wedding, and the construction of our new living quarters, which would expand our house in the traditional style to form a corner between my parents' and Kazuo's rooms. I saw from the foreman's sketch that our marriage bed would be separated from Kazuo's room by only a small sitting room.

I felt both elation and terrible confusion. How could I be think-ing about taking the American entrance exam when I was marrying Yoshiko? The Asian quota for American visas was completely inflex-ible, and students were not allowed to bring their wives. Yoshiko's mother was furious with me, only calming down when I reassured her that no one from the county had ever passed.

"And if I do go," I said, "it will be for only a year."

The old woman narrowed her eyes. "A lot can happen in one year."

"STOP WORRYING ABOUT it!" Yoshiko swatted at me with her purse.

She was standing in a pair of pink shoes, each trimmed with a tiny rhinestone bow. She walked back and forth in front of the mir-ror in the shoe store. "There. What do you think?"

"Pretty," I said, though the pairs she had tossed aside looked fine to me, too.

"Now," she said, "no more brooding, or I'm not going through with the engagement."

I considered for a moment. "How about if I take the exam after a year? It's too busy now, and I missed weeks of studying and I'll never pass it now——"

"Take it," she said. "Next year it will be even harder."

"But I promised never to leave you the way your father did."

She whirled around on her heels, the white skirt of her dress swishing around her calves, and put her hands on her hips. "Take it," she said. "I'm not a child anymore. I can take care of myself." She turned back to the mirror. "You already saved my life before. I know I can trust you."

"I thought you liked the idea of a radio shop," I said, feeling stung. "Would it make you so much happier if I had an American degree?"

"I will be happy when you are happy," she said, tossing the shoes into their box, where they fell with two dull thuds. "Will you be happy with a radio shop?"

THE NEXT TIME I saw the pink shoes, they were peeping out beneath the hem of Yoshiko's matching taffeta dress as she sat on a stool in the middle of her parents' immaculate living room. Her hair gleamed in the lamplight, and her eyes darted about, taking in my father as he sank into her father's armchair and gesticulated, making sophisticated proclamations about the utility industry's current inability to keep pace with modern development. He crossed his legs, dangling a silk slipper from his toes above the gleaming floorboards. He had only slightly wrinkled his nose at having to walk through the dressmaker's shop to climb the stairs to the house. He was, after all, an elected representative of the working class and could not afford to show disdain for those who lived above their shops and were illiterate.

Yoshiko's father, Swe-mu, sat on the couch with an easy smile, his eyes wide and sparkling like Yoshiko's, crinkled at the sides. Far from exhibiting the lowliness of his status in my father's view, he was trim and dapper as always, his hair neatly smoothed into place. The hand he extended bore a gold watch on its wrist, and in his breast pocket a silk paisley handkerchief brought out the deep burgundy of his tie. He looked incongruously slick next to his wife, who bowed before my father with a tray of tea, her face angular, her gray hair pulled back in a knot, her equally gray dress of uncertain vintage. She glanced at me suspiciously.

My father claimed center stage even at my own engagement. I stood uncertainly behind the couch, resting my hand on its polished rosewood frame, which I suddenly realized was far finer and more beautiful than any piece of furniture in my parents' house. Yoshiko's parents, for all their troubles, had many things my parents did not: a lifetime of working in the lumber business, good taste, and a willingness to part with their money.

"Pretty," my mother acknowledged, looking, as we all did, at Yoshiko on her little perch as though at a parrot in its cage at the zoo.

In American movies I had seen rapturously romantic scenes, rings accepted in torrents of tears followed by passionate kisses and fade-outs. This was not like that. I felt instead like a guest who did not deserve to enjoy the party or even to have been invited. I was not worthy of this beautiful, doll-like creature sitting on a stool. I had tricked her somehow into believing that I was worth something. Because I had saved her life when I was eight and taken her mother's rice sacks out from under the nose of Nationalist soldiers, she fancied me her hero. And the only way I could prove myself would be to leave her for the other side of the world.

I watched helplessly as my mother untied a silk pouch she had retrieved from her purse and took out a ring—ornate, braided twenty-four-carat gold, set with a ruby of deep pink, large as a pecan. She closed her fist over it, hoisted herself up from the couch, and shuffled over to Yoshiko.

"Your hand," she said.

Yoshiko delicately extended her hand. My mother pushed the ring onto Yoshiko's finger and then sank back wheezing on the couch next to me.

Everyone clapped and took pictures. Yoshiko beamed, showing off the huge ring on her finger. I smiled back at her but felt hollow, knowing I would never be able to buy her anything like that ring again.

My mother then took out another jewelry pouch and presented Yoshiko with two gold necklaces.

Yoshiko's mother, Chiu-yeh, whispered to Swe-mu, "It's shameful they would not agree to bring more. It's nothing to them and we need the money—"

"*Ah-ah*," Swe-mu whispered back, glancing at me over his shoulder. "I'm not selling my daughter."

WE WERE FINALLY allowed to sit next to each other when it came time to eat.

"I hear," Swe-mu said, his expression charming and deferential, "that you will win the election to the People's Political Council by a landslide."

"Ah." My father wiped his face with the corner of his napkin. "Just among family, I'll say that our campaign has been going quite well."

Yoshiko's aunts and uncles exclaimed, eyes bright with admiration for such fame and power, "The People's Political Council!"

Swe-mu smiled. "And will you continue to represent the Young China Party?"

My father said nothing but put a slice of abalone in his mouth and chewed. He requested some more tea and washed down the abalone with it.

"Delicious, delicious," he said absently.

Swe-mu smiled again and nodded his dapper head. "I'm so sorry . . . I had heard rumors that—"

"It's true," my father said. He cleared his throat and took another slurp of tea.

"I mean the rumors that——"

"It's true," my father said again. "I have joined the Nationalists." He set his teacup down and stared straight ahead.

There was a momentary silence. I glanced at Yoshiko, who looked anxiously at her father. I had heard this issue discussed at home. My father was indeed a man of expedience, but in this case he had had no choice. The Nationalists would not tolerate someone of such popularity maintaining an opposing party affiliation, even if the supposed opposing party had actually been set up and was supported behind the scenes by the Nationalists. But this was not an issue that could be explained at an engagement party.

Swe-mu was looking down at his plate. He laughed lightly. I remembered what Yoshiko had said about her father, that he had refused to assume a Japanese name to get better rations. That he had abandoned his family for a year rather than be jailed by the Nationalist government. He was a man who would preserve his own value system at the expense of his family, and I hoped our wedding would not be the next casualty of his pride.

"The Nationalists!" Swe-mu said. "Well, I never thought my daughter would be marrying a——"

"Aren't you getting land, Mr. Lo?" my father said suddenly.

Swe-mu looked up, blinking. "Land?"

"I seem to recall the former magistrate told me, before he was killed. Land, next to the lumberyard. Isn't it yours?"

Swe-mu smiled and shook his head. "I'm afraid that's my brother's property."

"Perhaps so," my father said. He was looking off into the distance as though completely absorbed by the topic, but I knew that he, the savvy politician, had thought of it just in time, as a distraction. "I don't know why I remembered him saying it had some connection to you and your name. Why else would your name be——"

"Well, that land used to belong to all of us . . ."

"I know a lawyer," my father said. "Perhaps he'll look into the matter."

Swe-mu recovered himself and laughed. "I assure you there's nothing to look into." He scratched his head. "I'm sure my family would have told me if we had land coming to us. I assure you that if there are any sudden changes in my finances, I shall let you—"

My father coughed to cut short this embarrassingly forthright statement.

"A month is too short to have a wedding dress made," my mother said, turning her head toward Yoshiko. "You can have mine. I was your size, before all the children."

"*Hou!*" Yoshiko smiled.

My mother glanced at Yoshiko, and her expression softened. "Take your time before you get pregnant," she said. "Spend some time being happy."

The cold platter reached me at last, and I bit into a piece of duck, chewing busily in the uneasy silence that followed. Marriage had seemed the most natural thing in the world, until today.

13

"Okay, Saburo. Where is it?"

"*Sa-huai?*"

"The dress!"

"What dress?"

"Your mother's dress! Don't you remember?"

I stopped in my tracks. It was the evening before our wedding and we were on Chungcheng Road in front of a clock shop whose owner was pulling down its corrugated iron front for the night.

Yoshiko stared at me. "She promised me, remember?"

"Yes . . ." I remembered. I also remembered my mother's fury in the intervening weeks when she discovered that Yoshiko would not be accompanied by any dowry to speak of, other than her clothes.

I looked at Yoshiko helplessly as hurt, disappointment, and panic played over her delicate features. One by one, the shop owners around us pulled down their metal doors and turned their keys in the locks.

"Oh, I knew I shouldn't have relied on her! It's just that my parents asked her about it and she reassured them . . . I can wear one of my reception dresses," she said, biting her lip. "I have a cheongsam. It's burgundy brocade, with silver, very pretty . . ."

I was failing her already. My parents would ruin her life before she even stepped in the door.

But suddenly, Yoshiko leaned in toward me, eyes shining. "I have an idea!"

AND THEN MAGICALLY, in the morning, she was my bride. To an explosion of firecrackers she stepped out of her house by my side, regal as a queen, her head adorned with a white tiara and glittering topaz earrings. Her lips were deep red, her cheeks lightly rouged. Her dress was a suffusion of white gauziness, in the Western fashion, with a round neck and little sleeves, draped with a lace shawl that was fastened over her bodice with a pearl brooch. The skirt was full and trimmed with real red roses.

Yoshiko's mother had served her a ceremonial meal — her last, in accordance with tradition, as a member of their family. We pulled away in our hired car toward my parents' house. Behind us trailed four more cars displaying her clothes and jewelry — a very modest dowry.

Yoshiko dabbed very carefully at her eyes and smiled at me.

I touched her gauzy shawl in amazement. "Where did you get this?"

She laughed. "The seamstress's daughter. We found a rental dress and she sewed all night."

"You can do anything, can't you?"

"Of course. And so can you."

WE FOLLOWED MY father's massive form across my parents' great room to the Tong family altar. Yoshiko's eyes, while dutifully downcast, traveled across the dull floorboards from the dusty windowsill to the patched ottoman by my father's chair. I had not realized before seeing my bride here that our house could have been cared for any other way than it always had. Now, seeing Yoshiko arrange her skirt and kneel doubtfully on the floor, I saw that the cursory efforts of my exhausted mother and her overworked maid could not match the pride of place and home that made Yoshiko's house shine. Our floor was darkened and dull; the brass fixtures on our lamp were tarnished; the chest of drawers on which the family altar rested was chipped and scratched through its veneer. As Yoshiko knelt, I caught a glimpse of her shoes—incongruously sparkly and deep pink. Amused, I tried to catch her eye, but she was somberly placing a stick of burning incense between her palms and bowing her head before the large scroll behind the incense pot, where my father pointed out our family tree, illustrated with the faces of kings, princes, and princesses. I did the same, breathing in the scents of the incense smoke and the large purple orchid pinned to my lapel.

We squeezed past my mother's piles of old shoes and newspapers in the hallway on the way to the dining room for our welcome meal. Yoshiko clutched at her shawl to keep it from being marred by the dust and ink.

My family name promised riches and aristocracy, yet how much poorer in some ways was our home life, compared to the one she knew.

At our reception I watched her, glamorous as a movie star in the shimmering reception gowns her friend had sewn for her over the past few weeks. She smiled graciously, circulating through the banquet hall with a tray of tea, serving all my father's relatives, his business associates, his political connections, key local members of the Nationalist Party. In return, they placed red envelopes of money onto her tray. Each time she came out with a new tray, she wore a new dress and was rewarded with new red envelopes.

I heard my father, Taoyuan's newest and most popular representative to the People's Political Council, lecturing at the next table, where Kazuo sat with a sour expression on his face.

"There are hierarchies, overlapping hierarchies," my father said, clearing his throat. "Within the family, within the community, within the government infrastructure, it is like a series of grids. You must learn these grids and work them well in order to use them as so many ladders. If you try to escape these grids, you will fall."

Yoshiko walked up behind my chair, and I stood up to meet her. She was wearing her brocade cheongsam, embroidered with silver, and she smiled up at me, her skin pale against the burgundy. I took her tea tray for a moment to give her a rest, my fingers brushing the soft skin of her arm. Her dress hugged her body, accentuating her curves, and I wanted the reception to be over, to feel that soft body under the stiff brocade.

She looked into my eyes and laughed.

The table behind her — my friends from junior college — began chanting together.

Yoshiko glanced over curiously. "What are they saying?"

The chant rose. "Give me back my one dollar! Give me back my one dollar!"

I laughed and waved to the table.

"Is that a drinking song?" Yoshiko asked.

I shook my head. "They used to visit you in the pharmacy."

She laughed so hard she had to wipe her eyes.

WE LEFT THE next morning for our honeymoon, staying in a Japanese-style hotel overlooking the startling aqua blue of Sun Moon Lake.

We made love on our futon, our ardor interrupted only occasionally by the unheralded whoosh of the shoji screens as the hotel maid, clad in a kimono and bearing a tray of tea, entered the room and provoked a flurry of flying bedclothes.

"*Hai!* Why don't they knock?" Yoshiko giggled from under her sheet as the maid left.

At night we lay on the bare tatami, our bodies damp with exertion, our laughter ringing out into the darkness and melting into the screeching of the frogs in the marsh grass.

We traveled, huddling together on the summit of Alishan to watch the sun rise over the countryside where Yoshiko's mother had spent her childhood.

And then, too quickly, we returned, and the first piece of mail that Yoshiko received at our house was a note from her boss at the bank notifying her that she had been fired.

"What! Just because I got married?" She sat down with the letter on our new rosewood bed and almost fell off the edge.

"Didn't he warn you?"

"Well, he did say something about how none of the women there are married, but I never thought . . ."

"He wants that long line of young men."

"That's absurd. They never deposited more than a few dollars. I passed the exam to keep the books, anyway. I wasn't supposed to be just a teller."

I sighed. "You should have married a doctor after all."

She looked up at me fiercely. "I didn't want a doctor, I wanted you. Thank goodness you have that job at Taikong or we'll never get out of this house."

I said nothing but stood up and opened the new rosewood armoire that her father's carpenters had built to match the bed. They had built it unusually tall, for my height, and it was beautifully, solidly made, the hinges turning smoothly, the finish polished and mirrorlike, easily the finest piece of furniture in my parents' house.

"How much do you earn, by the way?" she said.

I opened and closed the drawers, feeling the wheels gliding on their runners, smelling the rosewood. It smelled like Yoshiko's parents' house.

"Saburo, how much——"

I sat down on the bed next to her. "Seven hundred NT," I said.

"A month?"

I gave a short laugh. "A year."

"A year?" Yoshiko looked up at me for a moment, her mouth open, her face flushed with heat down to the collar of her yellow silk shirtdress. "I made ten times that much at the bank!"

She got up and paced around the room. Then she rummaged in my bag and took out *Fundamentals of the English Language for Foreigners.*

"Here." She dropped it into my lap, then took out the chemistry and physics books and a couple of issues of *Life* magazine that I had borrowed from the United States Information Service office to read on the train to Sun Moon Lake.

"What do you expect me to do after I go to America?"

She shrugged. "Teach at Taiwan University. Be a scientist."

"It won't make me rich."

"We'll be able to live on our own."

"You just got here. Maybe you'll like it."

She gave me a look.

"What?" I said.

"I've seen how they treat you."

"You have?" I thought back on the brief times we had spent with my family. The engagement, the wedding, the reception, our first twenty-four hours as husband and wife. It hadn't seemed remarkable to me. "What did you see?"

"They ignore you. They're always talking about Kazuo. Calling you stupid all the time—"

"Not all the time—"

"I remember what you said, you know," she said, folding her arms, "the day of the air raid."

"What? What did I say?"

"You said no one cared whether you came home."

I went to open the window as I had so many times as a child, looking outside for my refuge, my escape. The wind was blowing, rustling the grass and the leaves of the bamboo trees outside. My mother had not beaten me for many years, but even now, a bamboo tree was not all beautiful to me. I remembered how a bamboo branch felt across my chest, across my flank, how it could scratch you raw, give you bruises.

She stood up behind me. "No one will care if you leave, either."

"No one from Taoyuan County has ever passed that exam," I said, one more time. "Even the ones who went to Taiwan University."

"So study," she said.

I STUDIED. THROUGH the cracks in the walls, the wind swept onto my desk, ruffling the dimly lit pages of my book. The exam that had loomed in my imagination since I was a child had been developed to winnow out 99.98 percent of test takers so as not to exceed the quota imposed on Taiwan by the United States. As a result, the test's scope was paralyzingly huge. I charted my subjects out by the day. I reviewed differential calculus one day, Western history through the Renaissance the next. I wrote out chemical equations and reread my chapter on quantum mechanics. I quizzed myself on past participles and, when I became bored with my textbooks, read *Modern Radio* articles on new capacitor models and transistors, which I had never seen. I borrowed *Time* and *Life* magazine issues from the United States Information Service office so I could read about real-life cowboys on cattle ranches, about Fred Astaire and Ginger Rogers, about many other famous actors I had seen in the movies, and about something called the International Geophysical Year,

> which will become the greatest and most ambitious example of cooperation in the scientific community the world will ever see. Starting July 31, 1957, leading scientists around the world, free and Communist alike, will coordinate their efforts to track signals transmitted from satellites orbiting the earth!
>
> There's just one small problem: getting the satellites into space. But that's just a matter of time, according to . . .

As I worked, Yoshiko slept on the futon, turned away from my tiny lamp, the light gently glancing off her hair and the soft contour of her cheek. I sat back, watching her rhythmic breathing. Even in her sleep, she held her hand over her belly, for we had learned, much to our surprise, that she had become pregnant on our honeymoon.

"No wonder you've been so hungry," I had said.

She'd frowned. "Yes, and because there's not enough food . . ."

I didn't tell her that we had actually been getting more than the usual rations of food from my mother. My mother seemed quite enamored of Yoshiko and had been taking her aside so that they could do chores together or so my mother could complain about her ailments and her lot in life.

Through the days, I worried—about failing, and about passing. There was the issue of leaving my new wife and baby. There was also a practical, monetary hurdle. Before I would even be allowed to leave the country, I would have to demonstrate to the government that I had enough cash to survive a year in America. Namely, twenty-five-hundred American dollars, or a hundred thousand NT.

"Where am I going to come up with that!" I said, looking up at the ceiling in the dark.

Yoshiko laid her hand on my chest. Moonlight shone on her cheek, the closed lids of her eyes, as her head turned drowsily toward me on her pillow. "Go to sleep," she said. "You have the richest family in Taoyuan."

But my stomach growled, long done digesting my meager dinner, and I knew never to assume I would get what I needed from my family.

14

Through the train's window I watched: the sky lightening behind a double-peaked mountain on Taiwan's northeastern coast; light shooting down the mountain's terraced shoulder and onto the sugarcane fields below. The sun rose, its rays stretching across the plains, and the rice paddies glinted as we curved into the explosive manmade growth of Taipei City.

I jumped off the train and rushed through the streets. They were framed densely with store signs on either side, characters stacked one on top of the other, three stories high. Above my head, Nationalist flags flapped from wires extending from one side of the street to the other. On the sidewalk, street carts steamed with sweet soybean soup and *you tiao*.

It was an hour before the exam, and already a crowd of jittery young men had gathered on the steps of the civic auditorium. I glanced up at the massive building. The Settlement Committee, including my father's friend the Taoyuan magistrate, had met here after the February 28 Incident to draw up and present their demands for democratic reform to Governor Chen Yi.

My stomach churned with nervous energy as I snaked my way up through the crowd, climbing two stairs at a time.

"Hey! Our whole study group! All going to MIT, right?"

Toward the top of the stairs, a plump young man in a leather jacket smiled at his circle of buddies and raised his hand. It was Kazuo's friend Li-wen, from the Anti-Communist Youth Corps. "I'll go to California Tech," he was saying. "I like the warm weather."

His friends laughed.

I turned away. No one in my family, including Kazuo, knew I was taking this exam. The last thing I wanted was for Kazuo to find out and ridicule me if I failed. I tried to move away through the thick crowd. It was growing by the minute and I could smell the different brands of soap and pomade. I crouched down and angled myself behind a chubby young man with a pompadour.

Li-wen's jacket squeaked as he tapped his forehead. "I've calculated it. They pass about one in five thousand, and there are two thousand at this site, so that means half a person here will make it to America. The question is, will it be the top half or the bottom half?" He punched the bony arm of the student next to him. "Or Professor here. He's about half a person!"

The group erupted in laughter, jostling their friend, the Professor, who smiled quietly and pushed his heavy glasses up his nose. The pompadour shifted slightly, opening a direct line of sight between me and Li-wen.

Our eyes met for a split second before I hastily turned away. "Eh!" Li-wen said, and he pointed to me. "Eh! Aren't you Kazuo's little brother?" Li-wen chuckled. "The one who went to Taipei Provincial Tech? I can't wait to tell Kazuo you were here! *He* hasn't even dared take the exam, and here *you* are."

I felt my cheeks grow hot.

Li-wen laughed. "Do yourself a favor, little brother. Go home to your sexy wife." He turned to his group. "This boy improves our statistics. We forget who our competition is.

"Eh," he called again to me. "I'm curious. How are the English courses at Taipei Provincial Tech?"

I heard someone snicker. I watched Li-wen's face, pudgy with rice cakes and pork dumplings. This was not the face of a man who would succeed in the New World. Above the sneering mouth, the eyes were small, dim, and afraid.

I stood up straight and pushed forward to face him. Toru's shots had made me a head taller than the other men. The laughter trailed off, and I spoke in English. "If I were to go to America, I would not have to worry about people like you standing in my way," I said.

The group looked among themselves for a moment. One of them nudged the Professor, but he shook his head.

Li-wen tilted his head to the side and raised his eyebrows. "Nice use of the subjunctive, little brother," he said. "My friends, this boy has been rehearsing that line for a week."

The group laughed again, and I turned away, heart charging.

A hand touched my arm and spoke quietly. "Good luck, little brother."

But I did not look back to see who wished me well. The doors to the building were opening, and I pressed up the stairs to go through them.

You wasted your life!

I found my chair and sat tall — tall as a cowboy poised atop his horse on the prairie, strong as George Washington's gaze carved in South Dakotan granite.

Stupid boy!

I shook my head and breathed deeply, blocking out the persistent needling of my self-doubt, the rustling pages around me, the click-clacking of hundreds of shoes sticking to and releasing from the tacky floorboards. I would work slowly and carefully, pacing myself as I would for a long-distance race. Steady as the wind over the Taiwan Strait. Rhythmic as Fred Astaire in a fox-trot.

I forced the cacophonous images from my mind. My pencil made strong strokes on the paper. I calculated the area under a curve, the speed of a falling rocket as it entered the atmosphere. My heart flip-flopped as I saw that the reading passages were not textbook

English but culled from *Life* magazine and the *New York Times*. Thank goodness I had gone through the trouble of parsing all those sentences about Elvis Presley's gyrating hips and Spencer Tracy's Catholic upbringing. Two rows down from me, the Professor scratched his ear and pushed his glasses up his nose with a quick, repetitive movement.

In the same hall where a plea for democratic representation had ended in massacre, my pencil moved, deliberate and unstoppable as a locomotive, across the paper.

I can go.

I will go.

I'll go to the United States of America.

A FEW WEEKS later, I tried to stop Yoshiko from jumping up and down on the train platform.

"The baby! Remember the baby!" I said. And I hugged her tight. Her body shook against mine, and I didn't know whether she was crying or laughing.

A little crowd had gathered. There was a banner overhead, white with black lettering.

"Has someone been executed?" I heard someone ask.

"No, it's the examination results, rice-for-brains."

I reread the banner. It said TAO-YUAN COUNTY: TONG CHIA-LIN.

Yoshiko laughed against my neck. "See! I knew you could do it!"

I clutched her tightly, feeling her breaths, quick and shallow, and her belly, swollen with new life's promise. For the first time ever, the world felt open to me, boundless. I could open my arms and jump into the sky. I could fly across the Pacific Ocean with one beat of my wings, the sun warming my back.

"I'm going to America," I said, amazed.

Yoshiko laughed, and I touched the fragrant softness of her hair. And then, in spite of winning the two things that I had longed for all my life—Yoshiko and my ticket to America—I despaired. In proving myself to Yoshiko, I was also abandoning her. I closed my eyes, clutching her hair, her body, still slight despite her pregnancy. How could I leave? How could I?

To my surprise, she pulled out of my grasp. She looked up at me, her eyes sparkling and ferocious.

"What is it?" I said.

"Do well in America," she said. "And bring me over, too."

I stared at her. "What about your family?"

"They'll survive. You are my family now," she said, her eyes filling with tears.

"We'll talk about it. I have plans. I could teach at the university —"

"Bring me over," she said. "Please. I've thought about it. I've seen how your family treats you. We'll have a better life. We'll be free —" She glanced around at the train platform, at the white banner flapping in the wind.

And though I had no idea how I would do it, I agreed.

"I will," I said. "I promise."

Part 2

1957–1962

15

I POSED ON THE tarmac with Yoshiko, who held our eight-week-old son, Kai-ming. Together with my parents, my brothers and sisters, and several of my uncles, we stood silently in the light wind while the photographer shouted directions over the plane's roaring behind us. My family's pride in my passage to America — their announcements to friends, their hiring of Taoyuan's best, or at least most expensive, photographer — had surprised me. Even Kazuo, to my great shock, had congratulated me while I was packing. He had done so while handing me a very large, heavy package, which I had initially thought was a gift for me.

"What's this?" I looked down at the address scrawled on the paper. University of Michigan, Ann Arbor. I had been rejected from that school, and I was confused for a moment, thinking Kazuo had forgotten where I was actually going.

"Oh, it's for a friend of mine. Would you mind hand-delivering it?"

"It's so heavy," I said. "Couldn't you send it?"

"It's not as special if you send it. And it might break. Eh," he said, slapping me on the back. "I guess that little Japanese *sensei* was right about you, little brother. You're on your way to the land paved with gold. You'll be the richest man in Taoyuan."

Kazuo's package was stuffed into one of my two suitcases, making the suitcase vastly overweight and costing me a tremendous amount in fines. My noting that it would have cost less to send the package by freight released a torrent of nasty words from my mother. *Your big brother asks you to do something, and all you do is complain . . .*

"One more!" the photographer called out.

Kai-ming struggled against his swaddling blankets and cried, pressing his fists against Yoshiko's breast. He was a sickly child, and Yoshiko had been unable to nurse him. In the bend of his tiny elbow lay a crumpled bandage from Toru's latest infusion. What worked for the father would work for the son. I needed to believe it.

The plane's engine started up with a grinding roar, and Kai-ming startled, turning his head to look beyond his mother's arms. Despite his ill health he was an unusually alert child, his eyes focusing almost from birth. Perhaps it would have been better if he were less aware. I touched his tiny hand and he looked at me with what seemed to be reproach. And then he snorted several times and erupted in cries.

"Don't worry," Yoshiko said. "You'll see your papa again soon."

Yoshiko deftly adjusted his blanket and rocked him, humming. She was a natural mother, and next to her I felt clumsy and incompetent. She and Kai-ming were already bonded in a way I could not even comprehend. I wondered sometimes whether Yoshiko had purposely made me superfluous to my son's needs. Yet when the plane's roaring increased, the unnaturalness of leaving my infant son hit me full force. I touched the side of his face, so soft and tender. I wouldn't touch him again for a year.

"You'd better go," Yoshiko said. The delicate skin around her eyes was drawn with sadness and fatigue. Kai-ming had been up all night with diarrhea. We had had to take him to Toru's clinic before dawn. I felt in my pocket for the piece of paper Toru had given me, the address of his old math teacher, who now lived in Chicago as a gardener.

"I can't leave you," I said.

"Of course you can. We'll be fine."

"He's sick. I'm supposed to take care of him. I'm supposed to take care of you. I——" I promised, I was going to say as I had before, not to be like your father, not to abandon my son to his deathbed. But she already knew what I was going to say and she interrupted.

"We have Toru. Don't worry."

"I'm not ready."

"Of course you are. You're better prepared than anyone has ever been. Who else would go practice English with all those American nuns and missionaries?"

"But I mean, he's crying——"

"He's always crying." She bounced him back and forth, her polka-dot dress swaying. Even with a newborn she wore heels and silk. "Get on the plane. You worked your whole life for this." She bit her lip, tears welling in her eyes. "You take care of us by getting on that plane."

I could hardly bear to see her like this—Yoshiko, so fiercely independent, reduced to relying on me. She had hoped to find another job for the fall, but my mother would not hear of it. My mother claimed she would lose face if it appeared that her daughter-in-law needed to work, but I noticed my mother's face softening when she and Yoshiko chatted at home, and I knew she also wanted my wife at home for company.

Be worthy of this girl, I thought to myself.

I got the money for you from my family, my father had said, *but it comes with certain obligations.*

"I only have enough money for a year," I said. "I can't even get a degree."

Her eyes glinted in the sun. "You will," she whispered.

I tickled Kai-ming's cheek, feeling desperate; Yoshiko had such ready faith in me. A simple smile from my son would do me good. He had just started smiling two weeks ago, which amazed everyone, considering how ill he was. But here, during our parting moment, his lips were resolutely turned down. "Kai-ming," I said helplessly, "grow strong."

The plane's propellers started to turn.

"*Lai*," Yoshiko said, drawing near. *Come.*

I put my arms around her and Kai-ming. She tucked her head under my chin, and I felt her tears falling on my throat.

THE PROPELLERS QUICKENED. I sat back, feeling the roaring beat against my back and legs—my arms, too, as I clutched the armrests. Out on the tarmac, the tiny figures of my family clustered loosely behind a white line painted on the concrete, their faces turned up toward the plane. In front, my father, feet planted far apart. My mother, hands on her hips. Beside them, Yoshiko swayed back and forth, holding the baby close against her neck, her hand over his ear. I waved, and she nodded, bouncing Kai-ming up and down.

The roaring of the engines grew so loud that the entire cabin shook, joints creaking, compartments rattling. The entire plane might burst apart—it would be the best possible end for me, to die a hero rather than the charlatan I felt certain I would prove myself to be. But then the plane lurched forward, roaring, and we passed the hangar and a cluster of idle fighter planes. And then we hurtled down the runway, flanked with grassy fields. A farmer, holding his water buffalo by the collar, looked up past the brim of his conical hat as we passed. I felt a sense of being suddenly, heavily dropped. And we were aloft. With a groan, the landing gear folded up into the plane's belly.

The plane banked over the countryside. Still pinned back against my seat, I peered out as the waving fields of grass—the fields that had represented the boundaries of my boyhood world—transformed into verdant Cartesian grids dotted with houses, with factories, with villages and ponds. Beyond, the central mountains stretched through the clouds, their emerald shoulders cloaked in mist.

"Beautiful island!" the Portuguese had exclaimed, seeing Taiwan for the first time. *Ilha Formosa!* And now I saw why.

Live in the isle of flowers that flatter
For the land is decked with colors of seven . . .

We continued our ascent. I saw the sparkling aqua blue of Sun Moon Lake nestled among languid green hills, the surface of the water rippling in the wake of a rowboat just by the shore where Yoshiko and I had honeymooned. The boat passed through the shadow of a cirrus cloud and then we rose still higher. The air thickened with clouds, and the only land I had ever known vanished from my sight.

I took a deep breath, smelling antiseptic, coffee, pomade. The clouds streaked my window with condensation. All around me on the plane, white men turned their long noses toward the window or spoke with one another over the beating of the propellers in their low, murmuring voices.

I was flying. I felt such despair at leaving Yoshiko and Kai-ming, the lovely family I had wanted all my life. And yet, as the propellers pounded, leaving Taiwan far behind us, and the earth itself became veiled beneath the layers of vapor outside my window, I felt the molecules of the air loosen around me and felt gravity lose its relentless grip. I was no longer that boy in secondhand clothes, Kazuo's detested little brother, dragging his feet home while he gazed up at the sky. I was in that sky, cutting my own path through the rippling patterns of clouds, through the layers of stratified gases, to a land where no one knew me.

In the vastness of the sky, I felt also my smallness. I was simply a man, dressed in a Japanese broadcloth shirt and a finely tailored wool suit that Yoshiko had insisted on having made so I would look just like the other men, all white, who sat in rows all around me. A man like any other. And when the plane landed, no one would know my name, nor that of my father, my brother, or even my hometown. From now on, all that mattered was the man I was now and the man I planned to be.

I looked into the clear blue over the clouds, a blue bounded only by the emptiness of space.

Perhaps this was how Yoshiko's father had felt, setting off on his borrowed ship for Japan, leaving behind 1947 and the insatiable demands of family life, which I had only begun to get a taste of. Of course he had sailed on to China, for why, having gazed at the watery, glimmering horizon, feeling the salt spray against his lips, would he willingly fetter himself again? Only for his family's sake, and he would never in a hundred years have fathomed that his strapping son would die . . .

And here I had my own son—not strapping at all, but sickly, a newborn, his arms a mosaic of variously hued bruises from so many pokes of the needle. What right had I to exult in my escape from the constraints of my life? But my reasoning was more sound than Swe-mu's, wasn't it? My departure truly for the betterment of our family?

I AWOKE WITH a start, looking out at the Tokyo skyline. Why had I bought so rashly into cowboys and the prairie, the indefinable promises of personal freedom? I could have chosen Japan as my destination, where every class was taught in the language and the culture of my childhood. There was no quota for Taiwanese to visit Japan. Yoshiko and Kai-ming could have visited me, and I could have visited home for the holidays, whereas my visiting home from America was out of the question. Never mind the formidable expense—returning to Taiwan before the year was out would mean surrendering my visa and restarting the application process from the very beginning with both the Nationalist and the American governments. And no one expected the Nationalist government to reissue an American visa.

We finished refueling and hurtled again down the runway, leaving Japan behind in the glinting blue sea. Such a tiny island, for all the grief it had given the world.

HALF-ASLEEP IN THE propellers' din, I rode my father's motorcycle through the streets of Taoyuan but found I was not going forward. I checked the throttle, the clutch, and found myself rising—

"Look! Look!"

Excited voices roused me from my dream. The man sitting next to me, a white man in a gray suit—they all looked the same to me still—was craning his head to see out my window. In the plane all around me, people looked out the window into the darkness and exclaimed.

"What is it?"

And then I saw it myself just outside my window—a green glow sweeping across the sky in all directions.

"It's the northern lights!"

My drowsiness vanished. I had read about auroras in *The Earth* and had never expected to see one in my lifetime. I leaned toward the window, holding my breath so it would not fog the glass. The light seemed so close I could almost feel its feathery yellow edges against the blackness of the sky. I wished that the plane could hover, that we could stay and watch the shimmering beauty as long as it lasted.

The man next to me spoke in English, his voice low and gravelly from smoking.

"Now, someday they'll tell us what causes that," he said.

"They know to some extent." I glanced at him. He was large, white, with a huge, bulbous nose that seemed lumpy. I recalled what I had learned from *The Earth*. "When the sun has flare, it sends gas over and this somehow interacts with Earth's atmosphere."

"Interacts how?"

I shook my head. "Something to do with the electrons." I fell silent and went back to watching the spectacular display outside, feeling foolish for being so vague, as this was all I had learned. I didn't realize that my embarrassment was mostly a by-product of my insecurity; no one knew much more about auroras at that time.

AFTER MANY INTERRUPTED dreams and trays of tasteless food and a midnight refueling stop in Hawaii, the plane banked over the ocean. I peered over the laps of my fellow passengers to see my fairyland. And there was the artificial angularity of San Francisco, its rectangular masses of concrete jutting into the sky. Even from the plane, I could see cars crawling along between the buildings and across the massive bridges. My heartbeat sped with anticipation. I felt in my breast pocket for my bus tickets, thick as books, and in my pants pocket for an advertisement I had clipped from an American overseas newspaper.

FOCUS
Friends of Chinese University Students
We will host you upon your arrival in the United States . . .

The plane tilted to the left, and the announcement came that we would soon land.

THERE ARE CERTAIN things we take for granted: the smell of the air, the feel of our clothes. Walking along the immense, shiny corridors of the San Francisco Airport's Central Terminal, I found my most basic physical expectations upended. The airport smelled curiously bland, as though the oxygen and nitrogen molecules themselves had been boiled and scrubbed clean. As I walked, my tailored shirt and wool slacks slipped against my skin, smooth as silk. I stepped down to the baggage carousel, my hand sliding along the chrome banister and leaving no imprint. I realized, then, how humid Taiwan's climate was, how it had weighed me down.

I passed through customs, and a gray-suited man in a fedora extended his hand to me. "Mr. Tong?"

I looked up in surprise into the man's eyes, which were as pale blue as a wildcat's. The pinkish skin over his nose wrinkled as he smiled.

"Pat O'Reilly," he said. "From FOCUS. Call me Pat."

"I'm Chia-lin," I said. The Americans in Taipei had advised me to go by my Chinese name here, as Americans were still sore over Pearl Harbor and disliked Japanese.

He gripped my hand firmly. I had heard that a firm handshake was important in America. I returned his grip in kind, my sleeve cuffs, for once, hitting just right at the base of my thumb, the smooth cloth of my shirt slipping against my shoulder. I had been annoyed with Yoshiko for spending so much precious time and money, for fussing so much over my clothing, but now I was grateful she had insisted on a suit that turned out to be just as fine as Pat O'Reilly's.

"I did not know if you would come," I said.

"Oh, sure!" He smiled, teeth brilliant. "Welcome to San Francisco!" *Oh, sure!* So friendly, so American.

Pat O'Reilly smiled and picked up one of my suitcases with surprising ease. "You'll stay with me tonight. I'm having some friends over. My dental assistant, Mary, and a Chinaman, like you."

"Oh, sure!" I said, smiling, though there was no guarantee this "Chinaman" would even speak my language. And feeling tall, debonair, and American, I picked up my other suitcase with the same casual movement that Pat had used.

But the suitcase was much heavier than I was ready for, and I felt a ripping in my lower back.

"You okay?"

I gasped in pain. "Fine." I had forgotten. This was the one with Kazuo's package.

"You don't look fine . . ."

I bent double, looking into the reflection of my grimace in the polished linoleum. This was not how I had hoped to start my year in America. I could almost hear Kazuo laughing. In a few minutes the pain receded to a dull throb.

"I'll call a bellhop. That thing's darn heavy. No wonder—"

"I'm fine," I said, standing up. Pat nodded doubtfully and led me out of the building. I followed, hobbling, through a set of glass doors to a sea of undulating steel—row upon row of cars, massive, gorgeous, gleaming like rockets. A spasm of pain shot through my back, and I dropped my suitcase for a moment to survey the sight. Chevrolet, Lincoln, Mercury. Names I had only dreamed about. They might as well have been rockets, as far as I was concerned. Each one was worth a life's savings in Taiwan.

Pat O'Reilly opened the trunk of a sky-blue '56 Chrysler with tail fins and heaved my suitcases into the cavernous interior. I pressed the shiny chrome handle on the passenger door and sank into a seat so plush that I ran my hand along it, imagining how Yoshiko would love to ride in a car like this, how she would smile. Then my back clenched as I settled in, and my image of Yoshiko vanished.

Pat settled beside me and reached for the keys sitting in the ignition. He hesitated, then looked up at me. "We've got a couple hours before dinner," he said. "Care to see the Golden Gate Bridge?"

"Oh, sure!" I exclaimed.

"Redwoods, after. How about that?" He turned the ignition, and the car purred to life. Despite my excitement, my head was heavy with fatigue. I turned the smoothly oiled arm of my window crank, and cool air blasted into my face. I blinked, watching the pastel-colored cars around us staying demurely within the painted lines on the road and blinking their directional signals. They slowed gradually and let each other pass when roads merged; it was so genteel. No one honked, and though I had expected no rickshaws or oxcarts in American streets, I was surprised at the complete absence of military vehicles.

Beside me, Pat puffed contentedly on a pipe, the corners of his blue eyes crinkled in a smile below the rim of his fedora. His left palm rested on the steering wheel, and his right manipulated the gearshift with casual skill and obvious pleasure.

He explained he was a dentist and had gotten involved with FOCUS through a "Chinaman" he had met at church. "I enjoy it," he said. "For the most part you people from Taiwan are very polite, very educated. For some reason we don't get the people who come to the United States to wait tables or work a Laundromat, though there are plenty of those already here, believe me."

"We have to pass exams to enter United States legally," I said. "Also, you advertise in English-language newspapers. Uneducated people will not be reading these."

"True." He glanced at me in surprise. "Your English is pretty good, you know."

"I prepared," I said. "I contacted every American in North Taiwan to practice conversation. I talked to many nuns and missionaries."

"So you're a churchgoer?"

"What? Church? No."

"Well, many of your people become churchgoers here. It's quite common. You should try it out."

I had learned that the best thing to do when someone proselytized was to ignore it and pretend I didn't understand. I did so now and he parked in silence.

I stepped out of the car, and my mouth dropped open at the massive bands of steel arching over the San Francisco Bay. Tiny cars moved across, their passage suspended by wires as graceful, as musical, as the strings of an ancient harp. And again I was struck by the massiveness — not just in physical size, but in conception, in boldness, and in ego. This was a country where such things could happen, where an engineer might be shown plans to build the longest, tallest bridge in the world and make it beautiful, too, and where he would say, "Oh, sure!"

Pat was gesturing for me to move. "Picture," he said. "Look sharp!"

The bridge behind me, I gazed into the lens of Pat's snappy Kodak Signet.

These United States, I thought. Impressive.

I FOLLOWED PAT'S lanky footsteps through the Muir Woods. Everything in this country was massive; even its trees were primordially large, their trunks reaching toward the mesosphere, their tops swaying in the cool breeze, converging at infinity. I breathed in the sweet air, unable to stop myself from filling my newly elastic lungs. The oxygen seeped into my meager blood. Already, I was stronger.

AS TO WHY Pat's house was pink, or why a wealthy dentist would buy a row house sited on such a hilly, albeit quiet and tidy, street; as to why Pat marched with one of my suitcases right into his house and up the stairs to the bedrooms with his shoes still on his feet — these were mysteries whose answers I could not fathom. I simply kept my own shoes on, too, and marched up, teeth clenched at the pain in my back as I hauled the other suitcase up behind him. I was determined to keep my eyes open and learn as much about America as I could, and if that meant doing certain things that made no sense, so be it.

Pat was widowed or, I later realized, more likely divorced, and left me with my suitcases in his son's vacated bedroom, cool, carpeted, dominated by a huge and extremely tempting bed draped with a guitar-print comforter, the walls plastered helter-skelter with posters of Nat King Cole and Billie Holiday. I changed my clothes and walked around the room to avoid falling asleep. While I paced, the doorbell rang twice, heralding visitors I could hear talking downstairs. Pat appeared again to bring me down and, when I declined liquor, set me up in the strangely odorless kitchen with a glass of 7UP. "There's some ice in the fridge if you'd like," he said, and he excused himself to the living room.

I stood in front of the refrigerator, gazing in amazement at the mammoth thing—turquoise blue with chrome accents, like Pat's car. It hummed assertively, and when I pulled open the door, an interior bulb illuminated chrome shelves of shiny, brightly colored boxes, bottles of milk, drawers filled to the brim with apples and oranges. I opened a special compartment on the inside of the door, thinking the ice might be in there, but instead I found a dozen eggs, nestled perfectly. I should have known there would be a special compartment for eggs, that any American household would be assumed to have a dozen eggs on hand at all times.

I heard a rustle behind me, and like a naughty child, I quickly shut the egg door. A hand with red lacquered fingertips reached past me and opened a door over the shelves.

"The freezer's here. I'm Mary, by the way, Dr. O'Reilly's assistant."

I turned to face her and jumped at the sight of her green eyes, glittering in the light of the refrigerator's bulb as she scanned the freezer. All her colors shocked me—the pink of her face, the bright freckles on her nose, her curled orange hair. She looked very young, and far from looking like the movie stars I had seen on the screen, she resembled a little girl wearing her mother's clothes.

"There." She dropped two pieces of ice into my glass of 7UP, which I'd placed on the counter. She picked up the bucket and smiled, her lips painted to match her nails, her teeth small and white. "Come on into the living room."

Her shoes clacked away on the black-and-white linoleum and then were muffled by the carpet. I followed her.

Unlike the kitchen, the living room was monochromatically white, with hardly anything on the walls and a thick white carpet covering the entire floor. There were furnishings such as I had never seen: a white vinyl sofa, a wrought iron and glass coffee table, matching end tables in teardrop shapes, a large, ornate stereo cabinet. Mary stepped soundlessly across the room and dropped ice into Pat's glass and that of the "Chinaman" he was now conversing with, a self-effacing, slight man in a very modest suit jacket. Their conversation lapsed for a moment, giving way to the soft sounds of jazz, as Mary refilled their glasses.

I stepped toward them. After so many hours on the plane, I longed to take my shoes off and relax. Instead my leather soles slipped over the carpet's thick pile, depositing microscopic dust particles from the Taiwanese streets onto the pristine nylon fibers. I was in limbo — inside, but wearing outside shoes. It was evening, but to my body it was earliest dawn. I was in America, walking toward another Taiwanese, whom I wanted to meet but also wished had not come, as I was eager to meet Americans and converse with them on my own. My head swirled with excitement, with confusion and fatigue.

"Chia-lin, this is Professor Hong."

We shook hands.

Pat turned back to Professor Hong. "Really? Within the next year?"

"Of course, of course," Professor Hong said. "Thousands of scientists all over the world are counting on this."

"Now, aren't the Russians claiming they'll beat us up there? I heard just last week there was some crazy Russian saying they had intercontinental missiles right now that are powerful enough to blast satellites into orbit—"

"Well," Hong said, "anyone can say anything. Russians just announced they will launch a satellite, fifty kilograms. This is simply too heavy for today's rockets. It's impossible feat."

"I think you're right. Those Commies are full of bluster." Mary smiled as she passed around a silver tray of some kind of vegetable stuffed with white fatty paste that stuck to the insides of my mouth. I washed it down with 7UP, and the combination of stickiness, extreme sweetness, and the sting of carbonation made me gag.

"Where you from?" Hong said. He smiled, but his eyes, watching me, were sharp and wary. "Taipei?"

I swallowed, throat burning. "Taoyuan," I said. "And you?"

"Kaohsiung."

He nodded and was silent, looking down into his drink. I was surprised at his unfriendliness. I would have expected him to take me under his wing.

Perhaps he assumed I was ignorant.

"I heard you were talking about satellites," I said. It felt a bit odd to be speaking to a Chinese man in English. "Is this your field?"

"No." He looked up. "I am physicist only. Teaching at San Francisco State. But I have friends who study the atmospheric science, at University of Michigan."

"Michigan? I'm going there tomorrow!"

"To Ann Arbor? When are you flying out?" Pat said.

Hong looked up at me with interest. "You study at University of Michigan?"

I felt a twinge of embarrassment. "Oh, I'm just visiting Michigan. I'm actually going to study at the South Dakota School of Mines."

The doorbell rang and Pat excused himself.

Hong kept looking at me out of the corner of his eye. "You taking Greyhound bus to Ann Arbor?"

"Yes!" How had he known? I looked down at my breast pocket to see if my tickets were sticking out.

Mary gasped. Hong laughed, his eyes crinkling warmly. "I did same thing—to Tennessee! Poor boy. Those travel agents in Taiwan, they know nothing."

"I should say so!" Mary stood with us, now holding her own drink. "It'll take you a week to get there!"

I felt myself flush—embarrassed, despite Hong's kind tone, that I was in fact ignorant. "I'm tired of flying," I said irritably. "The propellers are so loud they give me a headache."

"Sure." Hong nodded generously.

"I thought there are turbojet engines already in this country."

"Turbo what?" Mary said.

"Not for commercial airlines, not yet." Hong laughed, and somehow the gentle way he patted my back made me realize that he was sorry for embarrassing me and meant me well. "Don't worry, you will enjoy this ride. I enjoyed mine. It's amazing landscape."

I was just looking up at him in gratitude when his eyes widened at something behind me. All the warmth drained from his face, and he quickly took his hand from my back.

I turned to see what had so alarmed him. And nothing in all my borrowed issues of *Life* or *Time* had prepared me for what I would see at that moment. For there stood Pat O'Reilly in the doorway with a short Chinese man in a pin-striped suit — a man whom I recognized, with his thick, pursed lips, his thick black glasses frames, as the very same Mainland goon who had lurked in the musty corners of my father's house during my father's stint as mayor — the security general's son. Pat gestured toward us, introducing Mary and Hong. "And Chia-lin, who's just flown in from Taipei. And this, folks, is Kuo-hong. I just met him yesterday through one of our parishioners, and when he heard about FOCUS . . ."

My stomach clenched, and I felt, redoubled, that strange sense of limbo, of unreality. What was this Nationalist agent doing here? I quickly turned my head away, and as I did, my eyes met Hong's.

"I know Hong very well," Kuo-hong was saying, his voice unctuous but heavily accented. "Very smart man. And he your friend?"

"No," Hong said quickly. "We meet here, a few minutes ago."

"Chia-lin, what you study?"

I kept my eyes on my glass; it had a raised design on it in the shape of a penguin in a field of daisies, which I had not noticed before. I did not think Kuo-hong had paid much attention to me at my father's house, as he had been hovering over my father most of the time, but it was possible he had observed me in passing. Though I had done nothing wrong, no good could come of letting someone like Kuo-hong recognize me. Hong's alarmed reaction only confirmed what I felt myself, and I longed to ask Hong what he knew.

"Electrical engineering," I said.

"Looking kind of familiar," he said. "Where you from?"

Pat offered Kuo-hong a drink.

Kuo-hong walked over to me and chuckled, clinking my glass with his. "Study hard, Chia-lin!" He leaned close, peering up at me. His face was ruddy, smelling of alcohol, dried plums. There were good Mainlanders, I knew. One had saved me from expulsion, and many had died during the White Terror, falsely accused of Communism. But I felt an instinctive revulsion at this agent's proximity. His kind spit on the sidewalk and destroyed whatever or whomever they did not understand. They did anything for money, nothing without a bribe.

"Don't forget to stay out of trouble!" he said, smiling, and he left.

I FOUND A moment alone with Hong after dinner. We were sitting in the living room, where Pat and Mary had settled us with a plate of cookies. I tried to think of a way to determine Hong's allegiances and ask about Kuo-hong without putting myself at risk.

Sweet potato or pig?

The vinyl of the couch squeaked under me as I leaned forward and picked a cookie off the top. It was plain and white.

"They look like *moachi*," I said, indicating the cookies.

He smiled at this Japanese-Taiwanese word and spoke in Taiwanese. "Unfortunately they are not *moachi*." He bit into his cookie.

I smiled, too, relieved to hear my native tongue. The fact that Hong spoke Taiwanese did not automatically mean that he was against the Nationalists, of course, but it increased the probability. He relaxed as the burden of speaking English was lifted.

"You knew Kuo-hong," he commented. "I saw it in your face."

"He's a security officer," I said. "My father was a member of the People's Political Council for a time and they were all over the house."

His face darkened and he looked at me shrewdly.

"Originally my father ran against the Nationalist Party," I said. "He ran for the Young China Party when he was mayor. But when he was elected to the Political Council, he became so popular that the Nationalists felt threatened by him and made him switch to the Nationalist Party. They made threats of some kind, I'm sure. He quit his position just before I left home, actually, because of it."

"Oh?"

"He couldn't stand all the secret agents and the name-calling. My uncles were absolutely furious, after all the family money he spent on the campaign."

Hong looked at me sideways for a moment. "What about you? What are your politics?"

"I don't care about this party or that," I said. "I just want to be free."

Hong scratched his head. "Why should I believe you?"

I shrugged. "Why would I make up a story like that? That's why I came here, to get away from it all."

"Well, you see now, you haven't." He sat back, looking at me, and folded his arms. "When I came to America, I felt I was free, too, and I became so entranced with this sense of freedom that I wished to bring this feeling back to my homeland. So I helped form a local group to discuss Formosan independence, Formosa being the European name, the non-Nationalist name, for our country. These groups are growing here, you understand. Any organization you see that uses the name Formosa is pro-independence."

"Pro-independence? You mean, independence from China?" I lowered my voice instinctively.

"Of course," Hong said. "From anyone. Why shouldn't the Taiwanese rule themselves? Why should we submit to the Mainlanders? Why should we let Western powers decide who rules us or buy into this claim that the Nationalists are the true leaders of China, that the Communist Party is just a temporary problem? This is like saying England is the true leader of the United States. Of course no one says that. Because England lost the war. Well, so did the Nationalists. It's ridiculous."

I bit into my cookie and almost gagged, both at the cookie's sweetness and in alarm at these words, which I had certainly thought to myself but had never dared to speak.

"But," Hong continued, "the Nationalists are also increasing their presence here. They control every Chinatown." He looked at me. "They are desperate to suppress the Formosan independence movement here and maintain American support for Chiang Kai-shek, without which they are nothing. This is why I was not so warm to you initially, because I never know who is an agent and who is not. I hope you were not offended."

I assured him I was not.

"After a while I noticed Kuo-hong appeared everywhere I went. My mail was being opened. I first noticed this when I was helping to arrange a talk at Stanford University by the great political scientist Peng Ming-min."

A kettle whistled in the kitchen, and we both glanced to the door.

Hong leaned forward, looking at me intently. "I've been blacklisted. My wife and my brother have both lost their jobs in Kaohsiung, and though I have a green card, I can't get them over."

"Ah!" I exclaimed. "Even in America they do this?"

"They do," he said. "They cannot do anything directly to me, but they can do all the damage they want at home."

"Ah!" I sat back, thinking of Yoshiko and Kai-ming on the tarmac, of my promise to her.

"Don't worry," he said, seeing my crestfallen face. "Just be careful. Now you know."

WE WERE SERVED cake dusted with pure powdered sugar.

I swallowed, the cake so sweet it stuck in my throat. How had I not suspected that the Nationalists would be here, too? But I smiled politely as Pat and Mary joined us in the white room.

Pat wiped the powder off his lips with a paper napkin. "Now, what's this I hear about you taking a bus to Michigan?"

I explained about Kazuo's present.

Pat and Mary looked at each other incredulously.

"You must really love your brother, and love him true," Mary said.

"Or you've offended him in some way."

"The latter," I said. My bitterness at seeing Kuo-hong loosened my tongue. "I married the girl he wanted. Also, he can't come here."

No one blinked an eye. Perhaps people said things like this all the time in America.

"Why don't you just send it?" Mary said.

"Could do it," I said. "But I already have my tickets."

Hong laughed. "You are a good Chinese boy."

"You're crazy!" Mary exclaimed.

Pat watched me for a moment, puffing on his pipe. "I'll help you book a flight. We'll just ring up the airline."

"That is very nice of you," I said. "I enjoyed my flight here—I even saw the aurora borealis. But now, I look forward to seeing this country." And, I almost added, I'm not a rich American, like you.

"By—Greyhound?" Mary said uncertainly.

Hong laughed again and patted my arm. The English slowed him down and he paused, formulating his words. "Tell you what. Since you go, meet my friend at University of Michigan. Ni Wen-chong. Shoots rocket into the air, study the atmosphere. Very smart guy, got PhD at University of Illinois, now doing his postdoctorate. You go see him, he'll take care of you."

Rockets. Atmosphere.

"Yes." Hong smiled at my expression. "Since you like turbojets and aurora borealis, perhaps this will interest you?"

"Of course!"

Pat laughed genially. "I think we have a future rocket scientist here."

"Ni Wen-chong," Hong said. "And perhaps you could give this to him." He pulled an envelope out of his pocket. "Going to mail it, but hand delivery will be better, just as your brother says." He laughed, but his eyes met mine pointedly. "You do it?"

I cannot say that I was in any way naive. I had seen Kuo-hong and known why he was there. I had grown up in a milieu where dissent from the government was expected to bring a sentence of death, and I was the son of a man who would slam the door on his friends and shuffle to the side of the man carrying the biggest stick. Professor Hong represented, for me, the Taoyuan magistrate, the university professors, the young students dragged off to become prisoners or mere inked characters that dripped in the mist above the train station. I should have feared any association with the man. But something shifted in me. Perhaps it was the clean white carpet or the odorless American air, free of any lingering traces of history, or perhaps it was my innate self-righteousness, untying itself from its bonds, for I felt, rising above all else in importance, Hong's essential goodness, his own righteousness and his rightness. I had worked, fought so hard to get here, because of what Toru had told me while he assaulted the venom that ran through my veins: that America was the land of personal freedom, the land of making your own choices. I was here, and Hong needed help.

And I wanted to meet Ni Wen-chong.

"I'll do it," I said. And I took the envelope.

16

I LOOKED OUT THE window. For a moment I saw my eyes reflected back, as wide and watchful as they had been when I fished in the paddies. And then the suspension wires of the Bay Bridge whipped past, the soaring towers anchored unfathomably deep in the bay's muddy bottom. I stared, knowing I might never see these sights again: the San Joaquin Valley with its neat rectangles of green, its vineyards and cotton fields stretching in straight lines to the base of the Sierra; the conifer-studded shoulders of the Sierra Nevada; and then, plunging down, the arid monotony of the Nevada desert, punctuated only by cacti, their arms raised in perpetual salute. If I scoured these landscapes I might find the secret to succeeding in America, the secret to getting a master's degree in electrical engineering in half a year. I had not even told Yoshiko the conditions of my year's funding. To get the money from the family, my father had promised his brothers that I would study pharmacy after one semester of electrical engineering at the South Dakota School of Mines. Taikong had no need for an electrical engineer, and my uncles had no desire to indulge my personal aspirations. They had spent enough money on my father's political campaign. And unfortunately I had received a scholarship to an undergraduate pharmacy program at Baylor, and no scholarship to the School of Mines.

"Reno!" The bus brakes screeched, and the driver, tossing on his stately-looking cap, jumped off the bus. The other passengers jumped off behind him and hurried after his lanky receding figure into the squat building by the highway. I assumed they were after the restrooms, as the bathroom on the bus — very impressive to me, as I had never seen one — was somewhat cramped and unpleasant smelling.

I stepped off the bus, wishing I had not skipped the restroom at Truckee. But it was not the restroom that had everyone running.

In the building's darkened interior, our lithe and otherwise respectable bus driver leaned on a long silver handle. With his other hand, he fed quarter after quarter into a machine with spinning cartoon drawings of fruit. The quarters glinted in the dim light, each one representing the equivalent of my daily wage at Taikong. Behind the driver, the passengers waited, peering over his shoulders, hands jangling their own quarters in their pockets, waiting to pour them into the machine, too. It made me ill to watch and to hear each quarter drop into the machine. I walked away. I actually did need to use the restroom.

At the ticket counter, a man in a Greyhound uniform slouched over an issue of *Life*. Extralong hair from the back of his head was brushed over a bald patch on his crown.

"Excuse me," I said. "I need to go to the bathroom."

He gestured, not looking. "There."

"Yes," I said. "But one sign says 'Whites Only' and one says 'Colored.'"

He glanced up briefly at my face. "Use the white bathroom. The other one's for niggers."

He returned to his magazine.

I watched him turn the page, casually, confident in his prejudice. It was universal: my people, the descendants of Han Chinese, had been suppressed on Taiwan by the Spanish, the Dutch, the Japanese, and the Mainland Chinese. We in turn suppressed the Hakka minority and the aborigines. And yet, walking into the bleach-scented white bathroom, I was amazed to think that a person might not even be allowed to enter a bathroom because of his race, that no amount of antiseptic could scrub away the traces of a man's trespass there enough to satisfy a white man's delicate sensibilities.

We crossed the Utah border into a tortuous landscape as red and alien as any scene from science fiction. And I caught my first, albeit distant, glimpse of snow on the peaks of the Rockies, so barren and angular compared to the lush mountains of my homeland, as we wove between them.

We stopped at Post House restaurants with log-cabin facades and cafeteria-style interiors. I shuffled through the line, bending my ear close as the person in front of me ordered and repeating the same words when I was asked. *Cheeseburger with fries. T-bone steak. Pork chop with mashed potatoes.*

My stomach churned at the fatty aromas and the unaccustomed surplus of protein, and I thought guiltily of Yoshiko having steamed bread and rice porridge with the vegetables she'd pickled herself.

The food servers squinted at me, though I spoke as clearly as I had with Pat and Mary. One man frowned and threw his spatula down. "I'm not serving a gook."

"Huh?"

His coworker stepped forward and said to me, "Sorry, sir, he's a vet. I'll get that for you. You want coffee with that?"

"No." Coffee cost a nickel, the equivalent of a bowl of noodles and a steamer of *shio mai* on Gongyuan Road.

For days we traveled, and I saw neither the answers I sought in the landscapes hurtling by nor any Asian face but the reflection of my own greasy, yawning visage in the window. I began missing my own bed and Yoshiko's soft embrace within it. Kai-ming could have learned to roll over by now.

Somewhere in the Nebraskan plains, the endless sitting began to exacerbate the pain in my back, and I moved the plush reclining seat back and forth every few minutes, trying to get comfortable. I was still eager to see Ann Arbor and the school too mighty to admit me. But what an obliging fool I was, to deliver Kazuo's present by hand! Were it not for the promise of meeting Ni Wen-chong, I might well have taken a bus in the reverse direction.

By Lincoln, I was more resentful than not. By the rest stop in Omaha, I was convinced that Kazuo had known full well what he had asked me to do, and by Des Moines I knew for certain that Kazuo had consulted a map of the United States and planned this detour for me as revenge for his having lost Yoshiko.

17

I DRAGGED MY SUITCASES onto the wet sidewalk of West Huron Street in front of the Ann Arbor Greyhound depot. The air was cool but fresh, smelling of wet earth, and I breathed it in gratefully after a week confined to the staleness of the bus.

In contrast to San Francisco, Chicago, and many cities in between, Ann Arbor was quite small and quiet, with low buildings and large maple trees lining the road, branches newly budded and shivering in the gray drizzle. Cars were plentiful, the reflection of their rounded noses slipping calmly over the curved surfaces of the windows flanking me. We were near Detroit, and I had no doubt that this area benefited from its proximity to the car-manufacturing center of the world.

How odd, then, to see an old yellow Volkswagen Beetle come chugging down the street. Who would buy a German vehicle in this area? As it came closer, I saw that the driver was Chinese, and then the car stopped, slightly away from the curb, just in front of me. It idled loudly, obviously lacking a muffler, and the air filled with the stench of burning petroleum.

The Beetle's passenger door opened, and out jumped a plump

young man who straightened the collar of his leather jacket with a familiar movement.

I stared into his small eyes and realized it was Li-wen.

He laughed. "Professor!" he said. "Get this man some smelling salts. He didn't know his brother sent him halfway around the world to see me!"

And there was Li-wen's emaciated friend with the horn-rimmed glasses, leaning against the car and nodding nervously at the pavement. I realized he had been the driver. "It has been a long time . . . ," he said.

How had I not known? I had simply not recognized the family name on the package.

I felt anger flash up from my feet to my neck. "How did you get here?" I said to Li-wen. And I meant it in more than one sense, for I distinctly remembered that no name like his had been announced on the radio with those who had passed the entrance exam.

He raised his finger. "How does one get anywhere? It's all in who you know." He tapped his finger to his head. I recalled his position with the Anti-Communist Youth Corps. No doubt some Nationalist official had helped waive some requirements for him. "Come, we're in America now. Let's let bygones be bygones and beat these American bastards at their own game."

I had little choice, and I went with them.

THEY WERE NOT yet degree candidates but merely took courses in the graduate department of electrical engineering; this much I gleaned from their elliptical speech. They were sharing the dorm room of a true graduate student who was also an alumnus of Taiwan University. The square, cramped room smelled of sesame oil and stale fish — such a contrast to the ivy-covered facade of the building, the broad walkways through campus shaded by oak and redbud trees. I had little desire to stay and urged Li-wen to open his present as soon as possible so I could venture out.

Li-wen sat on a couch between piles of magazines, pillows, and packages of dried seaweed. He pulled lazily at the brown package, talking to the Professor and his host.

"This is damn heavy. What shall we have for dinner? That pork loin?"

Finally the brown paper was gone, revealing a large glass vase.

A *vase*!

We all sat staring at this thing I had lugged, day in and day out, gritting my teeth as pain shot down from my back all the way to the sole of my foot, through bus terminals halfway across North America. It was a perfectly ordinary vase with some etched flowers around the rim; there must have been similar ones all over the world. Even across the world, my brother played me for a fool.

Even Li-wen was embarrassed. "The bastard! He thinks by torturing you with this he can make up for insulting me. You wouldn't believe what he called me when he found out I was coming here. Talk about a sore loser."

I said nothing. If not for Ni Wen-chong, I would have smashed that vase.

Li-wen glanced at me, setting the vase on a leather trunk that functioned as a coffee table. "Well, there's not a scratch on it. For all that, little brother, we at least owe you first dibs on choosing what's for dinner."

"You may cook whatever you choose," I said, "but perhaps you can help me find someone I'm looking for."

"And who is that?"

"A postdoctoral fellow."

"In what?"

"Double E."

His little eyes looked up. "What is his name?"

"Ni Wen-chong."

"And how do you know him?"

"He's a friend of a friend," I said evasively. Despite Li-wen's sympathizing with me about the vase, I did not trust him. "How do I find him?"

"Here." He tossed me a stapled booklet. "There's the directory. But it's dinnertime now, so no one is in the labs at the moment. At least none of the Chinese." He laughed, patting his belly.

Reluctantly I hung my suit on the back of a door to wait for the morning. Dinner was as could be expected from three bachelors in a foreign country, though after so many days of eating hamburgers and mashed potatoes, I was glad to have rice again, and to be able to examine another refrigerator; even in this nearly squalid dormitory they had one. I opened and closed it several times, admiring the clever design, the feeling of suction on its closure. To think that even students in America had refrigerators, while in Taiwan, middle-class families had just started to buy iceboxes! Yoshiko's eldest uncle had just started a new ice company.

I opened and closed the refrigerator once more and noticed some notebook paper held to the front of the refrigerator with a magnet. On the paper was an address: Bryn Mawr Country Club, 6600 North Crawford Avenue, Lincolnwood.

The Professor, whose name was actually Sun-kwei, was filling a teakettle at the sink.

"What's this?" I indicated the address.

"They pay well for dishwashers," Sun-kwei replied. "That's how everyone makes money in the summer."

"Washing dishes?"

"*Hyo.* That's how it works."

They cleared a space for me on the couch, which smelled of mildew and soy sauce. I slept, dreaming I was sleeping on my futon in the northern countryside during the war, Yoshiko at my side. And then I was fishing, a carp swimming at my feet, but when I bent to reach for it, I couldn't move my arm. It was in one of Toru's splints, a large-bore needle sticking out of my vein and dripping blood.

I cried out. As I rose into consciousness, I reached for Yoshiko but found only the rough back cushions of the couch, and my arm jammed beneath.

18

Ni Wen-chong's laboratory was locked. I stood in the linoleum hallway knocking on the door and trying to peer into the lab between the posters taped to the window. The poster on top had an emblem I would come to see everywhere — a blue gridded globe orbited by a satellite: SYMPOSIUM ON SCIENTIFIC ASPECTS OF THE INTERNATIONAL GEOPHYSICAL YEAR, APRIL 1957 . . .

I stepped onto a low molding and pulled on the locked door handle to boost myself up. And in that moment of pulling my chin up to the top edge of the poster, I was again a schoolchild, standing atop piles of broken desks to watch the Nationalist soldiers scavenge the very outlets off the wall.

But I was no longer that provincial child spying on a force that I was helpless to resist, and the room before me now was empty of people, soldiers or otherwise. It shone, laboratory benches beckoning with piles of shining steel equipment — capacitors, battery testers, and a large machine with round glass screens and a reel-to-reel tape standing at the ready. Above, on the wall, hung a framed picture of three men in a barren, windy landscape, flanking a rocket. The images from my past slipped away, and I saw that my future was here, in this room.

"You see?" Li-wen said behind me. "There's no one here, I'm

telling you. Let's go have lunch. We have some *shio mai* from Chicago."

"They'll take a long time to defrost," Sun-kwei said. "What about the leftover pork chops?"

I had been putting up with them all morning. First, they had said Ni Wen-chong did not exist. Then, after I found his name listed in the University of Michigan telephone book and found his building in a brochure about North Campus, they said that the Aeronautical Engineering Department was too far away, that it required a car, that North Campus hadn't even been built yet . . .

A door opened at the end of the hallway, and a group of young men appeared, carrying clipboards, their shadows flitting across the pool of reflected light on the linoleum. I jumped down from the window when I saw that one of the men was Chinese. How many Chinese guys could there be in this department?

I ran down the hallway, feet clattering. "Ni Wen-chong! Ni Wen-chong!" My voice echoed.

The man stopped, propping the door open with his shoulder. He was slim, compact, holding his clipboard under his arm. He looked at me in annoyance as the rest of the group galloped down the stairs. "Please," he said. "We're late for the launch." He spoke, to my surprise, with a Hong Kong accent.

"The launch?"

He started hurrying down the stairs, the tapping of his shoes against the concrete stairs echoing in the stairwell. I ran down after him.

"I'll be back in the lab at one thirty," he called. "You want help with class, Rodney can help you. He's in the student lounge."

His head bobbed up and down, disappearing from view.

"I have something for you," I called out, my voice bouncing from wall to wall. "From Professor Hong, in San Francisco."

His footsteps stopped. "Professor Hong?"

I caught up to him and handed him the letter. He glanced at me, his eyes sharp and appraising.

He tucked the letter into his shirt pocket and turned to go downstairs again.

"Wait!" I called out. "I want to see the launch!"

He glanced up at me. "Then hurry." And he ran down the stairs.

I hurried after him down the stairs and outside.

It was a brilliant day, cool and calm, and the drizzly skies of the day before had cleared to a crystalline blue. As I rushed after Wen-chong, my feet swished in the grass, its smell so sweetly pure compared to the complexity of the earth around my parents' house. In the distance a large group of people clustered around a pickup truck. All around them was such a display of nature's indolence, of fields turning blade by blade from brown to green, of trees slowly awakening from their winter's slumber to unfurl their tiny buds, that it was difficult to imagine the human industry that was planned here — the new engineering buildings, the music building, and now the . . . launch.

This did not look anything like the barren land I had seen in the lab photograph.

"You launch rockets here?" I said.

Wen-chong laughed briefly. "No, no. We do not destroy the campus. Model rocket," he said. "Real launches are at Fort Churchill. Manitoba. This is just for fun."

He laughed at my expression. "Partly to test our design. We want to make sure our recovery system works."

The door banged far behind us, and I glanced over my shoulder to see Li-wen and the Professor stumble out into the light, shielding their eyes.

"How do you know Professor Hong?" Wen-chong asked.

"I met him in San Francisco."

We approached the group surrounding the truck. A man with gray hair stood with his hand on his hip, looking down at a radio receiver attached to the top shelf of a metal cart in the grass. As we drew close, Wen-chong hailed him. "Professor Gleason!"

He glanced up at Wen-chong. "You have a schematic?"

"What?"

"Hear that?"

A loud hum came from the receiver.

"It'll cover up our transmission."

They unscrewed the back plate of the receiver and gazed at the tangle of capacitors. It looked to be a unit dating from the war. I had rescued similar ones from the trash during my college days.

"Who put this thing together? Les? Didn't he leave for White Sands?"

"Hm. Where he put the schematic . . . ," Wen-chong said. "What model number?" They turned the receiver back around.

I leaned over the gray-haired man's shoulder and turned the volume down all the way.

The hum remained. All this American higher education and they couldn't diagnose the simplest radio problem in the world!

The gray-haired man squinted back at me in surprise. "That's right. Still humming. Wen-chong, tell me what that means."

Wen-chong looked down at the radio and then sideways at me.

"Capacitor," I said.

"Who is this guy, Wen-chong?"

"Friend of Peter Hong's."

The professor straightened up and looked me in the eye. He was taller than me, with a broad forehead and kind eyes. He took a pair of horn-rimmed glasses out of his pocket and put them on.

"I'm Chia-lin," I said.

"John Gleason." He shook my hand. "Fix this in an hour and I'll take you out to dinner."

I smiled. "Twenty minutes."

Professor Gleason laughed. "I'll time you," he said.

WEN-CHONG AND I pushed the receiver back into the building and took it up the elevator. In the lab he rummaged through little metal drawers. I glanced at the photograph of the rocket at Fort Churchill, and at the gleaming equipment around me. My heart raced, but I sat down to examine the receiver's circuitry, following the flow of electrons — zipping through wires, handing off the charge inside each capacitor in a kind of molecular relay race.

"Here!" Wen-chong threw a new capacitor and a roll of solder onto the counter beside me. He laughed. "I know Gleason. If you're one minute late, he won't take you to dinner."

"Who is he?" I grabbed a pair of wire cutters and snipped out the faulty capacitor. Circuit broken.

"Gleason? You don't know? He's the most important man in atmospheric research. He's one of the lead scientists for the IGY."

"The what? Where's the flux?"

"Oh." He trotted over to a tall metal cabinet by the window. "The IGY? The International Geophysical Year, of course. It starts July thirty-first. Haven't you heard?"

I checked the soldering iron, which I could tell from the smell was almost hot enough. "I have read about it," I said. "A little bit."

"Oh, of course," Wen-chong said. "You're from Taiwan. They're late entrants. The only reason they entered at all was because they heard China was involved."

"Entered what?"

"The IGY! The greatest example of cooperation in the scientific community the world has ever seen. You see, we must coordinate our efforts to learn more about the earth. If we send transmitters into orbit, there have to be receivers around the world to track its signal."

He bent over to watch me and I asked him to hold the new capacitor in place for a moment. I could hear his wristwatch ticking next to my ear. Twenty minutes was just enough time to change a capacitor with my own equipment. What had I been thinking to wager that it would be enough time in a foreign lab?

"And what does Gleason do?" I asked.

"We study the ionosphere. We're planning to send up sounding rockets during solar flares to measure their effects."

"To figure out why we have radio blackouts?"

"Sure. And more."

The solder melted, creating a silvery liquid bridge for electrons to dance across. I was almost there. My heart pounded. This school had rejected me, I reminded myself.

We rolled the cart back onto the grass with two minutes to spare.

I smiled, jubilant, imagining myself across a restaurant table from John Gleason, imagining myself part of his lab, at the sounding-rocket launches at Fort Churchill, which Wen-chong explained was far up north, in Canada. Gleason had his back toward us, and as the cart bumped along the grass, he turned around and gave us a smile and a thumbs-up. "Work now?" he called.

"A-OK!" I called happily, but then my smile faded.

For there facing John Gleason, with big smiles on their faces, were Li-wen and the Professor.

I SAT ACROSS the table from John Gleason. So did Li-wen. The Professor sat next to Gleason, across from us.

I closed my eyes, breathing in the mixed smells of vinyl and disinfectant, and bit into a piece of raw lettuce.

"Taiwan University," Li-wen was saying. Though his accent was strong, he set his glass of Coke on the checkered tablecloth with pompous authority, a smile on his wide face. "Best university in Taiwan. Two of us, educated there." He waved his finger between himself and the Professor.

I wanted to punch Li-wen between his little beady eyes. But I was old enough to have realized by now that my outbursts of anger did not always serve me well, and I forced myself to keep chewing my lettuce.

"Oh yeah?" Gleason asked with interest. His hair hung down over the sides of his forehead, almost to the top of his glasses. "Where is that? Taipei? Is that a government-run institution?"

I took another bite of salad, really just a mixture of uncooked vegetables with a too-sweet, gooey sauce on top. I chewed slowly, deliberately. I should have known Gleason would lump me together with all the other "Chinamen" and invite them, too. I soothed myself with the thought that I was having the best experience I might have hoped for at this school—a nice dinner that I would never have been able to afford on my own, with a famous atmospheric scientist. I would write Yoshiko about my amusing adventures in an Ann Arbor steak house with a moose head mounted above a painted styrofoam fireplace, with waitresses wearing red-and-white checked dresses with frilly aprons.

". . . formerly the Taipei Imperial University . . . twenty-two departments . . . "

I sawed my steak into bite-size chunks that bled pinkish red. To my surprise, the meat was tender and tasty. I would tell Yoshiko about this, too. It amazed me that, somewhere along the way, American women had discovered they could just as well please their families by throwing whole slabs of meat into the pan and raw lettuce into a bowl, while women all over Asia spent the prime of their lives chopping, mincing, and marinating, crimping and steaming and stirring over a hot fire until their feet ached and their backs bent into a permanent hump.

Yoshiko could have a better life here. If only I could get her here. My mind slipped again into reviewing, as I already had a hundred times, the conflicting parameters—my promise to bring her over, my father's promise that I would study pharmacy for Taikong, my year's limit in funds.

I took a sip of ice water, the ice cubes tumbling and sliding along my upper lip, cooling me.

"We know so little about Free China," Gleason was saying. "I know there's always squabbling between them and the Communists about representation."

"It is just temporary situation," Li-wen said. "Soon Chiang Kai-shek will go back to Mainland." He smiled without any hint of irony.

"Sure, he'll beat the Communists, if Madame Chiang has any-thing to do with it," Gleason said. "I saw her speak in 1943. That's one feisty lady! Beautiful, too. Tell me, are the Chiangs popular back home?"

"Of course!" Li-wen said. "They have done so much for Republic of China." He went on to list all the economic gains, the superb infrastructure . . .

I felt my anger rising up again. Gleason showed such curiosity and openness of mind, and here was Li-wen giving him the full measure of Nationalist propaganda. How could Li-wen, a Taiwan-ese, say such things? My father had said similar things during his campaign, but he knew his audience had lived through February 28 and the White Terror. They understood what the truth was, and that it could not be spoken.

"Railroads were built by the Japanese," I blurted out.

Li-wen's leather jacket squeaked as he turned to look at me side-ways, the traces of a smile still lingering on his face.

I had never spoken such words before, but now that they were out, more followed in a heady rush. "Schools, too," I said.

Gleason's eyes shot back and forth between us.

The Professor laughed nervously and shook his head. "Schools, no, no, no. . ."

"This is true, of course," Li-wen said, turning back to Gleason. "But who is running schools and railroads after the war? Not Japa-nese." He skillfully went on to tout the Land to the Tiller Act, which had robbed my family of the land my grandfather had toiled his whole life to buy.

That was enough. As soon as Li-wen paused to put steak in his mouth, I interrupted. "What kind of rockets do you use for the real launch?" I asked Gleason, my voice unnecessarily loud. "Solid fuel? Liquid fuel?"

Gleason looked at me in surprise. And then his eyes brightened. "Solid. It's a two-stage rocket. We developed it here at Michigan.

It's designed to be portable, easy to use by a research team." He took off his glasses and pointed them in the air. "Something you can do when you can use your head. You can't just use those V-2 rockets from Germany . . . American industry is completely fractured. Here you've got the air force and the army going off in completely different directions, and then there's private industry doing their own thing . . . They've basically been reduced to using German design. And German equipment, actually. Higher education here is so theoretical, people don't even know how to construct a simple circuit."

Li-wen laughed heartily. "Simple circuit! Yes, yes."

"Rocket!" said the Professor, smiling and pushing up his glasses.

"Some things you have to learn on your own," I said. "They don't teach you in class."

Gleason nodded. "That's right. That how you learned?"

"Yes," I said. "I took some interest in building radios. I built the radios, read the magazines, fixed up broken ones . . ."

"Oh, well, that's swell," Gleason said. "That kind of initiative can take you places. Take Tom, he's the guy behind the model rocket. Fooled around with model rockets since he was a kid. Now he's doing real ones, and he sure does know what he's doing."

Li-wen gave his hearty laugh once more. He patted my back. "Because his school. Vocational."

Gleason glanced at Li-wen again. "What's that?"

"He goes——"

"I went to vocational school," I said. "They did have some class on radio repair, but the class is not enough to know how to build on your own." I glared at Li-wen, but he busied himself sawing his steak.

"That's right," Gleason said. He put a chunk of meat into his mouth and chewed for a moment. "Why'd you go to vocational school, Chia-lin?"

I hesitated. "I was a bad boy."

Gleason laughed. "I can't believe it. You're the politest young man I've met."

I told him about the wall-drawing incident in middle school and my subsequent expulsion, though I omitted the political circumstances, which seemed too complicated to explain. I had never told anyone but Yoshiko about my expulsion before, and I felt a tremendous relief at telling this kind man, who seemed more perceptive by the minute. I didn't care that Li-wen and the Professor were listening, too.

"Well," Gleason said, wiping his mouth with his napkin, "if something like that happened to my son at school, you can bet I'd have that principal's throat in a jiffy. Harmless prank like that. Child abuse, really. You're not a bad boy, just playful and honest."

I smiled down at my steak, so overcome for a moment that I could not speak.

"Different society, of course," he said.

I nodded.

"What school did you say you were going to here?"

I looked up. "South Dakota School of Mines."

"Oh, that's right. South Dakota. They have a doctorate program?"

"No."

The four of us chewed for a minute.

"Do you have opportunity in your lab for two graduate students?" Li-wen said, indicating himself and the Professor.

"Hm?" Gleason said. "Oh yes. Submit your résumé to my secretary at the office, and we'll see what we can do."

Li-wen talked for a few minutes about work he had done with one of his Taiwan University professors over the summer. I had no idea whether any of what he said was true, but his English was much better than I had initially thought and he sounded very impressive. He caught my eye and shrugged, as if to say, Too bad for you.

The waitress brought our tab, and Gleason laid his dollar bills on the table. As we were all pushing out the glass doors of the restaurant, I eyed the low clouds that swept over Ann Arbor. Drawing on that wall had cost me everything.

But on the sidewalk, Gleason turned to me and shook my hand.

"Get your master's from South Dakota, Chia-lin," he said. "Then come back and work in my lab."

And he walked away, the Professor on one side, Li-wen touching his arm and gesticulating on the other.

19

Dear Saburo,

I'm sorry it has taken me a couple of days to write my first letter. By the time this reaches you, you will be in South Dakota, so I will address this to your department office. I hope it reaches you.

After we dropped you off at the airport, your mother and I rode back in the jeep. Kai-ming was crying, and I tried to get him to sleep, but it was hard because he was hungry and I had run out of formula. Then I realized he had a fever.

So, with taking care of Kai-ming, filling dumplings with your mother, and folding your sisters' fancy underwear, I have not had much time to myself. Luckily, Kai-ming seems to be recovering, and so I have a moment to write you while he sleeps at my side.

His eyelashes are fluttering. He must be dreaming of something good—plentiful milk, perhaps, or a life without needles. I just gave him a bath and he has that warm, fresh baby smell. It's the first night this week he hasn't been sick. This morning your father rubbed his eyes and complained about all the crying last night, as though I should have been able to stop it for his comfort!

Though Kai-ming is good company for me, it is not the same

without you here. Your side of the futon is very cold at night, and I am lonely at the dinner table surrounded by all your family, poised with their chopsticks to snatch at the meat. Your mother keeps pulling me aside to confide things. She complains about your sisters and brothers. She says she always knew you were smart but she didn't know how to control you. She says being a mother is very hard and we should have waited longer. I think she has had a lonely life.

She also keeps telling everyone that you are studying pharmacy so that you will benefit Taikong. She says that you should raise chickens and send home a hundred dollars every month. Where does she get these ideas?

When we said good-bye, you did not seem convinced that you could get your degree and bring me over. But you can. It can be done.

Love,

Yoshiko

It can be done.

"That letter came last Tuesday. When you're done with that, I need you to fill out a few forms."

I looked up, the sudden movement sending pains down my spine, which had stiffened unbearably from the multiple bus rides back from Michigan.

The secretary for the School of Mines Electrical Engineering Department, Mrs. Larsson, was peeling thin sheets of paper from a large machine on her desk and placing them in front of me. She wore a pink dress with a little jacket on top, and her eyes were such a transparent blue that I saw the light shining through them from the window as she looked to the side. Her hair was white blond, like Marilyn Monroe's, with carefully sculpted curls. I had not realized that people actually looked like this except in movies. I stared, watching her eyes flickering back and forth, catching the light—not necessarily because I thought she was beautiful, which it was possible that she was, but because I had never seen anyone up close who looked so alien.

The papers were warm, their chemical smell mingling with the smells of the coffee and the sugary pastries that were nestled between the copy machine and the adding machine on her desk. No abacus here.

The papers curled up as I tried to sign my name.

"Here." She flattened out a sheet for me with her hand. "Darn Thermo-Fax," she said. "I love it and I hate it."

"What's that? It makes copies?"

"More or less. Saves me a lot of typing, anyway." She gathered up the curling papers and shoved them into a file drawer. "There." She turned and smiled at me, her eyes flickering up to meet mine, her pupils startling black disks.

"How does the machine work?" I asked.

She opened the lid to show me the glass bed. "You put the paper you want to copy here, and this special paper on top, and the infrared shines through."

"Ah, infrared. I have read about these machines."

"Here. I'll show you." She took Yoshiko's letter and placed it on the glass.

As the machine hummed and she peered down at it, I stretched out my neck, side to side, getting out the stiffness. I said, "I would like to meet the head of the department, Professor Beck."

Eyes flickering, she smiled. "Sure! But he's not in. You'll have to catch him at the end of the day." She handed me my letter and its curled, warm copy. "Relax and settle in, take a tour. Have you seen the area?"

I STOOD IN front of Mount Rushmore, remembering: Yoshiko sitting in the darkened theater next to me, the images of *Midwest Holiday* sliding across her face as she turned to face me.

I'd like to go there.

A plane flew in the vast blue overhead, casting a shadow that slid across the curving expanse of George Washington's forehead, stretched over the lock of hair above his left ear, and slipped in and out of the crevices of Thomas Jefferson's gaze. The plane flew on, its shadow dropping down below Teddy Roosevelt's chin and onto the forested slope below Abraham Lincoln's beard. And then the plane was in the open, glinting silver against the brilliant blue sky.

I had come to South Dakota because of these men. Because of them and this country, which they had chiseled out of boldness and idealism, I had left my home, my wife, and my child. Because of the Black Hills looming all around me, their rolling shoulders covered in sweet-smelling ponderosa pine. Because of the vast plains surrounding them to the horizon's end, and because of the big, bustling cities far out of sight, so full of complexities and riches and opportunities.

"Spectacular," a gravelly voice said behind me.

I swiveled around. Two men looked up at the mountain. The one who had spoken was older, white, peering through binoculars. He wore a khaki-colored hat with a wide brim and a matching vest with zippered pockets. The other man was young, about my age, with black hair. His skin was slightly darker than mine, and his arms were folded across his buttoned-up shirt.

The older man spoke again. "Though I respect your opinion on the matter, Bashir."

The younger man shrugged. "It's one of the greatest monuments in the world. You can't help being awestruck by it. And these are great heroes — heroes I was taught to admire. But it would have been nice if they hadn't been carved out of sacred Indian land by a member of the Ku Klux Klan."

"They're the ones you grew up with, right? The Lakota?"

"That's beside the point. The US gave this land to them by treaty, in perpetuity."

"Until it was convenient."

"Exactly."

The older man caught sight of me and whispered to Bashir. His whisper carried in the mountain air: "He one of 'em? An Indian?"

The young man glanced at me and smiled wryly. "Oh, he's no more Indian than I am," he said out loud, turning to face me. "Isn't that right? What is your ethnicity, if you don't mind?"

"Chinese," I said. "From Taiwan. I just arrived."

"Ah," he said. His eyes were black, astute. "How are those Nationalists?"

I was taken aback for a moment. No one had ever asked me that before—certainly not an American. "Difficult," I said, and I glanced around, as though an agent might be lurking behind a bush, under a rock. "How do you know about them?"

He shrugged. "I read the paper. Between the lines." He laughed, his teeth flashing. "By the way, I'm Bashir. This is Morris. I bet you never thought you'd end up at Mount Rushmore with a Lebanese and a Jew." They laughed together, and I did, too, though I had no idea where Lebanon was, or why it should be unusual for a Lebanese and a Jewish man to be friends. I felt, for the first time in weeks, more ignorant of history and geography than the people I was speaking to.

Bashir told me he was a second-generation immigrant, a civil engineering student at the School of Mines. Morris was a lawyer who knew Bashir's family. "Trying to win Bashir over to the law. No offense to you engineers, but if your goal really is to effect social change . . ."

I took a few steps away from the two men as they argued about the merits of the different fields. Not once did Bashir mention his parents.

I looked back up at the presidents. One man's symbol of patriotism, another man's symbol of betrayal and racism.

Nothing was ever as simple as it appeared. I had dreamed for so many years of escaping the narrow confines of my life by coming to this country. I had imagined that here I would be unbounded, free like this man, Bashir, to take whatever path I wished. In a way, it was true. No soldier would stop me in the street, no teacher would strike me for speaking out of turn. Paths in a thousand different directions were open and waiting to challenge me. All I had to do was step forward and I could shoot rockets into the sky.

But even here, gazing up at George Washington's serene visage desecrating the mountainside, I was a son, a brother, whose resources had been meted out. My father's conditions seemed unfair to me, but he had tried his best. Without the promise of pharmacy school, his brothers might well have voted to keep the money from me, and me in Taiwan. I knew, now that I was a parent, that all a father could do was his best.

Even without that promise to my father, would I have the courage to forge my own path in this alien land? Without question, it would be safer to follow my father's directions, to do a semester here, two semesters studying pharmacy, and then return. How would I get the money to survive longer? If I floundered, I would have no Toru to save me, no father to bribe the officials, no Yoshiko to tell me everything would be all right. If I made a misstep, I would fail, with no one to blame but myself.

But wasn't this what it was to be master of your own fate? What would this country be now if these presidents had taken the safe route? What would George Washington have done with one year in 1950s America? Studied what his parents told him to and gone home to do a job he didn't want?

Bashir and Morris waved and made their way back to the parking lot. "Perhaps I'll see you back at school," Bashir said.

"Good luck with your decision," I called.

He smiled and tapped his head.

He walked away, his gait self-assured. He laughed and slapped Morris on the back. And as I watched him, I decided that I would do as the Americans did. It was my life.

Full of excitement, I rushed back to the electrical engineering office. By the time I arrived, the previously blue sky had clouded over, and I paused just inside the door of the Engineering Building to brush the rain off the luxuriant wool of my suit.

" . . . young man's just got here from China. Been by asking for you, I hope you don't mind . . ."

I stood with Mrs. Larsson in the department office by Beck's door.

And then Professor Beck appeared, carrying a briefcase and wearing a yellow rain slicker and rain hat. Dark, graying curls peeked out from under his hat's brim. He studied me, his eyebrows thick and twitching, his eyes dark and sure as my father's. I caught sight of a row of modestly framed diplomas behind him.

I had long ago lost any reverence I might have had for authority figures. I respected them and understood that their position probably represented an accomplishment of some kind. But after all I had been through, I knew that every person was human, flawed and confined by whatever world he knew. I stepped forward without fear. "I'm Chia-lin," I said. "I just arrived from Taiwan and I want to introduce myself."

He shook my hand, looking me up and down from the top of my head to the soles of my Japanese shoes.

"Here this morning," Mrs. Larsson said, her dress swishing behind me. "Nice boy, and very interested in our automatic copy machine."

"It is a nice machine," I said. "Infrared."

Beck nodded.

Mrs. Larsson handed me a letter, which I saw was another one from Yoshiko.

"Nice to meet you, Chia-lin." Beck took a step toward the

hallway. He spoke with surprising gravity. "I'm sure you're a fine young man. Now if you'll excuse me, I have to make it home for dinner, or my wife will kill me. Been away for a week and she's been home with the kids."

His boots squeaked out the office door and down the hallway.

I had drunk in too much of the South Dakotan air to let him walk away from me so easily. I hurried after him, holding the letter in my hand. "I need to talk to you. I have a wife, too," I said. "And son."

He glanced at the letter, still walking. "Oh yeah? How old?"

"Two months."

He turned to me with a squeak, looking at me sharply. "You have a two-month-old? In China?"

"Yes, Taiwan."

He stood watching me for a moment, trying to see, perhaps, what kind of man would leave his newborn son for a year.

"It was my only chance to come to America," I said. "I want to bring them here. That's why I need to talk to you."

"What does that have to do with me?"

"I don't know," I said. "But you're the department head. Maybe you know a way."

He sighed and resumed his squeaky gait. I watched him despondently, but then he turned around, gesturing for me to follow. "Come on."

I followed him down the hall, out the door into the rain, and into the parking lot. He opened the passenger door of his car, a Ford station wagon, and gathered up books and papers from the seat. He backed up, arms full, and indicated the seat with his head. "There."

"Me? . . . Where are we going?" Could he be taking me to the immigration office? To a lawyer?

"To my house," he said. "You can have dinner with me and my wife, Rose."

He carried his load to the rear of his car and dumped it in through the tailgate. I stood by the open door, raindrops splattering on my head. I wasn't sure if he was making fun of me or just taking pity on me.

He indicated the seat. "Come. Be my guest." He looked at me, his eyes dark and impenetrable. The yellow brim of his hat quivered in the rain. "Chia-lin, we've had Chinese students for years. They sit in the corner talking among themselves. None of them speak up in class, they don't make eye contact, and not one has ever chatted with Mrs. Larsson about the copy machine or come by my office to introduce himself. Except for you."

He indicated the seat again, and I got into the car.

As he turned the key in the ignition, he said, "We'll talk to Senator Dickey about your family. But don't expect too much. There are restrictions for you Orientals."

I hesitated. "And I need to finish my master's in one year," I said. "I have received an offer when I finish, and I only have money enough for one year."

"No foreigner's ever done that." He looked sideways at me. "Take one day at a time."

20

But time was what I did not have. Time was what passed with each step of my foot through the well-mannered halls of the School of Mines. Each page I read marked another few minutes, each letter from Yoshiko another few days of not knowing how to fulfill my promises to her and to my parents at the same time. If I did not go to pharmacy school, I should at least send home the hundred dollars a month my family requested, as they had funded me in the first place. But if I continued at the School of Mines, I would not have a dime to spare, I would have no degree at the end of the year, no way of staying on, and no one would be satisfied.

Dear Saburo,

I am so happy for you! I received a letter from Professor Beck's wife, Rose, telling me about your dinner and how impressed she was with you. I told you the Americans would like you, because you're so smart and your English is so good.

Everyone is very impressed by the picture of you in front of your refrigerator, though they all comment that it is empty. Do you have enough money to buy food?

I cannot believe that one phone call could cost as much as your rent. Is that really true? Perhaps you heard your friends wrong and it actually costs five dollars, not fifty?

I went to the market with your mother today. She was so nice, holding my hand. Everyone at the market thought I was her daughter. So I told her about your visit with the Becks. I thought she would be proud.

And she said, "If he's doing so well, tell him to send us back one hundred and fifty."

I'm so sorry to have to tell you! I tried to reason with her, but she believes this nonsense about there being gold in the streets there. Don't even think about it. Of course you can't spare it. You have no income. Don't worry, just study, and everything will all come out all right.

I miss you all the time, and so does Kai-ming.

Love,
Yoshiko

I shared my cavernous refrigerator and the rest of my apartment with two Mainland Chinese bachelors — one who cooked everything with tomatoes, and one who cooked everything in pure soy sauce. Many dinners, I washed the sauce off my food in the sink while my roommates watched, one with lips stained permanently pink, the other bald and sweaty-palmed. They kept to themselves and remained within the Chinese community, and I avoided them as much as I could. I had come to America to meet Americans, not people steeped in the old culture and ways of thought. If Yoshiko were here, she would be out in the world with me. She wouldn't hole up like these men. I knew that.

I studied hard, trying to rectify the deficiencies of my education. What Li-wen had said to Professor Gleason was true. I had had vocational, not academic, courses. I knew circuitry, not theory. I was many years behind.

But all of America lay outside my door. And so, when Professor

Beck invited me to go for a hike with him and his friends in the Black Hills, I said yes without hesitation.

His friend, a geology professor, picked me up that Saturday, pulling up in front of my apartment in a beautiful white Buick. He hopped out wearing shorts, sunglasses, hiking boots, and a special hat with snapped-up flaps. He pulled down his sunglasses, and his eyes traveled from my Japanese broadcloth shirt to my freshly shined dress shoes. "You're going hiking like *that*?" he said.

I was not about to spend my family's money to buy an outfit just for a day hike. I had visited Yangmingshan with Yoshiko many times in dress clothes. Not everyone was rich enough to have special clothes for every situation.

A couple of hours later, though, as my leather soles slipped on the rocks with every step along the trail, I thought it might have been worth splurging at least on a pair of sneakers. I hurried to keep up with Beck and his friends as they disappeared up the mountainside — and slipped, jamming my toes. Branches of pine swiped me in the mouth and brushed against my button-down shirt. It was April, and I had thought myself warmly dressed, but as we climbed higher up, it was cooler, and the sweat from my exertion evaporated quickly in the wind.

I wished they would wait for me, but no one waited in America, it seemed. I was forever chasing people — Ni Wen-chong, Gleason, Beck.

I scrambled up a low rock face on my hands and knees to a path overhung by birch branches that glowed in the afternoon sun.

And then I was in the open. The sheer beauty of it stopped me short: the cool, mirrored surface of a lake, reflecting the surrounding cliffs, the tiered green branches of pines, and the sky above. Three bighorn sheep, their horns curled round their ears like decorative finials, stood in the water at the far end of the lake. I breathed in the American air.

Beck approached me, swishing through the tall, wheat-like grass in his hiking boots, and handed me his canteen to share, as I had none.

The rest of his party sat on a cluster of rocks by the lake's shore, pulling snacks and drinks out of packs stuffed full of equipment.

"You brought nothing?" Beck said as he drew near.

"This is how I hike in Taiwan," I said.

"Think you can make it to Harney Peak?" He looked at me, his expression unreadable, shaded by his khaki hat.

I wiggled my toes. They felt black and blue. "Sure," I said. I had no map or compass to guide me back. I indicated the lake, the bighorn sheep. "It's very beautiful."

He nodded and turned to the lake, his profile silhouetted against the glittering surface of the water.

He looked back at me. "I can lend you a blanket. It'll get cold."

I imagined clambering over the rocks with a blanket over my shoulders. "I'm fine," I said. "Have you heard from Senator Dickey?"

"I have not. You'd best write him yourself."

I nodded. I had been thinking of suggesting this myself. "My wife was very glad to receive a letter from Rose," I said.

"Yes. She likes you."

"My wife was so happy that she told my mother about it and my —" I caught myself before I told Beck what my mother had actually said. "Unfortunately my parents still want me to go to pharmacy school."

"Well, that would be a shame," Beck said. "Since you're a good engineer."

"I have no interest in pharmacy," I said. "But it's my family's business, and they are the ones who paid for my year here."

"I understand," Beck said. "But it's your life."

I smiled. "This is the American point of view."

He shrugged. "Isn't it yours?"

"Maybe," I said. "But you told me I couldn't get my master's in one year, and I have no scholarship, so —"

"I didn't say that, Chia-lin."

One of his friends called to him and he turned to wave back to the group. They were getting up from the rocks, screwing shut their canteens and brushing off their shorts.

"Chia-lin, I said no foreigner's ever done it. That doesn't mean you can't."

"But I don't even —"

"You don't even what?"

I fell silent. I had never told him I did not have a bachelor's degree. He was kind to me, in his gruff way, but I couldn't be sure that expelling me for misrepresentation would be beyond him.

"Have confidence in yourself," Beck said. He took back his canteen, from which I would have liked to drink more, and went back to his friends. He waved to me over his shoulder. "Come," he said.

THE WIND, SMELLING of pine and wildflowers, swept across Harney Peak.

I shivered as the wind penetrated the damp fibers of my shirt. I stumbled along after Beck's group on the bare granite. My feet throbbed and pain shot down my leg, my toes slipping into every crevice and depression on the path. I tore my eyes away from my feet to see the others enter a stone tower at the top of the peak, and I crawled to a spot just below the entrance so I would see them when they exited. I could go no farther. I sat down to rest and look out at the panorama.

The world lay below, an ocean of ponderosa pine punctuated with granite peaks, sloping down to pale green valleys where houses clustered, tiny and brave. In the distance, mountaintops marched to the horizon — pale, misty, infinitely layered. I could see the curvature of the earth. And up above: the sky, its vast cauldron of swirling atoms tinged golden by light shot from our star's fiery surface, past Mercury and Venus and all their moons, through the black nothingness of space, to reach us.

The earth turned. On the other side of it, the sun's rays would soon reach the horizon and filter through the red curtain by our rosewood bed. Kai-ming, lying by his sleeping mother's side, would stretch his tiny arms and, eyelids fluttering, turn his head toward his mother, his shock of hair squished flat against the underside of her arm.

I took Yoshiko's latest letter from my breast pocket. It flapped loudly in the wind. I hadn't had a chance to read it before we left. I so longed for Yoshiko's presence, for her laugh, for her touch, and this piece of thin, fluttering blue paper was a poor substitute.

Dear Saburo,

I have some bad news.

My sister Leh-hwa was hit by a truck. She is still alive, but as my mother says, she might have been better off dying and coming back as an ant or a catfish or some other animal that knows no pain. She has several broken bones and bleeding inside her body. Her husband is so busy drinking and fooling around that he doesn't even visit her in the hospital. I'm sure it was because of worrying about him that Leh-hwa failed to watch her step in the street.

I went to visit, and my mother said I was dressed like a doctor's wife.

I was wearing that red dress with white polka dots and that swingy skirt. I bought it with my own money from my old job.

And then my brother Kun-ji, who didn't even come to the hospital right away, came into the room and pulled out a chair for my mother, and they turned their backs to me. They were jealous, I suppose, and it made me sad. I have had people ask if you're sending me money, and it's possible my family assumes you do and they wish they had a bit of it, too.

It's because of that hundred fifty dollars you sent to your mother. I told you not to send it. Your sister used it to buy six

pairs of black shoes from New Rose. No wonder everyone
thinks you're rich.

I folded the letter back up and put it into my pocket, looking
glumly at the vista at my feet. The sunlight deepened to orange,
setting a lake afire in the valley below, and here, on the highest peak
in the United States east of the Rockies, I was not John Wayne, not
some genius electrical engineer. I was the stupidly obedient son of
parents who knew no end of greed, the buffoon who didn't know
to wear proper shoes for a hike, the lone boy at sundown, stepping
between the sunlit rice paddies toward home.

I heard Beck's voice and stood up, toes throbbing, pain shooting
down the side of my leg. He walked toward me from the tower. As
he drew near, he looked out at the panorama. "Nice view."

"The sun is setting," I said. "Shouldn't we get home quickly?"

He looked at me for a moment, his hat flapping in the wind. "I
thought you knew," he said. "We're camping."

I HAD NEVER known how hard the ground could be. Beck
gave me his blanket and a plastic sheet, explaining that he was already the third man in his friend's two-man tent and had no space
to offer me. I hesitated, not knowing whether to put the blanket
and sheet over me for warmth or under me to protect me from the
hard rock. In the end, I put the plastic between me and the rocks,
the blanket between my face and the bugs.

I swatted bugs that buzzed in my ear, and fuzzy moths that landed
on my neck, and I sat bolt upright, hearing the rustling and cracking that might mean moose or bears or whatever large creatures
roamed the American woods. The moon was out, and it shone on
the pointed roofs of all the little tents in the clearing around me.
Inside those tents, I knew, everyone was laughing. I was nothing
but an amusement for these people, all snug in their tents, laughing
at the funny Japanese, Korean, Indian, or whatever they thought I

was. One of them could easily have let me into their tent. But that would have meant snuggling right next to me, and how could they do that if they couldn't even use the same urinal as a black man? How could they ever scrub off my germs?

Who was I fooling? I was never going to belong here.

21

Y OU'RE MAKING A MISTAKE," Beck said.
    "Perhaps."
"No — to the side . . ."
We were knee-deep in the cool, swirling waters of Rapid Creek.
Evergreens dotted the grassy banks rising on either side of the water. Beck pulled my arm down from over my shoulder.
"This isn't tennis, Chia-lin. Now, cast."
I flung the rod awkwardly to the side. The line whirred out and
landed with a little plop in the rippling water. I lost my balance in
the current for a moment and stumbled, my waders squeaking as
the legs rubbed against each other. I had borrowed the waders from
one of the American graduate students after asking, this time, what
equipment I needed. Harney Peak had been two weeks ago, and I
was still sore from head to toe.
"You're not a pharmacist," Beck said.
"I'm not American." I reeled in my line, still bitter from spending
that night under a bush. I still played along, though. Played the part
of the funny Chinaman making a fool of himself in the South Dakotan outdoors. "I borrowed the money, I need to pay back. I have a
full scholarship to Baylor, and it's useful to my family."
"Master's in pharmacy?"

"Bachelor's."

"You already have a bachelor's."

I said nothing.

"What's one year of a bachelor's going to do for you?"

"Make my family happy."

"Why did you even apply to pharmacy programs? Let me guess. Because your parents asked you to."

I cast my line. In Taiwan I had viewed myself as something of a rebel. Here, I was nothing but a patsy.

"That's better," he said. "Hard to believe you never used one of these." He reeled in his line. "What about Gleason and ionospheric sounding rockets and all that?"

I reeled my own line in, silent, thinking of my excitement in Ann Arbor. Perhaps that would have been my fate in another life. "Filial piety," I said. "You Americans obviously don't know anything about it."

"We do," he said. "And we reject it. For the most part. You know, it's too bad I can't give you a teaching fellowship."

"Why can't you?"

He was quiet for a moment. Had I been too bold?

"Well," he said, "you've only been here two and a half months. You've done well but you haven't done anything special, engineering-wise. It would look like favoritism."

"Special? What would I have to do?"

He paused for a moment, adjusting his fishing hat. "Research."

"Research? With you?"

"Not with me. We're going to Sweden this summer, visit my wife's family."

"Oh." I looked down at the water. Beck's teasing, his flippancy, irritated me. My life was at stake and he played with me like a toy. He knew very well that the other engineering professors I'd had did no research.

A dark form glided below, following my line, but when I pulled up my hook, it was empty, dripping water that sparkled in the sunlight.

Beck pulled a leaf off his reel. "What about Gleason?"

"He told me to come back after I get my master's," I said.

"So? I'll give you a recommendation."

I thought of Li-wen and the Professor. "I would be embarrassed," I said.

He looked sideways at me, one eye hidden by the brim of his hat. "Chia-lin, anyone who can hike up Harney Peak in wing tips can take a little embarrassment."

"He might say no. Then my chances of working with him will be ruined."

"And if you go to pharmacy school and head home?"

I said nothing and cast my line.

"To the side," he said. "Don't cast so wildly. You'll hook me in the head."

"Maybe that's what I'd like to do."

"Watch it."

"We're not catching anything," I said.

"Don't give up so easy. Fishing's all about patience. You can't just go in and grab 'em by the throat."

"Actually, you can," I said. "But it is more dangerous."

22

WHEN I CALLED GLEASON'S department at the University of Michigan, I was told that his graduate student positions had been filled for the summer many months ago.

"Totally filled?"

"Filled."

"May I speak with Professor Gleason, please?"

Pause. "I'm sorry. He's very busy."

Dear Yoshiko,

I have some bad news of my own. What my parents have been saying has turned out to be true, after all. I can't get my master's and I'll have to go to pharmacy school. I got a full scholarship at Baylor University, so I'll be able to save up money. I'll make a lot of money over the summer and I'm sure when I get back they'll pay me more at Taikong. We'll make enough capital to open that radio shop in Hsimenting in no time.

"I need to make a lot of money this summer," I told my roommate. He had been at the School of Mines for several years in its master's program. I did not normally confide in him, but I did not feel I could broach this topic with Beck.

He paused to wipe the sweat from his hands and the top of his head with his napkin. He had cooked our dinner, a large lump of pork boiled in undiluted soy sauce. I had already rinsed my piece in the sink, but when I put some on my tongue, it still drew all the saliva from my cheeks. I took a long sip of tea.

My roommate cleared his throat. "Then you will have to work at a fine establishment."

"How do I apply?"

"Apply?" he scoffed. "What you do is, as soon as classes end, you hit the road for Chicago and knock on the door at all the restaurants to get a job washing dishes."

I looked at him incredulously. It hadn't just been Sun-kwei after all.

My roommate pointed his chopsticks at me. "It's what all Chinese students do. My advice is, you go early, because the best jobs go first."

I took a sip of tea, imagining all of Taiwan and China's intellectual elite tripping over each other for the opportunity to wash dishes. For this we devoted our lives to study.

"What day is your last exam?" he asked.

"June twenty-eighth."

"Ah . . ." He shook his head. "Many of the jobs will be taken."

I put down my cup of tea, watching him shovel pork and rice into his mouth. So accepting of the status quo, so lacking in curiosity. The ultimate product of a patriarchal society intolerant of questions or backtalk.

"Mark my words," he said. "You'd better take that exam early."

A few days later he appeared in my doorway, smearing his palms against the doorframe as I punched at the typewriter, squinting at the classifieds in the *Chicago Tribune*.

"Dear Sir," I typed. Return, return. The machine dinged with reassuring familiarity. Part of my job at Taikong had involved correspondence with foreign pharmaceutical companies.

"What are you trying to do?" he said.

"Apply for a job," I said. Ding.

He shook his head. "You're wasting your time."

THREE WEEKS LATER, I hitched a ride with a Chinese graduate student who was driving to Chicago's Chinatown to stock up on food and cooking supplies. We all took turns making the thousand-mile journey for Japanese rice. Uncle Ben's was not the same.

They dropped me off at Zenith, where the recipient of my letter, a man in a white button-down shirt, handed me a radio across the table. "It's broken. Fix it."

"YOU'RE FIXING RADIOS in a factory?" Beck's eyebrows wrinkled together. He sat behind his desk, his feet up on a filing cabinet, his hands clasped together on his stomach. Mrs. Larsson, in an electric-blue dress, bustled in to place a folder on his desk, then hunted around inside a drawer.

"Pay is very good. It's better than being a dishwasher." I was a bit stung at his reaction. Gleason would have been more impressed. "Not everyone can fix radios, you know. I had to take a bus down and interview and pass their test."

Beck cocked his head, looking sideways at me. "What was their test?"

"Fixing broken radios. I did it easily, and the others could not."

"And you're going to Baylor at the end of the summer."

"Yes."

Beck scratched his head. "I don't know what to say. I guess you must love your parents."

"It's not about love. You Americans are always talking about love."

"What is it, then?"

"Duty. Honor. Respect."

"Well, who's respecting and honoring you?"

I hesitated. "My family will. My son will," I said. "I think."

"You think?" Beck folded his arms. He looked at me for a long time, and while he did I thought wistfully of Mount Rushmore and Bashir and how I'd wanted to be like him — unencumbered, confident.

"Well, enjoy pharmacy," Beck said. "And remember that in America, we can change our minds."

I walked out of his office, head reeling. Mrs. Larsson was standing by the door and caught my arm. "Where are you staying?" she said.

I turned to her in surprise at her low tone, my eyes glancing over her neckline, which revealed a lot more than Yoshiko's ever did, both because it was lower than anything Yoshiko would wear and because there was more to reveal. She looked at me, eyes glittering blue, the black discs within them moving back and forth. I could smell her perfume, powdery and sweet. "What?" I realized at that moment that while she often talked about her children, she had never once mentioned her husband. But the hand on my arm had a diamond ring on it.

She pulled her hand away under my glance. "To forward your letters," she said. "Here. There's one for you today."

Dear Saburo,

Leh-hwa made it out of the hospital, and my mother is taking care of her at my parents' house. Leh-hwa is back to her usual self, complaining constantly.

I had dinner there today. My father got a beautiful red snapper for me. Of course, he can't afford such luxuries, especially with Leh-hwa at home again, but he was standing in front of the fish cart jangling the coins in his pocket, and the fishmonger snared him because the fish were fresh, on ice. Ice is so big now.

My uncle's new ice company is so successful he bought a car, while my father has been puttering around in his charming way, smiling and laughing and accumulating more and more expenses.

So I was enjoying this red snapper that my mother steamed

with ginger and scallions, some roast duck, and spare-rib soup. It was such a pleasure to have so much delicious food! Then my father announced to me that his brother had finally agreed to let him into the ice company. Finally!

I said, "Do it!"

My brother's wife, Ying, had been giving me sour looks all evening and she gave me an especially sour one then.

My father told me then that his brother was making him buy into the company, at a very high price, and my father would have to sell the house.

I said, then sell it. His brother's company is doing so well — everyone has iceboxes now. This is my father's one big chance.

Ying was arguing with me, saying soon everyone will have refrigerators like you, not iceboxes.

Well, but this isn't America, right?

It really isn't fair of my uncle. He kicked my father out of the lumberyard, and now he's making my father buy into the ice company. But what can you do? He's the eldest.

My brother started saying that the house is so valuable, in such a great location on Chungcheng Road, and how much it will be worth in ten years.

My mother said, "In ten years we'll be dead. You can't eat the house. If you want to keep it, get a decent job."

Kun-ji did not look happy at that. To tell the truth, I made many times more than he did when I worked at the bank, and it was a big blow to my parents when I left home. You don't make much working in a cannery. If only my older brother were still alive, things would be different entirely.

I kept telling my father he should sell the house. He's been there for so many years and hasn't gotten anywhere. They never make enough money from rent. They're just surviving. All the other buildings have more and more stories, and their house is the only one that has just two floors. It looks funny and people laugh at them. And now he has this chance to actually make money.

My father nodded and I think he knew I was right.

Ying was so mad she slammed her chopsticks down on the table.

Countrywoman! If I were her, I would get a job instead of complaining all the time.

But I should tell you, don't worry about these things here. Don't worry about what your parents want. No one here cares what you study, and it doesn't make any sense to leave South Dakota and go to Baylor. Get your summer job and go back to the School of Mines. All they care about is whether you are sending home money, but please don't do that, either. They have plenty and you don't. The world is open to you there. Don't let this Old Country squabbling and greediness tie your hands behind your back.

By the way, your mother has a soft heart. When I was talking about Leh-hwa almost dying, she started talking about your little brother who died, and how she should have taken him to a different doctor, or taken him earlier to the hospital. She said he looked a lot like Jiro and was a very good boy, very sweet and obedient, and not so headstrong like you! She actually got a little teary talking about it. She said she was so exhausted all the time when all of you were little that she couldn't think straight.

Now Kai-ming is crying, so I'll have to go. I think I can understand how your mother felt, as I have only one child and I am completely exhausted.

Love,
Yoshiko

23

I SAT AT THE end of the assembly line at Zenith, puzzling things out. I chased the images of Mrs. Larsson out of my mind, ashamed to be ogling a foreign woman while I had a wife and baby at home. I thought instead of lying with Yoshiko at Sun Moon Lake, limbs entangled, laughing while we watched the shoji screens. I thought of the indescribable pleasures of our rosewood bed, the surprising softness of Yoshiko's skin. These pleasures were real, and they would be my reward when I returned to Taiwan.

But was this job to be the pinnacle of my engineering career? A silent radio dropped into my box and I unscrewed the metal back to poke the wire innards, testing circuits, going through protocols I had developed in junior college. I untangled, connected, reconnected, and replaced missing parts, and when I plugged it in again, Marian Anderson's rich voice rang out in snippets over the clanking of tools and the whine of the conveyor belts.

God bless America . . .

How much could I accomplish at Baylor in a year? Could I jam my schedule with courses? Was there a special short course of study for foreigners who had already been to college?

Imagine. My family at my feet.

I screwed, unscrewed, added missing components, removed extra ones. Marian Anderson was silent and then crackled back to life, the waves of her voice intersecting with the waves from the other radios behind me that were being tested, plugged in one after the other.

While the storm clouds gather far across the sea . . .

"More for the dead bucket." An avalanche of mute radios fell into my box.

The electricity galvanized the tips of my tinkering fingers, and I worked as efficiently as a machine. The longer I worked, the more my thoughts rose above my mechanized routine and hovered in the realm above, where radio waves bounced off steel office towers and skittered across the vastness of oceans; where a computer could calculate the velocity of a rocket exiting the earth's orbit. Practical, theoretical — I could do both.

What a shame, then. What a shame.

I RENTED A single room for the summer at the Chicago Formosan Club, which was run by pro-independence Taiwanese. The club was in an old bus depot with a glass door entry and a front desk where our mail was held. My room was just large enough for a twin bed, a small table, and a chair.

Dear Yoshiko,
    I have not received a letter from you for some weeks now.
Perhaps there is a delay in the mail?

The lack of news from Yoshiko turned my fantasies to dark ones. Was she concealing something? The silence became unbearable. To rouse myself from my anxious solitude I made arrangements to visit Toru's old math teacher, a man by the name of Chen Kong-hsu. Toru had described him as brilliant, eccentric, a man who defied convention and had given up a significant career as a mathematician to work as a landscaper. I missed Toru and looked forward to meeting his mentor.

I walked up the path to Chen's row house. I had guessed which one was his. Where all the other yards were sparse, his burst full: a profusion of deep pink roses scrambled up the trellises flanking his door, peony bushes lined the front path, and the red-tipped leaves of a bright green Japanese maple ruffled in the wind. The path itself was uneven, some of the bricks missing or cracked, and white paint crumbled off the doorway and the door itself, which was inset with stained glass. But the plants were meticulously maintained, glossy-leaved and rounded in form with hardly a weed between.

Chen Kong-hsu greeted me perfunctorily and brought me into his dining room overlooking the garden. The dining table was covered with books, and he pulled out a chair for me, settling into another one facing mine by the bay window. A flip-flop dangled from his toes as he crossed his legs.

He was indeed very eccentric in appearance, at least for a Taiwanese. He had a thin, gray beard and thick, round glasses. He wore dungarees cut just below the knees, the edges white and frayed, a T-shirt, and a baseball cap, from which long hair peeked out in the back. He cocked his head, studying me without reservation. He should have offered me something to eat or drink, but he did not seem to abide by any societal norms.

"Toru speaks highly of you," he said. "I just got a letter from him last week."

"Oh." My stomach fell. So the mail was not delayed. Why had Yoshiko stopped writing? My head swirled for a moment, imagining letters falling from the mail trucks, the plane, pages falling into the water — or worse, Yoshiko's hand crumpling the pages, the pages gathering dust on the desk by our bed. And then I drew myself back to the moment. "Toru has been very kind to me," I said.

"How?"

"He saved my life twice," I said.

"How so? Do you have a chronic illness? Diabetes? Cancer?"

"I was bitten by a snake," I said. "And I was malnourished."

"Malnourished? Why? Are you poor? How did you get here, then—on a boat?"

"No," I said, somewhat impatiently. "Not on a boat. I flew."

"Don't scoff. I came here on a boat," he said.

"Oh." I looked around at the piles of books, a jumble of horticulture, mathematics, philosophy, art history. In the corner of the room was an easel with a half-finished oil painting of a nude American woman. I was irritated at his intrusiveness, his rudeness, and I wondered at his sanity.

"I hid in a box," he said, wiggling his toes. "Sailed into California."

"Why?"

"I was tired of the Japanese."

Since he eschewed all semblance of politeness, I decided to, also. "You don't miss math?" I said. "You're happy as a gardener?"

"I still have mathematics," he said, pointing to his head. His glasses blinked in the light from the bay window. "But mathematics is an inhuman field. Too much, and you become separated from reality. Whereas landscaping connects me to the world. When you choose a plant, you need to keep in mind the culture of the organism— the type of soil, the amount of sunlight filtering through the neighboring plants, the amount of shelter from the wind, the macroclimate, the latitude. There are just as many variables as in any mathematical equation, but the answer in the end is a living thing, a thing of beauty, rooted in the earth."

He uncrossed his legs and led me out through his garden, pointing at each plant and proclaiming its names in English and Latin while I feigned interest.

"Now this," he said, pulling out a large, gangly potted plant with two long buds on it. "You know what this is?"

I peered at it. "Midnight orchid?"

"Yes. So you do know something."

"I know a lot of things," I said, annoyed at his condescension. "It's about to bloom."

"So it is," Chen said. "Perhaps today."

My parents had always had a party on the day their midnight orchids bloomed. It had been a political networking opportunity like everything else.

He brought me into the kitchen and poured me a cup of tea. "There you go, Saburo. It's whole jasmine flowers. A friend of mine dries them and ties the petals together like this, reconstructing the flower." He sipped, sitting back and looking at me across his small kitchen table, the side of which he had stacked with books and papers to clear a small rectangle for our teacups. "It's interesting— you and Toru, holding on to your Japanese names like some badge of pride."

"It's not a matter of pride," I said, flushing. "It's just my childhood name."

He cocked his head and adjusted his baseball cap. "It's truly fascinating to me how the Taiwanese hold on to the vestiges of Japanese colonialism, after all the Japanese did to us."

"You haven't seen what the Chinese have done."

"I've heard. People go on and on about February twenty-eighth. Well, the Japanese killed just as many people in their early years. Tens of thousands at least."

"But the Japanese were more straightforward. It was like a war, not like 1947, where the Nationalists just eliminated people on a list, dragged them out of bed into the street."

"What about 1902? Taichung?"

I recalled learning about this. "They killed a bunch of rebels."

"That's right. The Japanese government offered amnesty to any rebel who surrendered. Invited them to a celebration dinner. Wined and dined them. Killed them all. Three hundred and sixty of them. Very straightforward. One of them was my father."

He took a drink of tea and set the cup back on the table.

For the first time, I felt ashamed of my Japanese clothes.

He continued. "The Taiwanese have been subjugated so long they don't even know how to express their own identity. All they can do is express loyalty to different regimes."

I stared at him, remembering our welcoming parade for the Nationalist soldiers. How we had cheered for them, waving our little Nationalist flags, because they were not Japanese.

"There were some months before the Nationalists came," I said, "after the Japanese surrendered. We studied Taiwanese textbooks at school. I saw a John Wayne movie. My family had big parties where we sang Taiwanese folk songs."

"Your only taste of freedom in Taiwan."

"My father knew the whole time that the Nationalists were going to crush us."

"He's a smart man. You know, I know why Toru likes you," he said, resting his hand on his pile of books. "You're just like him. Aware of convention but burdened by it."

"Burdened by it?"

He nodded. "Yes. I do hope you end up happier, though."

I walked back to the Formosan Club.

Happier than Toru? I had never even considered whether Toru was happy. He was always simply there, healing, fixing. Burdened by convention? What had Chen meant? The man was surely not right in the head. I had gone into his house hoping for some kind of camaraderie and walked out feeling ruffled and irritated.

I pushed my way through the glass front doors of the Formosan Club.

Brilliant, yes, Chen surely was, and his point about the Japanese was well taken, but . . .

"Well, how do you like that? It's Tong Chia-lin!"

I stopped short, my shoes squeaking on the linoleum tile. For there, on a torn gold velvet sofa, drinking tea and eating honey-dipped donuts, sat Li-wen and the security general's son whom I had seen in San Francisco.

It had been Li-wen who spoke, and he beamed, arms folded

across his chest, so that the leather collar of his vest puffed out. The security general's son squinted at me through his thick glasses frames. "Tong Chia-lin? Oh, I remember him now. His father was Taoyuan's representative on the People's Political Council for an extremely brief time. Funny, I saw him in San Francisco with Professor Hong." He coughed meaningfully.

My hair stood on end, and adrenaline surged through my body, urging me to run. The very inclusion of the word Formosan in the title of this club implied opposition to the Nationalist doctrine and support of Taiwanese self-determination. These two men were not here on a friendly visit.

Li-wen set his teacup down on a chipped glass coffee table. "You look surprised as a rabbit at gunpoint. But really, we are the ones surprised. What are you doing in Chicago?"

"I have a job repairing radios at Zenith."

"The factory?" The security general's son raised his eyebrow.

"America has a lot of factories," I said. I wasn't going to let him imply that I was Communist. "What about you, Li-wen," I said aggressively. "What are you doing here? Aren't you working in John Gleason's laboratory?"

Li-wen laughed again and waved dismissively in the air. "That Gleason, all hot air. I'm working in a better lab with a superior computer, just down the hall. But it's too hot there in the summer for the computer to work. I have a job at a country club."

"Bryn Mawr?" I said.

He looked at me, surprised. "How did you know?"

"Sun-kwei told me they paid well for dishwashers. And I suppose that means Gleason didn't take you on."

Li-wen winced. "Brash as always. But I guess that's part of your charm. We're meeting my old classmate here." He had a sly look on his face. "He's here on vacation and loves Japanese food. There's a place with pretty decent sushi, if you'd like to come along and shoot the breeze."

I could think of nothing I would have enjoyed less. "I have already eaten," I lied. All Chen had offered me was that jasmine tea. "I'll go to bed. I'm tired from my day's work."

They nodded, and I turned away, feeling glad about getting the upper hand.

"By the way," Li-wen called, "I just got back from visiting home. Your home, I mean. Your wife looks terrible—well, for her. Coughing up a storm. Your brother says she's being treated with antibiotics, but I would guess antibiotics don't kill tuberculosis, from the looks of her."

"Tuberculosis!" I turned on my heel. "Who says she has that?"

This time, Li-wen looked genuinely surprised. "You didn't know?"

"I don't believe you," I said, though his surprise confused me. "She hasn't said anything to me."

He shrugged. "Women lie." He pointed his chin toward the front desk, which was dark. "By the way, you have mail."

24

M Y HEART POUNDED SO that I could barely work the key in my door. The door caught as I pushed it open, and I reached in to switch on the light, half expecting Nationalist agents to be standing under the dangling bulb, but the light revealed only the same quotidian barrenness of the days before — my single bed with its coarse brown blanket, a small wooden table, and a chair of orange melamine with uneven steel legs.

I closed the door behind me and looked at the letter from the front desk. It was from Yoshiko, forwarded by Mrs. Larsson. The original postmark was from almost a month ago. I examined it closely for signs that it had been opened before but could find none. I ripped it open so hastily that a picture fell out onto the floor. When I picked it up, a shock went through me. In the picture, Yoshiko wore a dress I recognized from our honeymoon — silk (I knew it to be red, though the picture was black and white) with velvet trim around the collar — but whereas on our honeymoon the dress had accentuated her curves, here in the picture, just a few months after the birth of our son, the dress hung slack. Shadows pooled beneath her cheekbones, so that she resembled her mother.

Kai-ming, glumly propped up on his mother's lap, also looked terribly thin and had bags under his eyes.

Li-wen had been telling the truth.

I paced back and forth, holding the picture, remembering my words in Jin-fu Temple.

I'll have you know I am not your father. I would not leave you to starve.

History would repeat itself. Yoshiko had chosen the one man who would do just as her father had done.

I took some slow breaths to calm myself and then stopped my pacing to read the letter.

Your mother has been forbidding me to tell you, but now I feel I must disobey . . .

Your mother is so stuck in her old frugal ways, never getting enough food. I admit I am proud, and I will not stoop to fighting over the dishes at dinner or beg your mother for more. As a result I have grown very thin and weak. For some weeks I have been coughing and coughing. When I cough I feel that my eyes will explode. Sometimes I cough so that I vomit what little food is in my belly. And at night I lie in bed shivering, though it is ninety degrees outside.

In the mornings, though, I feel better. And so over the past few weeks I kept convincing myself that I was better. I don't want to be sick now. Not when you are going to bring me to America.

Your mother has also noticed I am not able to keep up with her when we go to the market. She bought a black chicken to make soup, but of course I had to share it with the whole family and hardly got anything but broth.

But then I started coughing up blood, and my friend May-ying urged me to get an X-ray.

My mother dragged me down to the roentgenogram clinic. She held my arm so tight she left marks on my wrist. She kept saying, "You foolish girl! Don't you remember your brother?"

The X-ray showed tuberculosis. What bad luck!

I sat in Toru's office coughing and shivering, wrapped up in a

towel. My mother was hysterical, saying I was going to die just
like my brother, that it was your fault for leaving—though it's
not, of course! But I have faith in Toru. I have been in that office
so many times with Kai-ming and he has saved Kai-ming's life
that many times.

Toru moved around the office, opening all kinds of packages
with all kinds of needles and bottles. He gave me an injection
called streptomycin. It's some kind of miracle drug, something
new from the West. It cures everything, but very slowly. I'll need
to take it for four months!

My mother asked if I should go to the hospital, and for a while
Toru didn't answer. I thought it was because he was busy writing
something down in his book and he didn't hear her, so I repeated
her question.

But then it turned out he did hear the question and he was too
embarrassed to answer. Because he does think I should go to the
hospital, but he already talked to your mother about it when he
heard from the roentgenogram clinic, and she refused to let me
go. She said, if Toru can give me the medicine, why should I go
to the hospital?

My mother was so mad she was shaking her fists in the air.
She looked like an old witch, with her drab old clothes and her
face all twisted up. She kept saying, "Too cheap to pay for the
hospital! Two cars and a chauffeur!" Maybe it was my fault that I
had told her about your sisters' Japanese pearls and gold bracelets,
their alligator-skin purses and shoes. My mother kept saying
your mother was hoping I would die so they could get a girl with
a dowry. Of course I know your mother is not that bad, and she
really does like me, possibly better than she likes her daughters,
but she is very stuck in her old ways.

I got my mother calmed down and she called your mother to
offer to take care of me herself, at my parents' house. Closer to
Toru's office, she said, but she also meant cheaper than the hospital.

But your mother thought this would not look right. She sent the rickshaw to pick me up.

So here I am, back in our room. I can't work anymore. Every day my mother comes with a bowl of herbed chicken soup for me, and then we go to Toru's office for another injection. He says I really need three injections a day, but how can I go back and forth to his office three times a day? I have to take care of Kai-ming.

Every morning your mother chats with me, about her backaches, her stomachaches, and she says to me, "You must not tell Saburo that you have tuberculosis."

Isn't that strange? I asked May-ying what she thought. She said if you can't tell your husband you're sick, then who can you tell?

Her eyes were wet as she told me this, and I squeezed her hand. Poor girl! I didn't mention to you that when her fiancé went last year on military service in the South, he got a village girl pregnant . . .

So now you know everything. Your mother will be terribly angry with me for disobeying her, but I don't care.

Have you or Professor Beck heard from Senator Dickey? Please get us over soon.

The blood rushed to my head. My ears rang as though I had been slapped. What a fool I was! After twenty years, could I never learn? Here I was again, groveling to my parents, yearning for their love and approval, and they had struck me down one more time.

I put my hand to my head, knocking into the lightbulb by accident. Shadows careened around the room.

Duty, honor, respect—how much would Kai-ming respect me if his mother died on my account?

You're just like Toru, burdened by convention. I do hope you're happier.

I sat on my bed to read the letter again. I looked at my watch. It was early morning in Taoyuan, a perfect time to call, before my parents left the house. But the only telephone was in the lobby with Li-wen and the security general's son.

Why had they come here? Was it to watch me? It didn't surprise me in the slightest that Li-wen would work for whatever overseas intelligence network the Nationalists had here, but could it be a coincidence that he would be here with the very same agent I had come across in San Francisco? The fact that I had done nothing illegal did not reassure me in the least, not in the face of the Nationalists. The mere fact that I was staying in this establishment and reading its newspapers was enough for them to file some trumped-up charge against me.

I cursed Kazuo. If not for him, I would never have gone to Ann Arbor to meet Li-wen in the first place. But it was my fault for obeying my brother. Chen was right. The Americans were right. I was weak. A patsy.

I opened my door and poked my head into the hallway, still hearing the clinking of porcelain and the pompous voices of Li-wen and Kuo-hong echoing down the hall. I quietly shut the door and stepped over to my window. It overlooked a quiet alley that connected to Eighteenth Street, where I knew there was a telephone booth. I poked my head out into the steamy night and looked down, considering for a moment. About a ten-foot drop into darkness.

I climbed up onto the windowsill, pushed aside my radio, and paused, hearing the distant clattering of the Lake Street "L" mingled with the quiet sounds of the cars going by. And then I jumped.

I landed in a puddle, pain shooting down from my back to my knee, the warm water covering my ankles and splashing onto the front of my shirt. I smelled the faint odor of urine and quickly stepped out of the puddle and made my way down the alley to Eighteenth Street.

"Thailand?" the operator said.

"Taiwan." My reflection looked back at me from the walls of the telephone booth, my face haggard and dirty. I sweated, my Japanese shirt and pants clinging to my skin. "Formosa. Free China."

"But that's Asia!"

"Yes, it is."

"Sir, that's sixteen dollars for the first three minutes. I'm afraid I can't connect you, unless you happen to have fifty dollars in change."

Of course I did not. That was the equivalent of a month's rent.

"I have an address. It's my parent's house. Perhaps —"

"You can't charge this call, sir. I'm sorry."

I hung up and headed back to the alley, but when I got there, I realized my window was too high for me to reach. I looked around for a box or crate to step on, but there was none.

I made my way back up the alley toward Eighteenth Street. But just as I turned the corner, I saw them coming through the glass doors of the Formosan Club — Li-wen, the security general's son, and a third man I did not recognize.

I quickly shrank back into the alley, flattening myself against the wall. Had they seen me?

". . . not at all," Li-wen was saying. "Just humiliated me in front of the Americans, that's all. Got a light?"

There was some rustling. "Here. What were you doing inviting him, anyway?"

"I knew he wouldn't come. Too principled, even for free food. And the Americans fall for it, see, because they don't know how things stand at home. Whole lot of barbarians. . . Now, his brother, there's someone to reckon with, you'll see —"

"We'll be late for the restaurant," the security general's son said. "Where is this place you're talking about?"

"Sakura. It's this way, but it's far too unsafe to walk. We'll get a cab."

"But there are no cabs here. And it stinks of urine."

"We'll walk to that corner . . ."

Their voices grew even closer, and they crossed right in front of the alley. I crouched, turning to the wall. My arm moved up automatically to shield my face, and I was still, my nose pressed against stone that smelled, oddly in this city, of musty earth. I heard the screech of bus brakes and felt headlights sweep through the alley, filling me with fear, a primeval fear of discovery, of pain and punishment. And then I realized that I was in the habitual pose of my childhood, face in the dirt, bracing for my mother's next blow.

I jumped up and turned to face the street, come what may.

The bus roared off into the distance, leaving only the glimmer and the low purr of well-behaved American automobiles within their marked lanes, gently stopping and starting at intersections. The trio of Nationalists made its way toward the opposite side of the street and into a cab and were driven away.

I HURRIED TO the glass doors of the Formosan Club, the lobby of which was now empty. What would I say to Yoshiko? Nothing about Li-wen or Kuo-hong, of course. I had to convince her that I was doing well, that I wasn't making the mistakes she thought I was . . .

But when I tried the doors, they were locked. I felt for the keys in my pocket, but they were gone; in my anguish over Yoshiko's letter, I must have dropped the keys on the floor of my room.

The front desk receptionist would not be in until morning.

Ah, misfortune! I was still that distracted, careless boy.

I sat on the front steps of the Formosan Club. But they were hard concrete and my back seized with the pain of sitting so low down, so I stood again. Now that I actually had no place to stay, I no longer wanted to be taken for a vagabond, and so I walked. I had no destination. I simply headed down the street.

Yoshiko with tuberculosis! I couldn't bear to think of her, shivering and coughing, a prisoner in our bed. What would happen to me without her, and to Kai-ming? Frail as he was in her arms, he would surely die without her. I looked up into the night sky, and the lights from the city cast such a purplish glow on the heavens that it blotted out all but the very strongest stars. How unlike the sky over the streets of Taoyuan, which I had walked so many times, hand in hand, with Yoshiko. The life that I had fled so urgently seemed a paradise to me now. Yet it was my own people who had beaten me down so that I might abandon my own wife and child—my mother, my father, my brother, and Generalissimo Chiang.

My eyes ached with held-back tears. If only I could let them fall, they would sweep aside all the armies of Asia.

I walked, my toes squishing in the wetness of my socks, my shoes scuffing against the concrete in the dark. My shirt stuck to my back. I approached a streetlamp, and as I passed into its aura, I saw my shoes making wet footprints on the sidewalk, the muddy hems of my pants plastered to my ankles. The elevated train approached from the west, its roaring clatter echoing through the dark, and I suddenly felt, exposed as I was in the lamplight, that those on the train would see me as I myself had once seen the Taiwanese farmer in the conical hat—head down, stepping through the flooded paddies behind his water buffalo. I had felt myself above that farmer, had felt that by flying to the other side of the world, I would transcend his rote existence. And yet here I was.

The train disappeared and I walked on, neon signs reflecting in the puddles around me in the night as the sun glimmers on the paddies: ALL-NITE CAFÉ. MOWIMY PO POLSKU. JULIO'S COCINA.

It began to rain. I walked for blocks, letting the rain rinse away the mud and the sewer smell from my clothes. I took a reprieve under the striped awning of a groceteria that was still partially lit inside. Water dripped off the edge of the awning and collected in broken sections of the sidewalk.

I got the money for you, but it comes with certain obligations.

I thought of my father dropping a red envelope into the Mainlander's palm, Kazuo burning *The Earth*.

Japanese characters flickered in the puddles, neon pink. It was my mind, my memories, playing tricks on me. And then I looked up

and saw the sign in a restaurant window across the street, in both
English and Japanese: Sakura. The restaurant where Li-wen and the
agents were eating.

Curiosity drew me, and I crossed the street.

I leaned close to the glass and spied Li-wen at the back of the
restaurant with the security general's son at his side. Another man
sat opposite him with his broad back toward me. He reached out his
chopsticks to grab a piece of *nigiri* sushi with a movement almost as
familiar as my own.

Before I realized what I was doing, I had opened the door and
walked all the way to their table.

"Look who's here!" I heard Li-wen say nervously.

But I was not looking at him. I was looking at the man facing
him—at the broad, round face of my brother Kazuo.

His thick lips were open in shock, and his eyes, usually cold and
slit-like, were wide open. He wore a gray button-down shirt, and
his belly swelled so that I could see slivers of his pale skin between
the buttons.

The half-eaten piece of sushi dropped off his chopsticks, and he
looked at Li-wen. "How did he know we were here?"

"I don't know. I didn't tell him where."

"You look like a drowned rat," Kazuo said to me, recovering his
air of superiority. He picked up the piece of sushi that had fallen and
popped it into his mouth. As he chewed, the mole on his Adam's apple bobbed up and down. He looked at his plate, avoiding my glare.

My pulse pounded in my ears. I could hardly see.

We're meeting my old classmate. Here on vacation.

So this explained Li-wen's sly smile.

"Enjoying your holiday?" I said, a bit louder than was necessary.

"Have a seat, little brother," Li-wen said. "Have some sashimi.
The tuna is very good. Just like home. Or perhaps you've eaten
here before?"

"I don't eat in such expensive restaurants," I said. "I've been saving money to send home."

Kazuo looked embarrassed and took a drink of sake.

Even with the Nationalist agents there, perhaps because of them, because of all they represented, the anger surged up inside me and burst out. "So this is why my wife can't go to the hospital?" I said, my voice shaking. "So you can come here for vacation?"

Kazuo set down his sake and looked up at me coldly. "I'm not the one who makes those decisions. It's *Oto*——" He glanced at the security general's son, who was watching us with interest while he piled pieces of sushi onto his plate. "Our father and mother. I had an opportunity of a lifetime and I took it. The amount of money is a pittance compared to what they're paying for you. I'm only here for two weeks."

"I'm sure it's less expensive than a few weeks at the hospital, too."

"It is, actually. That hospital is damn expensive." He folded his arms and looked up at me. "Li-hsiang is getting treatment at home. She's fine."

"That's not what I hear." I glanced at Li-wen, who was looking sheepishly at his plate. He had set a piece of sushi for me on a little plate and set it out in front of me with a dollop of wasabi and soy sauce.

"Take it up with our father." Kazuo unfolded his arms and reached for another piece of sushi. Salmon with roe on top. "It has nothing to do with me."

I said nothing but watched him chew, the mole bouncing up and down, a piece of seaweed sticking out between his lips. I hated him at that moment more than I ever had.

But he was right. Loathsome as he was, he was no more than an instrument of our parents. I hated him because of them.

I turned on my heel and walked out of the restaurant.

"*Eh*, you forgot your sushi!" Li-wen called.

I turned back and saw him standing at the table, holding out the plate with its piece of tuna.

"I wouldn't trust the fish here," I said. "The ocean is hundreds of miles away."

Kazuo waved dismissively. "Don't forget about the Great Lakes, stupid."

I STEPPED OUT of the restaurant and into the street, my feet falling ankle-deep into the water coursing along the curb. As I crossed, the rain came down hard on my head, cold and elemental, pouring down my neck and over the scars on my chest.

The sight of Kazuo dining on fine food and sipping sake while my stomach was empty and Yoshiko succumbed to tuberculosis at home enraged me to no end. But I let my resentment fall, washed away by the rain. It was my parents, not him. It had been them all my life.

A taxi pulled up next to me, splashing me from the chest down. "You goin' somewhere? Wanna get dry?"

I looked at the driver, a thin black man wearing a beret and large plastic glasses. From what I had seen of the United States, he had surely known a lot more hardship than I had. And yet here he was, cheerful, eking out a living, helping a poor drowning Chinese man who would get the backseat completely soaked.

"Where you goin'?" he repeated. "You comin'?"

The Formosan Club was locked. The factory was closed.

"Yes," I said. "I'm coming."

THE WALKWAY SMELLED of roses.

Chen opened the door and watched me dripping onto his door-mat. His glasses blinked as a car passed by on the street, and I saw that he had brown stains on his T-shirt. "Saburo. You're back." He said my name, I thought, with some derision.

"I've been locked out. I need to use the phone."

"Ah. That explains it. Chinese usually flee from the elements."

The rain fell on my head as he considered me. He had already fulfilled his obligation to Toru by inviting me in once. I had the feeling this was the most his doorbell had rung for a long time.

He stepped back and waved me in. He put a couple of folded newspapers on a dining chair and indicated for me to sit. "Why were you locked out?"

"There were Nationalist agents there."

"At the Formosan Club? Why?" He settled into his own chair, facing me. It was as though I had never left, although I saw that he had brought the midnight orchid inside and it was sitting in a clearing between stacks of papers by the bay window. The giant white blooms had begun to open, and the room was filled with the powerful, sweet smell. The fragrance, seductive enough to ensure pollination during the eight hours the plant was in bloom per year, transported me back to the self-important parties in my parents' great room, where I would see the Taoyuan magistrate admonishing my father to be more optimistic, where my uncles would drink warmed sake and sing one sad Taiwanese folk song after another. My stomach grumbled in remembrance of the trays of shio mai, taro cakes, fried shrimp balls—foods normally forbidden to me but at parties up for grabs for all comers.

"They were waiting for me," I said.

"Why, what have you done?"

I shrugged. "Nothing."

"Did they see you come here?"

"No. They went out for sushi."

"How ironic."

Once again, seeing that he eschewed courtesy, I did, too. "I'm hungry," I said. "And I need to call Taiwan."

He raised his eyebrow. "Let's start with dinner." He got up and went to the kitchen, returning with a plate, on which he'd placed rice and a leg of chicken in some kind of sauce with an unfamiliar, deeply savory smell. He pushed aside a stack of papers on the dining table to make room for the plate. "Coq au vin."

I was so hungry that I did not argue. I ate with a knife and fork, the rich, unfamiliar flavors melting in my mouth. He set a cup of jasmine tea by my plate.

"You like it?" he said. "That's red wine. Chinese don't use that."

When I was done, I sat back. He was still watching me, sipping his tea, and I was acutely aware of his penetrating gaze, of the powers of his observation, his everyday brilliance. I wanted to call home, but I knew he already knew I did, and he was waiting for something before he offered. What that was, I had no idea.

"Why did you say Toru is burdened by convention?" I said. "Why do you say he's unhappy?"

Chen set his tea on the dining table and clasped his hands around his knee. "I've known Toru for a long time, since he was a young man. Always a good boy. Like you. He noticed things but kept his head down. Stayed out of trouble. A brilliant student. He had talent in math, but his parents wanted him to go to medical school, so he did. Of course, that's not unusual."

"Not at all." I felt a bit defensive about the man who had saved my life and my son's. "He's a good doctor," I said.

Chen nodded. "Of course. But he would have been good at many things. That doesn't mean he would have been equally happy doing them all. But this is not the point of my story." He took a sip of tea and wiped a jasmine petal off his lip.

"When he was in medical school, he met a lovely young nurse and fell in love with her. He wanted to marry her, but she was from a poor family. Her mother was the second wife of a merchant and had divorced her husband. Toru's parents did not approve of the match and said they would disinherit Toru if he married the girl."

I had wondered why Toru wasn't married. "So he didn't."

"He didn't. He's told you this before?"

"No," I said. "But he told me once, I had only one chance at life."

"And did you listen?" Chen looked at me intently.

I hesitated. "Yes."

"Good. Because I said much the same to Toru and he did not listen to me."

"He's alone," I said.

"He is."

"What happened to the nurse — the girl?"

"She married Toru's best friend."

For so many years I had thought of Toru as only a doctor. Of course he was a man, too. I remembered his agitation when I told him about Yoshiko.

"What about you," I said. "Why are you alone?"

"My wife died ten years ago," Chen said. "Pancreatic cancer. There was nothing to do. So you see I know both, having and losing." He got up and took my dishes into the kitchen, his flip-flops slapping against his feet.

I followed him into the kitchen. He stood at the sink, filling it up with soapy water.

"Did you know my wife has tuberculosis?" I said.

He looked over his shoulder. "Yes."

I stepped forward. "Why didn't you mention it?"

"I thought you knew."

"What about Toru? Why didn't he write me or wire me or something?"

Chen shrugged. "Who knows? Maybe he was told not to?"

Blood rose to my face. I was angry at Chen. Angry at Toru. Angry at Kazuo. And then I felt my anger melt away. They were not the ones at fault.

Chen finished rinsing the dishes, turned off the water, and dried his hands. He glanced shrewdly at my face. "Come. The orchid is still opening."

I followed him out to the dining room, where we sat in facing chairs by the flowerpot. The blossoms had indeed opened slightly more, revealing the long, powdery stamens at their core, the scent of the orchid blooms mingling with the traces of savory red wine.

"My parents won't pay for my wife to go to the hospital," I said. "But they paid for my eldest brother to come to the United States for vacation."

"Hm." Chen struck a match and lit a pipe, his toes tensing in his flip-flops. He puffed, waving out the match, and wiggled his toes. "Why do you think that is?"

I considered. "Because they think he's worth everything and I'm worth nothing."

"Have they always thought so?"

"Yes." I felt a twinge in my chest.

"Do you think that's true?"

"No, of course not. I'm the one who passed the exam."

"Self-worth is more than an exam." He puffed, looking at me through the smoke. And then he started shuffling through the books, papers, and magazines on his dining table. He pulled out a telephone, yanking a length of wire from the piles, and set it before me. "Remember what Toru told you. Don't lose the girl."

For a moment I was speechless with relief. I put my hand on the receiver. It was cold and solid under my palm. "I'll pay you back right away," I said.

"You'd better. Landscaping doesn't pay that well."

25

I HELD THE RECEIVER, awaiting the operator's cue. I waited, hearing clicks, hisses.

"Just two calls ahead of you, sir."

My ear was sore, and I shifted the receiver to the other side. Chen got up and left the room, his feet flip-flopping.

"Okay. Now, sir."

I waited, hearing more clicks. And then:

Brrrr-brrrr. Brrrr-brrrr.

They would no longer be sleeping, as it was now past nine in Chicago. The sun was rising high over Taoyuan, oppressively hot, baking our dirt road into fissures, dulling the colors of the earth so that even the cranes flew low, close to the water in the paddies.

Brrrr-brrrr

"*Ue?*"

I pressed the hissing telephone receiver to my ear, but the distortion of sound was so great it was impossible to discern even the gender of the person who had answered.

"*Eh*," I said. "It's Saburo." My voice, translated from sine wave to radio wave, was broadcast over the Pacific Ocean. It went so far across the earth that, were it not for the band of electrically charged particles called the ionosphere, it would have shot straight through the atmosphere into space. It was the ionosphere that re-flected my voice back toward the earth and around its far curvature toward that tiny green island — Isla Formosa, Republic of China, Taiwan — where the waves were funneled into a succession of ca-bles and wires running through the cities, through the fields and the paddies, through a small hole behind the heavy front door with the old lock, to snake along the wall and reach the dull black phone by my father's chair.

"Is that really you?"

"Of course it's me," I said. "Who's this?"

"It's your mother, stupid."

Some of the frequencies escaped through the ionosphere into space, leaving a sound not true to life. The words, though, were true, and they echoed.

Your mother mother, stupid stupid.

I saw her standing there in her old gray dress and plastic slippers, no longer holding bamboo branches, clutching the phone instead.

"Li-hsiang needs to go to the hospital," I said. My radio waves crashed into hers, intersecting, passing through, driving toward home.

"What did she tell you?"

"She needs to go to the hospital."

"What did she tell you?"

"I saw Kazuo here," I shouted. "Take her to the hospital!"

I was handed to my cousin. And to another cousin. I was a novelty.

"Is that really you?" they said. *Is it you you you . . .*

Finally a woman's voice came on the phone and told me she was all right.

The voice was nasal, echoing, and harsh and did not sound like Yoshiko's at all. I found myself saying, "Is that really you?"

"*Ai!* Who else would get on the phone and say she was your wife?"

"Are you okay?" I shouted.

"What?"

"Are you . . ." I paused, listening to the echoes. I wanted to tell her so many things—how I missed her, how I regretted everything. But the line crackled, echoed, popped.

Let me let me have it, I heard in the background. *Give me give give me . . .*

"Yoshiko?"

"What?"

"Go to the hospital," I said.

I was still hearing *ospital-ospital* when she started to speak, so all I heard of what she said was *expensive-pensive-pensive.*

"Go to the hospital," I said slowly, loudly. "Or I'll come back to take you there."

Her words came quickly, blended together.

No! Your visa no! the money you won't get back in don't!

"Go to the hospital, then! And tell my mother a funeral would be more expensive! Get well," I shouted into the echoing space, "and I will get my master's and bring you to America."

26

I settled up with Chen and took a bus to Ann Arbor. I needed to talk to Gleason and I was never going to get past his secretary on the phone.

His laboratory was once again locked and quiet, and I ran up and down the halls peering into the windows. A door opened suddenly, hitting me on the forehead. I reeled backward in surprise.

"Oh! It's you!" Ni Wen-chong appeared in the doorway, pushing a cart that held what looked like a large column of jumbled transmitter components.

"Where is everyone?" I said. "Did I come at a launch again?"

Wen-chong laughed. "Well, yes. A real one, this time, at Fort Churchill," he said in his clipped Hong Kong accent. "You have quite the nose for launches. I stayed here to fix the telemetry unit. Actually, come here." He opened the door and pulled the cart back into the laboratory. It rattled, banging against the door, and Wen-chong steadied the metal column with his hand. "I wasn't able to fix it, and I was just going to drive it up, anyway, which would have made Gleason quite furious, though the data-collection device seems to be working properly. See, it all has to fit into the payload compartment, and we had to make modifications." He spoke quickly, anxiously. "I don't know what happened."

"When's the launch?" I asked.

"Wednesday morning." He laughed.

"Oh, so there's plenty of time."

"Not at all. It's way up in Manitoba, middle of nowhere. Sub-arctic, you know, there's not even a road. It takes days to get there. You can't just throw this equipment onto the baggage carousel, you have to use ground transport, and I don't have access to a car with a trunk large enough to contain all this." He looked at his watch. "There's a train from Winnipeg to Fort Churchill on Sunday. I'd really have to start driving today to get up to Winnipeg—"

The phone rang and he quickly trotted over to the wall to answer it. "Yes, Professor Gleason. Yes, well, no, not yet . . . "

I pulled up a chair and sat in front of the cart. In addition to the transmitter components, there was also a long white metal cone pierced with a metal rod that had spheres at each end. I had never seen anything like it.

". . . someone here to help now," Wen-chong was saying. He looked at me sheepishly. "Yes, I'll make the train, don't worry."

He hung up and trotted over to where I sat. I pointed to one of the spheres. "What's this?"

"It's a Langmuir probe," he said impatiently. "To measure the electron density. It works fine. It's this that's not working properly." He pointed to the column of transmitter components. "I don't know why he's so worked up about it. We can get the information we need so long as we recover the nose cone somewhere. What do you think?"

"I need a tester," I said, "and a soldering iron. Is this a pulse-code modulator?"

"Of course. The iron's right here," Wen-chong said, plugging it in. "Now, whatever you do, remember to do a solid job with the soldering. The vibrations are terrible during liftoff. Here. Let me help you set that upright."

The transmitter column had transistors and parts I'd never seen before except in textbooks and *Modern Radio*. What was I doing attacking this thing with a soldering iron? This man had a PhD in electrical engineering and he couldn't fix it. And if I wrecked this equipment, everything would be ruined. Their experiment, the launch, and, it went without saying, my future in atmospheric science.

I wiped off the tip of the iron, then picked up the solder coil and unrolled it, straightening out the end. The metal was soft and as pliable in my warm fingertips as the string I once twisted out of grass when I was a boy, making wings from scrap, wondering about that strange girl who thought me clever.

I bent toward the column and saw the circuits, the little electron highways looping and intersecting. I touched them, and the electrons skipped under my fingers. Where they paused, I pointed my soldering iron and made a bridge for them, the molecules of copper, lead, and tin jumbling together in the bubbling flux and rearranging their bonds into a new compound, so that the electrons zipped along smoothly, around and back, corralled together here and there into organized streams of electricity.

At 4:30 p.m. we checked all the components. Wen-chong, seeing the needle jump on his receiver, gave me a clap on the back. "Ah! Well done."

I sat back, relieved. Things were going my way now. They had to.

He picked up the phone to call a rental car agency, but it was a small branch and they had no cars left.

"Damn this infernal college town!"

I watched him scratch the back of his neck and call an out-of-town agency, carefully logging his call in a notebook labeled "Long-Distance Calls."

I was tired, and my back ached. I was tempted to find a hotel and go to bed—but how much more exhausted were Yoshiko and Kai-ming?

Wen-chong hung up the phone, cursing.

Now was not the time to rest.

I stood up. "Wen-chong," I said, "let's go buy a car."

27

I'LL LET YOU HAVE it for four hundred."

I looked out the showroom window into the parking lot. The horizontal blinds had been pulled up, all the better for me to see what was at stake. Wen-chong stood by a sky-blue '54 Chevy, his hand caressing the gleaming curve of its side-view mirror.

"Previous owner was an old lady. Hardly drove. That's a great deal I'm giving you, Mr. Tong."

I turned toward the salesman. He sat at his desk, tapping his box of cigarettes against the table. His hair was long and white and fanned out to the sides. His large brown eyes searched mine. "Four hundred. It's a beautiful car, isn't it? Takes a—"

"Okay."

"What?"

"I'll take it. Four hundred dollars."

The sides of his mouth turned up slightly, then opened into a big wolf smile. "Well then! Nothing I like better than—" He coughed. "How much you putting down, Mr. Tong?"

"Putting . . ."

"To finance."

"What?"

His eyes fixed on mine. "You mean you got it in cash?"

"Of course." I patted my pocket.

The lupine smile. He pulled a sheaf of papers from his drawer. "All right. I'll need your license."

"No driver's license." No one I knew had a driver's license back in Taiwan; it was virtually impossible to pass the exam.

The smile disappeared. He brought out his cigarette lighter from the pocket of his blazer. "Auto insurance?"

"Huh?"

I felt a sense of panic. The car would slip through my fingers. I wouldn't be able to buy any car at all. We wouldn't make it to Manitoba. This pink-faced man, who was trying so desperately to light the wrong end of his cigarette, was going to stand in my way because of rules I didn't even understand.

I reached into my pocket and pulled out my wad of bills. As I counted them out on the table, the salesman's eyes fixated on them. I thought of my father and his red envelope.

These people are obviously desperate and corrupt. There's only one way to deal with people like that.

My father the cynic. The survivor. I gave the pile a little push toward the poor salesman. He probably had a family at home waiting around the table. Waiting for his commission. We were all caught up in the same game, just trying to stay alive.

"Four hundred," I said.

The salesman rapped his fingers on the desk, eyeing the little pile of money. He blinked, then stuffed the money into his shirt pocket and closed the papers back into the desk. The teeth shone again. "Deal."

WEN-CHONG SETTLED INTO the passenger seat next to me and pulled the door shut.

I fondled the steering wheel, chrome and white. I had my own rocket now.

Wen-chong looked sideways at me, his face obscured by the night. "He sold it to you even though you don't have a license?"

"Yes."

"That's illegal."

"Really?"

"And how come you had four hundred dollars in cash with you? Why did you come to Ann Arbor, anyway? Are you some kind of overseas agent?"

"Oh no! I loathe agents. I came to work for Gleason," I said.

He looked at me sideways again as I turned out of the lot onto the darkened highway. "You need to turn on your headlights."

I paused, fumbling at the knobs. "I brought all my money. Everything depends on what I do here."

"Did Gleason invite you?"

"Of course not," I said. "But I need to do research this summer."

"We're full. We don't need any more students."

"I know."

WE DROVE WEST, then north, the highways stretching on for a thousand miles into the darkness.

"How do you know Professor Hong?" I asked Wen-chong.

"My father was an economics professor at Peking University under the Nationalists," he said. It was his turn to drive, and the light from the streetlamps slid rhythmically over his trim, almost child-like frame. He sat on a tote bag filled with papers so he could see over the dashboard. "He moderated the student protests there — he just opposed the civil war and the fascist nature of the government's crackdown on the Communists. He wasn't Communist. He was an economist, after all.

"But I'm sure you know the Nationalists don't make such refined distinctions. One day when my father was giving a speech at a student rally, disguised government soldiers stole in and threw a hand grenade. It went over his shoulder and exploded in the hand of a poor literature student who had picked it up from the stage and tried to lob it back. A piece of the grenade lodged in my father's neck. After that, my father took me and my mother and fled to

Hong Kong. It was just in time. Shortly thereafter, as the Communists began to win the war, the Nationalists cracked down on university students and those professors who had aided them.

"In Hong Kong my father had nothing. The University of Hong Kong did not even have an economics department at that time. My mother had worked as a seamstress in Peking, and her skillful labor supported us in Hong Kong. But my father was unhappy and booked passage to Canada. It was there, at McGill University, that he heard Peng Ming-min, the Taiwanese political activist, speak about self-determination, and in the audience was our Professor Hong, although he was only a student at that time."

"I see," I said. "He's a friend of your father's."

"Not only," Wen-chong said. He glanced in the rearview mirror and switched lanes. "Many years later my father died. That fragment of grenade was always getting infected and he would never stop working long enough to get it removed. He said he wanted to keep it to remind himself never to become complacent. And one day the infection overwhelmed him and he died."

I watched Wen-chong as he drove, but his expression was unreadable in the dark. So much suffering there was in the world!

"By that time my mother and I had joined him in Canada. Hong became like a father to me." His voice became gravelly and he cleared his throat. He gestured toward the road. "And speaking of Canada, here we are."

THE TRAIN WE boarded at Winnipeg lurched a lot more than any train I'd taken on Taiwan.

"It's the muskeg." Wen-chong, sitting opposite me, waved toward the landscape outside, what looked like plains covered with clusters of short pine trees. "Bog, basically. The permafrost layer prevents the water from draining properly and this vegetation grows on top. There's just gravel on top to make the tracks. Very unstable." Our car banged around a bend, and I winced, thinking of the transmitter I'd soldered together.

"Are you sure it wouldn't have been better to fly?" I said.

"Well," he said. He scratched the back of his neck. "I think the components are too heavy for the plane here. It's no Boeing 707, you know."

I looked back out the window. The train curved away behind us, one hopper car after another, filled with grain. All along the track, wooden utility poles leaned at forty-five-degree angles, propped up by wooden poles in gangly tripod form. The utility lines stretched, unbroken, to infinity on either end, so precariously supported that one storm, one unseasonably warm day to melt the permafrost below, and communication would be lost. I could die out here and Yoshiko would never know.

I turned back to Wen-chong. He was sitting and looking at his hands in his lap, his eyelids heavy.

"Tell me about your research," I said.

He looked up at me wearily. "Why?"

"Because," I said. "I want to do research, not just repair your equipment."

He sighed. "I don't have anything to write on."

I dug up the tote bag and pulled out a sheet of paper.

"No," he said. "That's our specifications and experiment design and such. You can't use that."

I looked at the diagram in my hand. "But this is the schematic for the transmitter! You didn't tell me you had this!"

"Oh." He looked sheepish. "I didn't realize we did."

"Well," I said, "we don't need it anymore."

28

AT LAST WE ARRIVED at Fort Churchill, stepping into air so frigid that it burned the passages of my nose and lungs. I saw with excitement that Gleason had arrived at the station with a pickup truck. Wen-chong and I waited at the cargo car for the boxes of equipment while the pickup backed into a space near us. The tundra stretched, barren, in all directions, punctuated only by small rectangular buildings.

"Here they are," Wen-chong said.

I grabbed the other end of a large box and looked around eagerly for Gleason. He was walking around the truck to open the tailgate, the wind ruffling the fur on the hood of his parka. He unwound a length of rope from a large ball in his hand.

The wind cut through the meager wool of my winter jacket, and I smiled at him, shivering, my hand resting on the box containing the nose cone. My fingers were already numb.

Gleason squinted up at me and cut the rope with a large knife. "What are you doing here?"

I felt a shock in my belly. I had thought him so kind.

Wen-chong stepped to my side. "He fixed the telemetry," he said. "And he drove me up in his car to Winnipeg."

Gleason silently wrapped the rope around the tailgate of the truck and began knotting it in place. Wen-chong went up to the truck to help him. They whispered to each other for a minute, and the wind brought their words to me.

"I can't be babysitting—isn't he that . . ."

"No, no, he's the one who . . ."

"Oh, I thought he was the other fellow . . ."

I watched despondently, my arms hanging at my sides while they tightened the rope.

When they finished, Professor Gleason turned to me, his face still somber. "I remember you now, Chia-lin. Didn't I tell you to come back when you had your master's?"

"Yes," I said. I trembled, only partly from the cold. "But I don't have time to wait."

He looked at me for a moment, drumming his fingers on the side of the pickup truck. "Get into the cab before you freeze to death."

THEY FOUND ME a spare parka and we unpacked the payload components in the blockhouse. Gleason and Wen-chong assembled the payload with their backs to me, Wen-chong throwing me nervous glances every once in a while. Had I traveled all this way to be treated as an intruder?

And then when they tested the telemetry, the dials were silent.

"Okay, wunderkind," Gleason said. "I thought you fixed it."

"It worked at the—" I began to say.

"The train ride," Wen-chong said. "Some of the connections must have come loose." He glanced at me, harshly this time. "I told you they needed to withstand strong vibrations."

I flushed.

Gleason pulled the schematic out of the tote bag. It had my writing all over it. "What happened to this? Now we'll never be able to fix it!"

Wen-chong looked at me.

"I did that," I said, feeling my old righteousness welling up. "We had no other paper, and I already know the circuits in my head, so I knew we didn't need any schematics."

Gleason stood up and faced me. "It doesn't pay to be arrogant, Chia-lin."

Arrogant! The blood surged through my head, my ears, to the frozen tips of my fingers. I turned away and stepped toward the door. It was middle school all over again. I would leave these ungrateful people behind me to flounder with their own equipment. See how they would miss me then! I could have been working all this time, making money to send home — straight to Yoshiko this time, or to her parents —

What was I doing? I had fixed those circuits perfectly well. I turned back and pushed past Gleason and Wen-chong to look at the payload assembly.

"There's nothing wrong with my connections," I said irritably. "You just assembled the units incorrectly. The inputs are all scrambled."

WE WATCHED THE launch from the blockhouse. The rocket went off smoothly, the earth literally shaking beneath our feet, and the team, including Gleason's entire laboratory plus three Fort Churchill technicians, cheered, watching the rocket roar off into the sky.

The telemetry needles jumped to life, and Gleason patted me on the back. "That's my boy," he said. "If it were up to us, Vanguard would already be up there."

"Vanguard?"

"Satellite. Guys are having a heck of a time with it. Supposed to go up in November, now they're saying December. But they'll do it. And imagine that — a man-made moon over our heads."

We celebrated by bonfire. On the shores of Hudson Bay, the fire crackled, sending sparks into the growing darkness. One of the Fort Churchill technicians who had helped monitor the launch knelt by the hot coals, cooking bread in a cast-iron skillet.

"Bannock," Gleason said. He slathered butter onto a piece and handed it to me. "The natives eat it." And then he walked away and sat by the fire. The others closed in next to him, and I remained on the outside of their circle.

I bit into the bannock. It was crunchy on the outside, and so hot inside that the steam burned my lips. Aside from the butter, it was plain and unseasoned — a simple combination of little more than flour and water. But here, in the flickering, smoky light of the fire, by the frigid waters that had slipped past glaciers and carried ice floes up and down across the Arctic Ocean to lap these shores, it was the most delicious food I had ever tasted. I ate it up, the crumbs falling down into the folds of my borrowed parka and onto the sparse grass and pebbles at my feet. I could have eaten ten more, but there was only one skillet, and the next bannock was still cooking.

We roasted sausages on sticks, and one of the graduate students said, "This is basically what we have to eat in Churchill — bannock and sausage."

There was general laughter. "And last week's newspaper," someone said.

"I'm dying for some fresh milk and a nice, fresh sirloin."

I bit into my sausage, and the hot fat ran down my chin. It was spicy and delicious. Yoshiko would have loved it.

I stood up and left the fire.

I made my way over the rocks to the edge of the bay. The night was growing darker and the surface of the water glowed in the waning light. The wind blew, and I smelled the salt in the air, the smoke from the bonfire behind me, and the bannock.

Rocks clattered behind me and I turned around to see a dark form approach from the group, silhouetted against the fire's light.

"You shouldn't leave the group in a place like this." It was Gleason. "It's dangerous."

I was in no mood to be chastised. I turned back to face the bay. Its surface undulated in the distance, toward the ocean.

"Those are belugas," Gleason said, drawing up next to me. "They come here to breed."

"They are lucky to go wherever they want," I said. "And so are you. I would be happy to feed my family sausages and bannock."

He was silent for a moment. The belugas disappeared, then re-appeared farther away, so that I even doubted whether I saw anything at all. "Chia-lin," Gleason said, "why did you come here?"

"My wife has tuberculosis," I said, and then my throat stopped me.

"And you want to visit her."

"No. Well, yes, of course.. But I can't. I wouldn't be let back into the US."

"You're trying to get her here," he said.

"Yes."

"I can't pay you, Chia-lin. I already filled my student positions."

Though I knew this, hearing Gleason say it was a blow to me, as buying the car had been a calculated gamble that he might bend his rules.

"But I can give you an unpaid internship. If you'll help us with the data from the launch, I'll put your name on the paper."

I thought for a moment. Getting my name on a major paper might be just the thing to get me that teaching fellowship at the School of Mines. But no income, in the most expensive country in the world . . .

"No money?" I said.

Gleason sighed. He took a step to the side and turned away. "Well, after you get your master's . . ." He started making his way back to the fire, holding out his arms for balance.

"Wait." I clambered after him. "I'll take your internship."

He looked back at me for a moment and then waved his arm. "Come on, then."

29

Nights, I stayed late at the lab, and when I returned to Wen-chong's apartment, where he so graciously allowed me to sleep on his couch for the summer, I lay in the quiet of the night, reading the latest papers on the newly burgeoning field of atmospheric physics.

I did also study at times under the magnificently arched ceiling of the Hatcher Library, and it was in the corner of the main reading room that I found a cluster of Taiwanese graduate students hunched dutifully over their textbooks. One of them was Sun-kwei, the Professor, whose nervous smile I studiously avoided, though I wondered what had become of his buddy Li-wen. I recognized also a student named Wei-ta, whom I had competed against in junior college in intercollegiate track meets. I remembered him as a good sprinter, and he was built like one — a bit shorter than me, with a powerful build. He had an easy smile and introduced himself as president of Michigan's Chinese Student Association.

"I remember you," he whispered over his book. "Horse, right? Taipei Provincial Tech? You beat me on the four hundred meter."

"Yes," I said. "But you beat me on the fifty and one hundred."

He invited me to his Plymouth Road apartment for dinner, and

I accepted happily, looking forward to an evening of reminiscing about track and field.

He had barbells in his guest bedroom and an old coffee table padded with pillows to make a weight-lifting bench. We took turns doing bench presses while Wei-ta's wife prepared dinner in the adjoining kitchen. My stomach grumbled at the familiar savory smells of ginger and garlic, sesame and allspice.

It felt good to be speaking Taiwanese with someone who did not appear to be a Nationalist agent and even had some social graces. Wei-ta's wife also seemed very friendly, and I wished Yoshiko were there with us, to laugh in her rich voice and shake her head as Wei-ta and I relived our glory days at the stadium.

Wei-ta led me to the living room, where his wife had set out cups of oolong tea and a dish of roasted peanuts. "I'm sorry, this place isn't much to speak of," Wei-ta said. "These places come prefurnished."

I glanced around at the pioneer-wagon curtains and imitation Navajo rugs, with their lingering smells of cigarette smoke and disinfectant. Yoshiko and I could live in an apartment like this. We'd be proud of our American home.

Wei-ta sat in an armchair and indicated for me to sit opposite on the matching plaid couch. He explained that he had tried to buy a house but was sure he had been discriminated against in favor of American buyers. He had determined to wait a year or two; the Chinese students had too little power, but there were many more blacks in the same situation in Ann Arbor, and they were mobilizing the Fair Housing Association for a housing ordinance.

"That sounds savvy enough," I said, slurping my tea. It was much better than Wen-chong's.

Wei-ta smiled and leaned forward as though he was about to tell me a secret. "Now, tell me," he said. "How did you get here?"

I hesitated, confused. "To Ann Arbor? I drove."

"No, no. I mean to America."

"I flew." I almost added "of course" but remembered Chen's arriving in his box, on a boat.

Wei-ta rolled his eyes and laughed. "Oh, come on. I mean, how did you get here without passing the exam?"

I felt my face flush. "What do you mean?"

"Listen, I've been running the Chinese Student Association for five years. Every single Taiwanese here went to Taiwan University. You can't tell me you passed the exam after vocational school. Was it some connection you had? A bribe? Whatever you did, I want to know. I've got a friend who wants to come, but he hasn't got the mental firepower for it, if you know what I mean, and he's not well connected."

My blood rushed in my ears. What a presumption! But I bit my tongue. It was probably true that everyone else here was from Taiwan University.

I put my teacup down, a bit too hard, so that it sloshed and spilled a little into the saucer. "Sorry to disappoint you," I said. "But I'm afraid your friend will have to pass the exam," I said, "as that's what I did."

He gave me a pointedly skeptical glance and sat back in his armchair, which looked suddenly dirty to me. "Didn't mean to offend," he said, though his voice was not very friendly anymore. I wondered if he had invited me for dinner solely to discover this purported secret of mine.

"Five years here and no PhD," I said, before I could help myself. "You're not even working on a thesis yet. Why is that?"

He smiled wryly. "I suppose you have the right to ask. But some have been here nine years. You have to pass the qualifying exam before you do your thesis, and no Taiwanese or Mainlander has ever passed it here. Though I suppose you could, Horse."

"I plan to."

"Go ahead and try. It's oral." He folded his arms, smiling again.

"Notoriously difficult. Professors from double E, physics, and math asking you proofs on the spot. They teach you how to do that at Taipei Provincial Tech?"

"Of course not," I said. "But apparently they don't at Taiwan University, either."

"True," he said.

"Perhaps the only thing that matters is what we do in America," I said. "People here can hardly tell the difference between Taiwan and Thailand, much less Taiwan University and Taipei Provincial Tech."

"True again." He nodded, then raised his eyebrow, cocking his head. "I prepare to be astonished by your trajectory."

NEAR THE END of my internship, Gleason informed me that I would be on his paper — not first author, of course, and not last. I called Beck's office immediately, readying myself for his dry note of surprise and approval. I had changed my decision, hadn't I? He had been absolutely right. I wasn't a pharmacist by any stretch of the imagination.

Mrs. Larsson answered. She sounded perfectly friendly and businesslike and I felt a jolt of shame at having ogled her when I left.

"I need to speak to Professor Beck. It's quite urgent," I said.

"Actually, Chia-lin, we were expecting Professor Beck back in a couple of days, but he just informed us that he'll be spending next semester in Marstrand."

"Where?"

"Marstrand. Have you ever been to Sweden? It's so lovely there by the sea, and Professor Beck loves to sail — "

"The whole semester?" My mouth went dry.

"Yes, he'll be back in January," Mrs. Larsson said. "It gets so cold there in the winter."

"But he told me I could have a teaching fellowship if I did research this summer," I said. "Now I'm on an important paper at the University of Michigan . . ."

"I see. Oh, dear. You'll have to address those concerns to the acting chairman now, Dr. Krauss. He'll be in tomorrow. You'd better hurry," she said. "The semester starts next week and you're not registered."

Damn Beck and his flippancy!

I hung up the phone and held my head. I had no idea who this Krauss fellow was, but hopefully he would be a reasonable man. I set to work packing my suitcases and readying myself for the long journey back to South Dakota. At least this time I had a car.

I THOUGHT IT would be better to wear my suit while I drove from Michigan rather than fold it up in my suitcase as I usually did. I'd be sitting in my own new car, not a smoky public bus. For the first couple of days, I enjoyed feeling like Pat O'Reilly, rocket windows down, in my fine suit. But the suit became thoroughly wrinkled after the first day and then stained with cheeseburger grease. Somewhere around Mason City I folded it back into my suitcase, and when I unpacked it in the next motel, I found toothpaste on it. I spent the next two nights trying to scrub the toothpaste off with rough motel washcloths.

By the time I arrived in Rapid City, the suit was a mess. I bought a clothes brush and brushed it off as well as I could before walking into Beck's office.

Professor Krauss looked at me over Beck's desk. He wore round glasses that made him look like an eighteenth-century philosopher. All around him were pictures of Professor Beck — Beck holding up a fish, Beck at the helm of a ship, Beck holding a baby. I thought it odd that Krauss would set up camp in someone else's office when his own office was just down the hall.

"What you say sounds impressive," Krauss said, his voice thin and gravelly, his eyes roving my suit. "But you'll need to submit an application and go through the formal process like everyone else."

"But Professor Beck told me — "

"Professor Beck is having a lovely time eating crayfish and drinking schnapps. While he enjoys himself, I'm chairman."

I kept quiet, hearing his sharp tone. He looked up at me, his face serious, humorless. No doubt he thought Beck a clown and resented his position.

"Mrs. Larsson will show you an application," he said.

Mrs. Larsson glanced at me as I came out of Beck's office, my face hot. "Don't worry," she whispered, putting a red-lacquered finger to her lips. "His bark is worse than his bite." She handed me an application. "And this came today," she said with a smile. She handed me a blue airmail envelope that smelled of her perfume. She turned her back to me and resumed licking envelopes. She obviously had no interest in me at all. I had just been vulnerable, had imagined things.

I tore the letter open.

Dear Saburo,

    It's very boring in the hospital. I'm in a room by myself so the other patients won't bother me. The food tastes terrible, but it's enough, at least, and I am regaining some of my weight. They come by three times a day to give me my medication, and once a day they record my weight.

I sighed, relieved and amazed. I had made one — albeit one very expensive — phone call. I had spoken out against my mother more strongly than I ever had. And now Yoshiko was in the hospital, getting what she needed.

    I miss Kai-ming terribly. Your parents have not brought him by, nor have they come by themselves. Only my family and my friends come, bearing me delicious treats that I have no appetite to eat.

    Your mother was so angry with me after your phone call. She said she told me not to tell you I was sick. Then she didn't say anything to me at all or even look at me until I left for the hospital. It was as though I was never there. I suppose there will be no more holding hands at the market. I think that she thought we were best friends and that I deceived her. I'm very sorry about that.

"Would you like to register now?" Mrs. Larsson said brightly.

"What?"

"You'll need to register to attend classes on Monday. You missed registration, but I'm sure they'd help you at the registrar's office. And—" She handed me a little slip of paper.

"And what?" I took the slip of paper.

"Rick's Laundry. He's the best." She winked.

I registered for fall semester, paying in cash. And I had more to worry about than Yoshiko, Kai-ming, and my mother. Because after registration and all I had spent on the car, the train tickets to and from Churchill, my summer's living expenses in Ann Arbor, and Rick's Laundry, I had $204.53 left for the entire year.

30

WHILE I HAD GROWN up considering eggs a delicacy, eggs were actually the cheapest source of protein I could find in America. And having learned from my childhood encounter with malnutrition, I dutifully supplemented my eggs with whatever odd vegetables I could afford at the supermarket. There would be no Toru here to rescue me.

I flipped an egg, but the protein stuck to the dented pan and the yolk spilled open. I tried to scrape the mess off the pan with the spatula, but it didn't come off and the egg looked even worse. I mixed it all up in the pan, hoping to make it into an omelet.

"Look at this!" My roommate held up the morning's newspaper, its letters smeared under his sweaty fingers: SOVIETS FIRE SATELLITE INTO SPACE!

"A satellite?" I stared at the grainy image of a metal sphere trailed by four spikes.

It wasn't possible. Everything I'd read had agreed with Hong's assessment, that the Russians were bluffing. Eighty kilograms to the Americans' projected one and a half, an altitude twice as high. Impossible.

Yet there it was.

I shut off the stove and scraped the partially burned mess of egg onto my bowl of rice. "I don't believe it," I said. "Those guys can say anything they want. The picture could be a fake."

"No, no! People have seen it!" my roommate said. "They're track-ing the radio transmissions." He laughed. "Except the frequency is different from what everyone expected. Tricky Russians."

I read the paper. It was true. The satellite was orbiting.

I walked to the window and looked at the sky, hung with cumulo-cirrus clouds. Above them, roving atoms tumbled in the wake of a beeping Russian sphere, their bonds jolted for the first time by this thing so weirdly smooth, so symmetrical, so man-made. Space was no longer pure, and that thought filled me with excitement, wistfulness, and fear.

Two days later I got a message from Mrs. Larsson say-ing that Dr. Krauss wished to speak to me.

As I walked by Mrs. Larsson's desk, she handed me a letter from Yoshiko:

Your sisters dropped off Kai-ming in my hospital room, saying they needed a break from caring for him.

He cried and cried. He clung to me but his grip was so weak.

He looks so thin. I told them they must take him to Toru. But what can I do if they do not?

Krauss's door was closed.

"He'll just be a few minutes." Mrs. Larsson smiled and turned up the volume on her radio, her eyes wide. "Listen," she said.

. . . *Soviets' launching of a one-hundred-eighty-four-pound satellite two hundred miles above the earth, traveling eighteen thousand miles per hour . . . This does not, according to the president, in any way mean that Soviet technology is superior to the Americans', and there is no cause for concern . . .*

"Scary, isn't it?" she said. She pointed straight up. "They're up there."

"It is scary," I said, though at the moment I was more worried about my wife's and my son's health than whether the Soviets were on the path to world domination. "Have you heard from Professor Beck?"

"Oh yes! He sent me this." She held up a jar. "Lingonberry jam. Would you like some?"

"No, thank you," I said.

"You're just being polite. You look hungry." She spread some jam on a cracker and handed it to me. "Mommies can tell."

I bit into it, and it was so sweet I almost gagged. A chunk of jam fell out of the corner of my mouth and fell onto my jacket sleeve.

"Oh no," I said. "Not again."

"Oh!" With a look of alarm, Mrs. Larsson leaped up and wiped the jam off my sleeve with a paper towel.

"How many children do you have?" I asked.

She put up two fingers. "Twelve and nine. They're with Grandma. Spoils 'em to death." She winked.

"They're lucky," I said.

Dr. Krauss's door opened. He frowned at me as Mrs. Larsson and I brushed the crumbs off my suit. Mrs. Larsson quickly switched off her radio, returned the carriage on her typewriter, and set to work typing.

Dr. Krauss let me into his office and sat behind his desk. I stood awkwardly looking down at him, fingering the sticky spot on my sleeve. There was a chair next to me, but he didn't invite me to sit in it. "One of the teaching fellows has had to leave suddenly," he said. "In light of recent events—with the launching of Sputnik—your experience with rocketry and atmospheric physics gives you an advantage over the other candidates."

I sat in the chair, relieved.

"However," he said, "I was reviewing your résumé and noticed that you attended a technical institute. Was this a four-year college?"

"Yes, it was," I said, though I declined to mention that I had not attended high school first. "College is college," I remembered Yoshiko saying. Though it wasn't really true.

"Did you obtain the equivalent of an American bachelor's degree?"

This again! He was just like Wei-ta. My stomach clenched, but I stayed quiet for a moment, calming myself down.

"It was not called a bachelor's degree," I said. "But since I'm doing well in the master's program, it must be equivalent." I crossed my arms, and I could feel my heart beating. I made myself smile. If Krauss's bark truly was worse than his bite, as Mrs. Larsson said, I had to be careful not to overreact.

"True," he said. "Though the terms of the fellowship state that the recipient must have a bachelor's degree." He rested his fingertips against one another and looked up at me.

I could not believe this was the end of my quest, after all I'd done.

I stood up and paced briefly beside my chair, then turned to Krauss. "I have learned that in this country you can change your mind. I can do this job. If you find I'm not doing well, you can take back your money and give the fellowship to someone else."

Dr. Krauss cocked his head, looking up at me. He slid a piece of paper toward me on his desk. "All right, Chia-lin. The fellowship comes with a stipend of sixteen hundred dollars a year. We'll refund the portion of tuition you've already paid. Next class is tomorrow. You do know electromagnetics?"

"Of course." I swallowed. I had never taken any courses on the subject.

"You'd better," he said. "Because there are a lot of other lads here who could teach it in their sleep." And then he sat back and smiled. "You're an interesting man, Chia-lin," he said. "I can see why Beck likes you."

He pointed out a folder on his desk. "Course description. Follow the book and you should be fine."

31

I WENT TO THE bookstore and picked up the introductory electromagnetics textbook listed in the folder. On my way out, I
flipped to the chapter I was supposed to teach the next day. How
had I managed to sound so confident with Krauss? I didn't recognize
a single one of the equations. I didn't even recognize the concepts
titling some of the sections.

I ran back to my apartment and sped through the first two chap-
ters. But the material was too dense to be skimmed and I was so pan-
icked I could hardly absorb any information. I reread the first chapter,
scribbling some notes onto a piece of paper, and tried to calm myself.
All I had to do was follow the book; the man had said so.

I did the first problem and got stuck. Luckily I had the teacher's
answer key.

Follow the book. Follow the book.

THE FIRST CLASS was a disaster. As long as I talked and
followed the book, I was fine. But unfortunately the students asked
questions.

"Pardon?" I said.

"*What?*" they said in reply to my mumbled, shamefaced explanations.

I stopped by the department office, hanging my head. Mrs. Larsson was bent over her copy machine. She wore a pink shirtdress with a full skirt, its buttons closed, thankfully, all the way up to her throat.

"No letters today!" she said brightly. "But the registrar's office called. They have your tuition refund."

"Oh, good," I said, feeling a pang of guilt.

"That's a relief, isn't it?" She winked over the dull roar of the infrared copy machine.

Infrared.

"Herschel!" I exclaimed.

"God bless you!" Mrs. Larsson said, feigning alarm.

"That's what we'll do," I said. "Herschel and Ritter."

"Sounds good to me."

"Where can I find some prisms?"

"Prisms?"

"Yes, you know—glass, to split the light."

"You mean, like this?" She turned to a large pile of papers on her desk and took a large triangular prism off the top. It was perfect.

"Well, yes. But it's yours."

"I just use it as a paperweight. But don't lose it. Professor Beck got it at a symposium. There are more like it in a drawer somewhere around here." She looked around and started rifling through cabinets. "Oh, here." She pulled out a cardboard box filled to the brim with identical prisms. "They're a little scratched. Will they do?"

"Very well." I took the box. "Now I need some thermometers and some ammonia."

She looked at me and put her hands on her hips.

"For science," I said.

FOR MY NEXT class, we spread out on the grass and reproduced simplified versions of Herschel and Ritter's discoveries of infrared and ultraviolet light. The students bent over their prisms, recording the temperature of the different parts of the spectrum and the part just beyond. Being outdoors with the Black Hills on the horizon made me feel like Wen-chong, like Gleason. It was the American approach to science. To break free from the textbook, to be free from convention. Of course, it wasn't Maxwell's equations, but we would have time for that . . .

"That's swell," I heard someone say. "It's hottest just off the red, just like the books say."

"Sure it is. But I did this in high school. There's a satellite orbiting the earth and we're doing experiments from 1800."

I felt my face flush, and I glanced around the grass to see if the other students were laughing at me. They appeared not to have heard, though I knew some of them must have, and I went back to work, quietly finishing recording my own data. I went around from one group of students to another, checking their thermometers. For the most part the students were very polite, smiling and nodding and dutifully recording their numbers. But now I knew what they were thinking underneath their pleasant, perfect American smiles. I was nothing but a fraud, and they'd exposed me already, in my second class.

I looked up into the sky. There was a moving glint of silver in the far distance, and I felt a brief moment of excitement when I thought it could be Sputnik, but then it transformed into a plane with a contrail. Somewhere up above that plane, far above the layers of atmosphere, was that silver orb, tumbling, beeping.

If only I had a good dipole and a forty-megahertz receiver, I could listen to that beeping.

"Aha!" I said aloud. A few of the students looked up at me. "Who would like to help track Sputnik's orbit?"

WE STILL HAD to learn the textbook, of course—I and the class. We couldn't spend all our time on the roof, and we had to coordinate with the other graduate students and professors who took interest in the subject. But everything we studied in the book

I tried to relate to Sputnik. The project focused my mind and gave me an incentive to learn the material well enough to teach it.

Yoshiko was worried.

Are you sure that's what you're supposed to do? Shouldn't you teach the material in the book, as the head of the department asked you to?

Partway through the semester, Beck returned. "What's going on?" he said. "Krauss says you're turning electromagnetics into astrophysics. Says you're popular but the kids aren't sure they're learning the basic material."

"I had to do it this way." I felt some remorse at deceiving him. "You see, my college was not really — "

"What's that to do with anything?"

"I don't know the material. I need to learn it this way. I need to teach it this way. Connecting it to practical applications."

He was unpacking bundles of Swedish goodies from a large bag onto his desk. "Well, that's not a very efficient way of learning theory. Here, that's for you. It's called a snowball. Brought a bunch home. Things damn near broke my back."

I opened the heavy little box in my hand. It contained a candle holder made of thick glass.

"What's more efficient?" I said. "I've been cross-referencing two different textbooks, too."

"Reading three different books is efficient? I don't know. Try the Socratic method, maybe."

"What's that?"

He looked at me, his hand in the bottom of the bag. "Why is the sky blue?"

"Why is — oh, the . . . uh, it absorbs the — "

"Exactly. You need to practice answering questions. Best way to learn. You'll know the stuff cold and you can teach it no problem." He took a box of gingersnaps out of the bag and unwrapped it.

"Who will ask me questions?"

He shrugged and handed me a cookie. "I'll ask you. You have to come up with the answers, though."

I bit into the thin cookie, tasting the sweet spiciness.

"How's your wife?" he asked, biting into his own gingersnap.

"I think she's better," I said.

"Better than what?"

"She had tuberculosis."

He stopped chewing for a moment. "You didn't tell me."

"You weren't here."

"Oh." He chewed a bit and swallowed. "If I'd known, I wouldn't have given you such a hard time."

"What do you mean?"

"Oh, well." He grabbed a bottle of liquor from the bag and headed out the door of his office. "Now you know you earned your fellowship. Mrs. Larsson! Schnapps!"

I followed him out of the office, and Mrs. Larsson handed him a letter.

"From Senator Dickey," she said. She took the bottle of schnapps and admired the label. "Ah, the real stuff," she said, smiling.

Beck read the letter and set it down on the counter silently, avoiding my glance.

My heart quickened. "What is it?" I said.

He touched the letter lightly with his finger. "The tuberculosis. Turns out they know about it, too, and that's a problem."

"What do you mean?"

"It's communicable."

"But how do they know? Who told them?"

"I don't know, Chia-lin. But they know."

32

I CALLED SENATOR DICKEY. I wired Toru. I called Immigration and Naturalization Service in Washington.

"We have to prove that she's been treated successfully," I said into my scarf. The wool was damp with my breath. Snow had soaked through the seams of my boots, and my feet were painfully cold.

Beck walked beside me, boots crunching on the snow-covered cornfield that extended for acres around us, the stumps of corn plants sticking up in rows the way rice sprung up through the water in Taiwan. How much better to be there—warm, at least, knowing your bearings, knowing nothing of this cold, confusing place that still seemed to me the frontier.

Beck wore a bright orange hat and an orange vest and carried two guns. I wore the same getup, plus the scarf, minus the guns. I was afraid of setting one off by accident. A little spaniel trotted at Beck's heels, and I stayed clear of it, too. I didn't trust dogs.

"Has she?" he said.

"She has one month of treatment left."

"Okay, so get all the paperwork together in a month."

"But then we'll be on the bottom of the pile!" I said.

He shrugged, shading his eyes with his hand. "Good cover over there," he said, pointing to a clump of trees. "This is about right."

He handed me a gun. "Quotas for Asia haven't changed, anyway, so why get worked up about it?"

I frowned under my scarf. "I just wonder how they found out."

"Her doctor tell? Here the doctors have to report TB to the state."

"No," I said. "He wouldn't have."

"You ready?" he said.

"To shoot?" I readied my shotgun.

"No," he said. "For tomorrow's class. What's it on?"

I put my gun back down. "Antennas."

He squinted, patting the dog, who sniffed the ground excitedly. "Okay," he said. "Tell me why car antennas are straight up and down."

I sighed, looking up at the sky — gray, uniform stratus clouds.

Beck's specialty: the simple yet impossibly hard question.

"Go on," he said. "Give me a good answer and you might have yourself a job."

"A job?" I said.

"Yeah. We need popular professors."

"I don't have my master's yet."

"You're getting it in June, right?"

"If I pass all my courses."

He gave me a weary look that said, Of course you will. "It'll help get your wife here, right?"

"But I don't want a job here. I want to get my doctorate, at Michigan."

"And how're you paying for that, big boy? Don't you need income to show the INS? Gleason giving you a scholarship?"

I was silent, squinting at the trees, wiggling my toes to make sure I could still feel them. Of course Gleason wouldn't give me a dime. The spaniel sniffed at my feet, and I moved away.

"Teach here during the year and take courses at Michigan over the summers," Beck said. "You know Tom Reynolds, right? Teaches signals? He's been doing the same thing for a couple years. You can carpool. Now, tell me about those antennas."

Dear Saburo,

Your parents finally came to visit me in the hospital. I had been there for three months and they came and stood by my bed.

Kachan wouldn't look me in the eye. When I asked why she had not brought Kai-ming, she said, "We are here visiting a friend. We did not come just to see you."

Can you believe that? Did I hurt her feelings so much? Of course I enjoyed her company, but I am not going to be so blindly obedient that I die. Maybe she thought if I stayed sick, I would stay in Taiwan and be her companion forever?

After a moment your mother looked around and said, "Hm. Your friends have brought you a lot of treats."

I said that I couldn't eat them all. What a stupid thing to say!

The next day, your sister Mariko showed up with two empty shopping bags from New Rose. She walked over to my bedside table, picked up the package of Japanese *moachi* right next to my nose — the *moachi* my father had brought for me — and plopped it right into her bag. Then she took the sugary bread that May-ying got from Ho Won in Taipei, the bag of preserved prunes from my mother, the Japanese rice crackers from the seamstress's daughter, the pears from my second aunt, and the red bean cakes from my elementary school principal. You always said she was the nicest sister, just a little spoiled, but she opened every single drawer and every cabinet door to find the gifts there, too, before she left, so that both shopping bags were bulging and there was not a single package left in my room. I swear she even looked under the bed.

When she left, she smirked at me, as if to say, Now who is *Kachan*'s favorite?

My friends ask how I enjoyed their treats. What can I say?

This is why I say, write Senator Dickey again. Get your PhD and get me and Kai-ming to America. I want to be free from this place.

                                                    Love,
                                                    Yoshiko

I crumpled the letter angrily and threw it against the wall. What had I done for my family to treat my wife this way? Was my mother acting only out of betrayal and jealousy? Or was she still punishing me for my little brother's death?

I smoothed out the letter.

Free. Was I free, here in America? Would Yoshiko be?

33

IN APRIL, YOSHIKO FINISHED her treatment and was released from the hospital. I got the medical waiver for her and shortly afterward received my master's, snapping my own graduation picture with a tripod. I only wished I could see my family's reaction when Yoshiko showed them the picture.

I took Beck's advice: I would work as a School of Mines professor during the year and study at Michigan over the summers. My income was enough to satisfy immigration requirements for extending my visa, and the extra years under Beck's Socratic tutelage would help me with my coursework at Michigan. If I studied at the rate of a certain Chinese Student Association president, it would take me twenty years to prepare for the qualifying exam, but my colleague who studied at Michigan, Tom Reynolds, believed I could do it in three.

"We'll take the exam then, at the same time. We'll be in the same position. I've already gone for two summers. I can't do it any longer—I'll be up to my ears in loans."

After graduation I gave him a lift to Michigan so we could split the drive and the motel bills, and we moved into a two-room apartment near North Campus. I had a desk and a refrigerator. That was all that mattered.

I found Wen-chong in the laboratory, working the ionosonde. He leaned back in his chair, stretching his arms. "Ah, it's you! Got your master's, I heard!"

I would be working on a project with him during the summers while I was taking courses. I planned to improve their rocket's telemetry design and somehow develop that into my doctoral thesis once I'd passed the qualifying exam.

As I spoke, the hallway door opened, and Li-wen's friend the Professor walked in carrying a clipboard. He smiled widely on seeing me and waved.

I stopped talking midsentence.

Wen-chong turned around. "Ah, you know Sun-kwei?"

"I do," I said.

"He's a good number cruncher," Wen-chong said.

I FOLLOWED WEN-CHONG down the hall to his office. His shoes made sharp clicking sounds on the linoleum, while mine, worn out from walking through mud puddles and clambering over rocks and snowy fields, were silent. "His best friend is a Nationalist agent," I whispered to him.

"Really?" he said, wrinkling his nose. "I don't believe it. He's harmless as a mouse."

"Perhaps he is," I said. "But he makes me nervous."

"Well then, be careful what you say. By the way," he said, "we have a launch in December. Can you make it?"

"I'm a professor now," I said. "I can arrange my own schedule."

34

INTO THE GREEN GLOW that lit up the Manitoban winter sky and waved over the cosmos like a woman's lovely hair blowing in the sea breeze, our rocket soared. Into the aurora borealis, probes at the ready, transmitters beeping. For science. For beauty.

Dear Saburo,

I took Kai-ming to Taipei, and all the passengers marveled at our boy. As soon as the train began to move, he jumped up in his seat, exclaiming, "But why are all the trees and buildings flying backward?" He had many questions about how the train works, and I did my best to answer them. I tell him he is so smart, just like his papa, a professor in America!

We are practicing English together. There's a course on the radio every morning, very early. I turn it on quietly so as not to wake anyone else in the house . . . I am glad your job is going well at the School of Mines. Can you really get a PhD just studying there in the summers?

I dreamed of Yoshiko sitting on the rocks by Hudson Bay. She wore a flowing white dress and sparkly shoes. Kai-ming jumped

around her, his feet slapping on the rocks. I strained to see his
face —

The phone rang, splintering my dream.

I sat up, finding myself in my Rapid City apartment, my night
table piled high with exams to grade and data from the December
launch. The snores of my roommates halted briefly.

I grabbed the phone.

"Saburo," a voice growled, "what's going on?"

My father! My stomach clenched at his echoing words. He ad-
dressed me only if I was in trouble. Calling me from Taiwan meant
very big trouble indeed.

"What?" I said.

"I'm trying to visit your little brother in Japan and they wouldn't
let me leave the country. They say you're a subversive."

"They" could only mean the Nationalists.

"It's not true!"

"Well, they think it is."

"What about Li-hsiang?" I said, panicking.

"Li-hsiang? Why talk about her? She's not sick anymore."

"But she won't be able to leave Taiwan."

"Of course not, stupid. You'd better come home. We gave you
the money for one year only."

The image rose to my mind of the waving fields around the
house in Taoyuan, the dark, wide floorboards inside, cool against
my burning belly. "This is my home," I said.

"*What?*"

"This is my home," I shouted into the receiver, tears springing to
my eyes. "I'm paying my own way!" The idea that he would hold the
money over my head when they had sent Kazuo here for vacation,
when he had sent my little brother to Japan, enraged me.

"*Ai!*" he said. "I had to reregister with the party to get my visa."

I spoke up again. "Then you can help get Yoshiko and Kai-ming out now," I said. "In addition to yourself. It's not good for you if I look like a criminal."

The line clicked and went silent.

IN THE MORNING I called Wen-chong.

"I have bad news," he said, before I had a chance to say anything. "They're trying to deport Professor Hong."

35

THEY'RE ALSO TRYING TO imply that you have some kind of conspiratorial connection to him," Wen-chong said. "The letter you gave me was traced."

"Well, that's absurd," I said, shifting the phone to my other ear. "I only met him once, by chance."

"Of course," he said. He hesitated. "But I think you understand how logical your government is. There's something else."

"What?"

"There's been an anonymous charge that you've been plagiarizing in our lab."

My face flushed. "Well, that's even more absurd. No one has ever done this kind of work before. There's no one to plagiarize from!"

"I know it, but Gleason wants to look into it. There are many labs in other universities, and he wants to make sure you're not duplicating something we just haven't seen. There's a committee that has to investigate any such charge, and they'll be contacting you. I suppose they'll have to talk to you by phone or fly out to South Dakota."

I hung up the phone in despair. Li-wen was trying to destroy me! I had no doubt this was all his doing. It was too much of a coincidence that the Professor had joined Gleason's lab just before these accusations began.

I SOMEHOW GOT through the last two weeks before the School of Mines' spring vacation and drove to Ann Arbor in two days.

I burst in on Li-wen and the Professor as they ate noodles in their dormitory room. They looked up at me in surprise. It smelled like stale sesame oil. On the counter behind their heads, Kazuo's vase stood, filled with chopsticks and spatulas.

"Well, it's Superman," said Li-wen after a moment. He waved his cup of tea toward me. He wore a denim button-down shirt. "Coming to save the day. I'm so glad you found us." He put some noodles in his mouth and chewed.

The Professor smiled and nodded.

"Why are you trying to ruin my life?" I said, heart pounding. "I have done nothing to you. I have a baby, you know."

"He's not a baby anymore, little brother," he said. "He's over two years old now. Clever little bugger. Tease him and he comes right back at you. Would you like some noo——"

"Stay away from my family," I said. "If you continue to play games with me, I can always mention to the INS that you entered this country illegally."

He chewed for a moment, looking down, and took a slurp of tea. "It's not me you need to talk to," he said finally. "Do you think I'm so soft? It's your brother."

"Kazuo?"

He shrugged. "Who else?"

"Why?"

He shrugged again. "He's jealous. Your parents are pressing him to marry some ugly rich woman, and your lovely wife is right there under his nose. And you're here in America, while he was too scared to even take the exam. It doesn't seem fair, does it?"

"I don't believe you," I said.

He leaned over and reached for an airmail envelope that was on the counter and handed it to me. I recognized Kazuo's handwriting.

I am grateful for your connections and all you've done, for I cannot abide the thought that he would have everything that should be mine. All my life I have done what I was asked. I have been the dutiful son, the diligent student. I have lived my whole life in fear of disappointing my parents. And for all that, I have earned nothing but a life of endless toil and a prospective bride who never smiles. While my little brother — the one who never cared, who talked back and flunked out of school — he is the hero, somehow.

"Are you all right?" Li-wen said.

I walked over to the bathroom, stuffing the letter into my pocket. I leaned over the sink and vomited. The edges of my vision began to darken, and I sat down on the toilet, head in my hands, panting. Towels hung on a rack just by my head, their stale mustiness reminding me of the futon in my parents' country house, where I had lain during the war.

After a minute, my vision returned, and a pair of green leather slippers appeared in the bathroom doorway. I looked up to see Li-wen holding a wet paper towel and a glass of water. I took only the paper towel.

He held out the glass. "It's not poisoned, my boy. We push papers. We're not criminals."

I took the glass, rinsed out my mouth, and spat the water into the sink. I used the rest of the water to rinse the vomit down the drain and wiped my face and neck with the paper towel.

He leaned against the doorframe, his mouth twisted. He put his hand in his pants pocket. "Your brother is a bit of a bastard," he said. He shifted his feet.

"He had the advantage his whole life," I said. "If he didn't end up with what he wanted, it's his own fault." I squeezed past Li-wen out of the bathroom.

"What are you going to do?"

I said nothing. Because I didn't know and wouldn't have told him, anyway.

36

Mrs. Larsson held a gingersnap in her teeth while she poured me a cup of coffee. She took the cookie out of her mouth and looked up, eyebrows arching. "What's that, Chia-lin?"

"May I use your automatic copy machine?" I repeated.

"Oh, sure!" she said brightly. "You've been dying to use it for two years now, haven't you?"

She gave me the cup of coffee, and I took a sip, the warm vapors opening up the vessels in my brain, calling things into focus. I'd been driving all night.

I handed her Kazuo's letter.

"Which side?" she said. She looked blankly at the Chinese characters, which described not only my undeserving nature and Kazuo's conversations with Tu Kuo-hong, the security general's son, but also Kazuo's favorite pulp novel series and his current infatuation with a certain well-endowed Taiwanese folksinger.

"Both."

"One copy?"

"Three."

"Three it is. Oh! There's another letter from your wife. Have a seat. It'll take me a couple of minutes, anyway."

Dear Saburo,

My father is selling his house to join his brother's ice company. My older brother and his wife are angry about it, but what choice does he have? My father is incapable of making it on his own, and his only chance at success is to join the ice company. His brother has made the price so steep. Imagine, making your own brother sell his house so that you can profit all the more! There's something deeply amoral about it, but this is the same man, after all, who stood by and did nothing while my brother died.

What can we do? My uncle holds all the cards and he knows it. My mother keeps saying we should find out what significance my father's name has, because she recalls my grandmother's saying the name had some value, but my father waves this off as another one of my mother's complaints.

"All done," Mrs. Larsson said. She handed me the warm, curling sheets of paper.

"How are your children?" I said. I longed to hear news of a happy American life.

"Oh, they're great," she said. "Getting all geared up for the end of school. They do miss their father, though."

"Where's their father?"

"He's passed on," she said. She handed me the envelope, eyes down, and lifted her chin slightly. "Korea."

TWO WEEKS LATER, I received a telegram from my father:

RECEIVED YOUR LETTER. WILL FIX.

It was hard for me not to read this as angry, both because of the stark format of the telegram and because I had always experienced him as angry. I wished I could see him face-to-face, for the one moment that he might be defending me against Kazuo. Did my father finally see my worth? Or was it simply the responsibility of a man for his underlings, like the time he had rescued me and *The Earth* from the Nationalist soldier? Was it just that he wanted so badly to visit my brother in Japan?

I heard nothing else for months except from Yoshiko.

Dear Saburo,

There has been a lot of strife here since you sent that letter to your father. I don't know exactly what you said, but your father has been irritable as an old bear, growling and snapping at Kazuo. Kazuo finally agreed to marry So-lan, that scowling girl with three downtown Taipei apartment buildings as her dowry. He and your father have been in a terrible mood.

But the house is full of activity, as Jiro has also found a bride, a bank teller named Li-sing, who wears bright blue powder on her eyelids and has been plying your parents with beer. Plans are for a double wedding. The phone rings again and again and packages are piling up all over the great room. I couldn't help noticing that two of the packages were very ornate and expensive wedding dresses for the brides . . . Well, expensive or not, my dress was much more beautiful.

I told Kai-ming he would have two new aunts by his next birthday, and he was quiet for a moment, then ran down the hall, shouting, "Oh no! I'm dead! New aunt! New aunt!"

Poor boy! His aunts were so cruel to him while I was in the hospital. For him these years have been very hard.

These years. My poor boy! And I didn't even know him.

I knew only *of* him. And all that I knew was in the gossamer blue airmail envelopes I received from Yoshiko. I told myself that this was enough, that I knew just as well as any father how high my son could count, how well he could throw a ball. I knew, from pictures, his delicate face. A photograph of him on one foot was enough for me to divine his sense of balance, his confidence.

But I knew what I told myself wasn't true. Yoshiko's words on

onionskin, a two-inch photograph—these were nothing real. As
the year stretched on and I received more letters detailing Kai-
ming's larger shoes, his height, now thirty-six inches exactly, his
hilariously bold comments (to a teasing uncle: "I'm the boss and
you'd better listen to me!"), I felt more and more that I had made
a mistake in leaving him. Probably Yoshiko alone was giving him
more love than I had received from my whole family as a boy. But
he wasn't getting anything from me except for messages and the
few small gifts I could afford to send. Between my studies in South
Dakota, in Michigan, and in South Dakota again, I arranged my pictures of Kai-ming—once so tiny, now one, now two, now wearing
a new birthday shirt with an orchid pinned to it, left over from my
brothers' wedding. Yoshiko's father had abandoned his children for
a year. Now I had abandoned Kai-ming for three.

"IT'S A BIT of a delicate situation," Senator Dickey said.

It had taken some doing to get myself into his office. Some
months earlier I had bumped into Bashir, the Lebanese student I
had met at Mount Rushmore. He was indeed now pursuing a career in civil service and had been working summers as an intern
with the South Dakota State Legislature. It was through his efforts
that I had obtained fifteen valuable minutes with a United States
senator.

The desk surface gleamed, reflecting light onto the double chin
of this man who had been chosen free and clear by the people of
South Dakota to represent them. He looked perfectly ordinary to
me—a white man with trim gray hair and rectangular glasses. Did
he have special skills of oratory, a special way of appearing as every
man's friend or father? Was his house filled with sycophants and
operants, whispering and persuading, while his children cowered
in the shadows?

Through the window behind him, snow fell, coating the pine
branches and making them sag. Pheasant-hunting season had come
and gone again.

"The government of your country, the Republic of China, has been allied with us against the Communists since the Sino-Japanese War." He cleared his throat. "So on the one hand we don't want to upset our allies. On the other hand, we want to discourage foreign governments from throwing their weight around in inappropriate ways within our borders—"

"That's right," I said. "Especially when some of their agents are not even here legally."

He took off his glasses and rubbed his eyes. Suddenly he seemed old and very weary. "Not here legally?"

"Yes."

"I suppose I should ask you who."

I was silent. Even after all the trouble they'd caused for me, I felt sorry for Li-wen and Sun-kwei. They were lightweights, really.

Dickey gave a little wave of his hand and sighed heavily. "Actually, I don't want to know." He sat back and fiddled with a golden letter file. "Any other reason why they should listen to me?"

"You're an American senator," I said. "They want to stay in the UN."

He looked at his watch, scratched his head, and sighed. "You know, Chia-lin, I'll tell you something. I really am not sure the US has any business meddling in Asia."

I swallowed.

"I mean, look what happened in Korea. Fifty thousand American boys dead, in some country most Americans can't even find on the map."

"But—"

"And all this squabbling between the Nationalist Chinese and the Chinese Communists. Who is the real ruler of China? Well, who cares? How is that our problem?"

I said nothing.

"But you're not asking me to fix that problem, are you, Chia-lin?"

"No," I said.

"Give me your information."

I handed him a stack of letters representing my odyssey through the United States. Pat O'Reilly, Ni Wen-chong, Professor Gleason, Professor Beck.

"You know," Senator Dickey said, taking my papers, "the thing that gets me about this case is that your own brother did this to you. Now, that's what makes me mad."

"ANY NEWS?" BECK said.

We sat on folding chairs on a vast frozen lake in Custer State Park, watching our lines freeze in the fishing hole. Other fishing parties on the lake had huts — heated ones, even. We, of course, had none.

Beck wore a red parka and a mink hat he'd bought in Czechoslovakia. I wore the new parka I'd splurged on at Sears. It was so cold the air hurt my lungs when I breathed in. It reminded me of Fort Churchill.

"My son has measles," I said.

"I thought he already had measles."

"I thought so, too."

"What about your wife?"

"They say the quota will be abolished soon. We just have to get me cleared of the political charges."

"You said your father's taking care of it?"

"I think so."

"And Senator Dickey?"

"I think he will help," I said.

I got a bite on my line. I pulled it up, and a silvery trout wriggled three beats on the ice before it froze. I pulled my fingers back up into my sleeves. No need to end up like the fish.

I drove us back over Iron Mountain Road, which hugged the side of the mountain with precipitous drops to the side.

"When are you taking your qualifying exam at Michigan?" Beck said.

"Oh, a couple years. First I'll teach signal processing this year so I can review that, then the next year I'll do — "

"Just take it. You're ready."

"But it's extremely difficult. It's oral, and they can ask you any-thing. None of the Taiwanese there has ever——"

He glanced at me sideways.

"One more year," I said.

"What happened to the plagiarism charge?"

"It's dropped," I said. "I'm very lucky. Otherwise, Immigration would say I do not have moral character and I could not stay or get my wife here."

"You're not lucky. I'd say you're not lucky at all——"

Suddenly a car zoomed out of a narrow tunnel into our lane.

"*Ai!*" I swerved and felt the tires skid on the icy road. The steer-ing wheel spun out of my grasp. I slammed into the horn and then against the door.

When the car came to a stop, Beck was leaning against me. He looked sideways at me and then moved back over to his side of the car. One of his mink ear flaps was over his eye, and he swiveled the hat back into place. "As I was saying . . . ," he said.

"We're on the wrong side of the road." I reached for my door handle.

"I wouldn't do that if I were you," Beck said.

"Why? We need to get out." I opened the door and shifted to step outside. But my foot didn't touch anything. I turned to look and saw the ground——a thousand feet below my dangling boot. We hung over the edge of a cliff, prevented only by the base of a half-dead tree from plunging down and crashing onto the glinting ice below. I recoiled into the car and began shaking. "My God," I said.

"You don't take no for an answer, do you?" Beck said. "Some-times that's good, and sometimes that's not going to work out well for you."

37

Dear Saburo:

    I got a letter from Senator Dickey saying that I have been "reclassified into the preferential portion." What does this mean? Will he let us in soon?

                         Love,

                         Yoshiko

I bought a little yellow house on Elm Street and filled its empty rooms with furniture from Sears and Montgomery Ward. For our bedroom, a double bed with a bookcase headboard for my bedtime reading. For Kai-ming's room, a small twin bed, as Yoshiko had told me he no longer needed a crib. There was a guest room, and in there I put a full-size bed with a very firm mattress — easily the most expensive bed in the house, because Yoshiko had told me my father was planning to visit as well.

I leaned out the window of the living room. Against the backdrop of the low, snow-covered hills that separated Robbinsdale from the School of Mines, the apple tree out back was beginning to bud, its branches swollen with the promise of sweet beauty after the frigid blasts of winter. Perhaps this fall my wife would be here to twist the ripe fruit off our own tree. Perhaps we could bite into the juicy flesh together — I, Yoshiko, and Kai-ming.

I opened the window. The grasses rustled, and the cool wind, spiced with new life, rushed into my body like an embrace.

AND AT LAST:

Among the gray and brown figures making their way down the stairs from the plane in Rapid City, in bold relief—black hair, fire-red coat—she appeared. She stopped for a moment on the stairs, scanning the crowd. She was dwarfed by the pale midwestern throng around her, her face thinner, her nose and chin more pointed than I recalled, though less skeletal than in the photograph of her at the height of her illness. I felt as I had when I was a boy at the Nationalist parade, spying her across Chungcheng Road between her father and her beloved brother; as I had peering through the pharmacy window the day before the meet, wondering whether she really was that same girl I had clung to in the air raid. But then her eyes found mine. And this was the difference between then and now: she was mine, and she came to me, stepping carefully down the stairs, her high-heeled legs appearing and disappearing between the flaps of her coat as she descended. Though she had flown for two days, her hair was styled in a glossy bouffant and her complexion was white and immaculate. She held the hand of a child—my impossibly big son, navigating his own way down the stairs, his face echoing Yoshiko's delicate features. As they climbed down, a camera bulb flashed in Yoshiko's face, and she and Kai-ming looked up in surprise at a stranger taking their picture.

They reached the tarmac, and we embraced, feeling the people rush by. She was slight in my arms, soft and vital, her breaths quicker than I remembered. I clutched her hard. I couldn't believe I had almost lost her. My nose in her hair, I smelled peach blossoms, the scent of life.

But I could not hold her forever. There were the people squeezing by, Kai-ming at our feet. I released her, and she smiled up at me, eyes sparkling, mouth bright and lovely. I had told her Americans did not have gold teeth, and she had gotten new porcelain ones.

I picked up Kai-ming and he held me at arm's length. The weight of him sent searing pain down my leg.

"Don't you recognize your papa?" Yoshiko laughed, that rich, womanly laugh that put me at ease. I smiled at my son, but he did not smile back. He blinked, his eyes scrutinizing mine, scanning my face, my hair. And the idea of him that I had built up from all Yoshiko's letters, of his illnesses, of his first steps, of the time he escaped from his crib and the time he rode the train, blew away like the merest wisp of vapor. Here in my arms was a four-year-old boy full of life, his fingertips brushing my shoulder, his body twisting unexpectedly as he glanced at his mother, and we had not one shared memory, not one shared smile. I did not know his movements, his expressions, his smell. I did not know my son at all.

He turned back to me. "*Amah* took my gun," he said seriously.

"What?"

A dark expression passed over Yoshiko's face and she touched the child's hair. "No need for that. Be happy. We're in America!"

I GLANCED AT Yoshiko as we drove, the bright coat throwing into relief the whiteness of her throat and the pink delicacy of her lips, smiling and half-open at the new world around her. The light reflected from the plains and played upon the luminosity of her skin. On all sides, the grass stretched to the horizon, forming a landscape vast and empty beyond the imagination of any boy or girl growing up on an island so dense with life as Taiwan.

"*Aiyo!*" she exclaimed. "There's nothing here!"

"That's right," I said. "But it's a good place to live. I'll show you."

The light caught the gold in her eyes as she turned to me. "I'm very happy," she said. She touched my arm and laughed so that her dimples showed. Then she looked down for a moment. "Your father's coming in May," she said. "For four months."

"Four months! Why?"

"He said he wants to see the country. But he seemed very serious about it. I think he wants to talk to you about something."

"But we're moving to Michigan in the summer. I wanted to take the qualifying exam in August and then work on my thesis."

"So he'll see Ann Arbor, too. He can help us move."

I had never seen my father lift a piece of furniture in my life.

"What about my studying?" I said.

"Study. If he wanted you to cater to him, he should have asked what was a good time for a visit."

I looked at her. She sat upright, looking straight ahead, and there was a bitterness in her lovely eyes that I had never seen before.

I HAD PIGS' feet and noodles waiting on the table at home because it was Kai-ming's birthday.

Yoshiko laughed. "I don't even know how to cook that myself!"

Kai-ming seemed satisfied, and he ran around the little yellow house as though he owned it. At nighttime, tucked into the bed I had purchased at Sears, he said to me, "My mama says you'll get me a new gun."

I found Yoshiko in our new bedroom, unhooking the clasp of her faux pearls in front of the bureau mirror. She unpacked her toiletries from a train case.

I sat on the bed, watching her. After so many years of yearning to have her in my bed again, I was impatient for her to be done with her preparations. But then she rubbed her eyes, and I could see now her fatigue, the weight of traveling so long with a child, of being in the opposite time zone. She had had an overnight connection in Seattle, and I had arranged for an acquaintance's wife to meet her and take her to a hotel for the night. If not for this stranger's coming to pick her up again in the morning, Yoshiko had told me, she would have missed her flight. She had slept so deeply she did not hear her alarm.

She pointed to a cloth-covered bundle on the bureau. "That's my money. It's a lot. We should put it in a safe place."

"I'll put it in the bank tomorrow."

She nodded, opening a jar of cold cream. "Your mother wanted it. She saw me packing and said, 'There's no need to take all your money to America. Just leave it with us.' "

I felt sick to my stomach.

"And then a day later, Kazuo came in and sat down to watch me pack. At first I thought he was being nice, helping me pack. He really hadn't been so bad recently. He plays well with Kai-ming and gives him rides on his back.

"He said, 'You're working so hard. You should take a break.'

"I thought that was very nice. But then he folded his arms over his belly — he's got a big one now. He said, 'There's no need to pack so much. There's gold in the streets of America. All you need is one dollar, and you can leave the rest with us.' "

Yoshiko turned to me, eyes flashing in the dim light. "Can you believe it? Do they think I'm stupid?

"After he left the room, I realized it was your mother. *Kachan* had asked him to talk to me. I was so angry I grabbed a fistful of cash and stormed into the kitchen. *Kachan* was there pickling cabbage, and she looked up at me with her mouth open. I threw the money on the table. 'Take it!' I said. I was so angry. And that made them stop bothering me. I gave them a few hundred. They have no idea how much I had stored with my parents."

I was speechless, both at my family's greed and at my wife's boldness.

"Kazuo makes plenty of money as a doctor," Yoshiko said. "And with So-lan's money, he has all the money he could possibly want. Your parents, too." She shook her head.

Ah, but no amount of money will be enough, when what you really want is Yoshiko. In a way, I felt sorry for Kazuo, and even for my mother.

Yoshiko continued dabbing the cold cream onto her face. With the anger in her eyes, she looked more like a warrior applying war paint than a lady performing her beauty routine.

"Kai-ming keeps talking about a gun," I said.

"*Ai!*" She clicked her tongue, wiping the cold cream off her cheeks with a tissue. "It was his favorite toy. My uncle gave it to him. You pulled the trigger and it went *tyak, tyak, tyak.* We were all ready to bring it onto the plane and he was out on the tarmac shooting with it.

"When it was time to board, your mother called for him to come over, and I thought, How sweet, she wants to give him a hug." She glanced at me. "But then she grabbed the toy gun and yanked it out of his hands. She said he wouldn't need it in America and she was going to give it to her nephew."

Yoshiko turned to me, her face dark. "Kai-ming started screaming. I took his hand and turned my back to *Kachan.* I wished I had a thousand backs to turn to her, a thousand chances to refuse to say good-bye. Kai-ming was crying so hard he couldn't walk, so I had to carry him. Him, my X-rays, my carry-on, and everything. I walked all the way up the stairs and onto the plane, all the way to our seats, which overlooked the tarmac, and not once did I look back at your mother."

She sat on the bed and blew her nose. "Why don't they love you, anyway?"

My head swirled.

"They used to tell Kai-ming you were dead, you know. They thought it was funny when he cried." She looked at me and grabbed another tissue. "I will never go back there," she said. "Not ever."

38

I WOKE IN THE morning to hear her singing in the kitchen, the song of the fisherman's wife. Her side of the bed was still warm.

Looking at the net, my eyes redden — such a hole!
I want to repair it but have not a thing . . .

Alone and miserable, my lover has gone hiding.
I sew but have trouble controlling the needle and thread.
My long needle connects West and East.
My thread is a bridge to the Milky Way . . .

I had watched her sleep in the moonlight. So many years had passed without her it seemed a waste of time to sleep when she was here, living, breathing, her eyelids fluttering. In the middle of the night, when it would have been noon in Taiwan, her eyes had suddenly opened and she had laughed to find me watching her. And I had reached for her, made love to her.

I walked into the kitchen, and she stood at the sink, smiling at me. Sunlight, reflected by the snow, poured in through the window, illuminating her face, catching the gold flecks in her eyes. I touched her waist, feeling its curve through her yellow flowered dress, and I kept my hand there, relishing the desire between us, the years of longing come to fruition, the future laid out before us like a sure path through the forest.

She turned, her waist tensing under my hand, and handed me a cup of steaming tea.

"From my father," she said. "The best."

I took a sip of the fragrant tea. It transported me to our courtship, to waiting in the living room with her mother. Waiting for Yoshiko to come home from work, waiting for the proper time for our engagement. Waiting for this.

"My father is doing very well now," Yoshiko said. "He has a nice new house and he's even been able to buy some land from his brother."

"So you were right about selling the house," I said.

"I was!" She smiled. "Even my sister-in-law is satisfied. My father said, 'Next time you come back, maybe I will have two houses' — "

A sudden sob cut off her words. The dream was over. She turned her head to the side and put her cup of tea on the counter.

Ah! What she had given up for me! In escaping from my parents, she had left her own. I looked down, crushed under the weight of what I had done to her.

Kai-ming came running in. "Ma! Why are you crying?"

He ran to her and wrapped his arms around her legs. He glared at me. He was fully dressed, even wearing his hat and parka.

Yoshiko laughed, sniffling. "Kai-ming, where are you going?"

"I'm going outside to play in the snow. Why are you crying?"

"Ah, don't worry. Your father and I were just talking about how much better life will be for us in America, you silly thing. You can't go out by yourself like that. Four years old and our first day in the United States!"

"It's not our first day in the United States. We were in Seattle yesterday."

She laughed, hugging him cheek to cheek, and beamed up at me. "You see? Kai-ming is amazing. He is my big, big boy. He protects me."

"Where is my gun?" he said, looking up at me. "Then I can do better."

"I'll get you a gun, Kai-ming." I smiled, but their closeness both touched and saddened me. It was a bond of love and hardship, the kind of desperate bond that grows when it is attacked, when a child is told for sport that his father is dead — a bond so steadfast, so unassailable, that I wondered how it could ever include me.

39

WE SPENT OUR FIRST months together preparing for my father's arrival. We bought sheets for his bed, a new TV. We bought these items with no small amount of resentment, which Yoshiko expressed with little disguise.

"Will he like this? Can we afford it?"

"Of course," I said. "There's still more on our credit card."

"I hope so. Or we'll have nothing to eat. Or maybe that will make him feel at home."

"Yoshiko! He got the money for us to come here, remember?"

"Believe me, I've heard that enough times to remember. Now he's coming for his payback."

I HAD LONGED for my family for so many years. Here they were, finally, and we argued.

"Saburo!"

Yoshiko appeared in the doorway wearing a frilly green apron, her face scrunched up. "Why are you making Kai-ming sit at the breakfast table for so long? It's time for me to make lunch now."

I stood to face her. "I told him to stay there until he finishes his egg. It's a sin to waste it. He's like a stick."

"He doesn't like it! I cooked it too long," Yoshiko said angrily. "Leave him alone!"

I loved my son, yet when I saw Yoshiko fold him into her arms and kiss him, I felt that such gestures were her domain. Wasn't that the difference between men and women?

The next day, I gave him a BB gun.

"Not a real gun! He's four! What's the matter with you?" Yoshiko cried. "You don't know how to behave with children at all!"

It was true. I once fought with her to convince her it was okay to leave Kai-ming by himself while we went to a dinner party. I had roamed the streets and paddies with Aki at that age. Why shouldn't my capable son be safe in his own house?

"He's almost five!" I said angrily. "People would laugh at us if we got a babysitter."

Knowing better, Yoshiko had fretted the instant we left the house and insisted we turn around. We entered the living room to find the boy sinking a fourth parallel slice into the black vinyl of our armchair with a razor blade.

"*Li kwa,* Saburo! You see!"

I did see, and I began to wonder whether my own upbringing had permanently snuffed out my ability to be a good father.

Overall, we were happy to be together, but the fights wearied me. I wondered at my wife's moods, which went from laughing and sweet to furious and back again with hardly a pause in between.

We fought, in particular, about my future. I was having second thoughts about taking a sabbatical year to get my PhD.

"It's too much of a risk. There's no way I can pass the qualifying exam and write my thesis in one year. All those people from Taiwan University have been there for years. What if I don't pass the exam? I'll have taken a sabbatical for nothing."

She frowned, scooping rice from her frying pan into blue plastic bowls. "Don't listen to those people. They're just trying to make you feel bad."

"*Hai!*" I clucked my tongue. "They're just telling the truth. They're still there, and they had a better college education than me."

The pan clattered as she dropped it on the stove. She shook a pink spatula at me. "They had a better education than you, and now you have a master's degree and you're a professor at an American university. That means you're smarter than them!"

I watched her in surprise. "Have you been talking to Professor Beck?"

"You're the one who told me what he said. Maybe you should listen to yourself."

MAY WAS COMING. We washed the windows. We took an extra trip to the Chicago Chinatown to replace the gamy-tasting pheasants in the freezer — the ones I had shot with Beck — with Chinese staples for my father.

Yoshiko lay on the couch, a damp towel on her forehead. She wore a lovely white dress with red roses on it, even though she had been cleaning, and the skirt draped over the edge of the couch onto the floor. "I don't know why I'm so tired," she said.

We found out two weeks later that she was pregnant.

"An American baby." She took my hand as we walked out of the doctor's office. "It will have a happy life." She smiled up at me, her face as bright as it had been in her childhood, before she had been left behind by her father, by me. I felt another pang of guilt at having made Kai-ming fatherless for his first years.

Everything would be different now. This child would set all my wrongs to right.

40

IN THE LAST DAYS before my father's arrival, I could not sleep and instead sat in the black vinyl armchair in the dark, running my fingers along the slices Kai-ming had made in the armrest. This seemed to me the reward for all my trials: that I should have Yoshiko and Kai-ming in America with me, that we should welcome another child into our new home, and that my father would come to recognize, in however small and reserved a way, the worth of my life.

I wasn't completely naive. I didn't expect him to smile and say, "I love you," as Americans did. I had never seen him smile and I would never expect him to embrace me; he never had. But perhaps there was some way — some subtle, casual way — that he could acknowledge my worth. That I was Kazuo's equal — even his own. I wanted to talk to him as father and son, yes, but also as a grown father to a respected son, man to man. I had not taken the path he wanted, but how much more glory I was bringing to the family by pursuing my own path! If I did everything right — passed my qualifying exam, wrote my thesis in a year — I would be the first person from Taoyuan with an American doctorate.

Yoshiko made sure his room was spotless. I moved his bed this way and that, back aching, to find the best placement in the room. When the day arrived, I awoke so early with anticipation that I watched the sun rise over the valley of neat little Rapid City homes.

It was a brilliant day, and I went by myself to pick him up from the airport, anticipating that moment when we would be alone together, the two of us. We had never been alone for all my childhood except when I faced him in his armchair. Someone else had always been in the way — my siblings, my cousins, his colleagues, Nationalist agents, soldiers.

I waited on the tarmac for his plane, and finally it came, touching its delicate, spinning toes to the Rapid City runway. All the passengers spilled out the plane's doors, and then he emerged, dwarfed by all the tall white people around him, his face as grim and self-important as an army general heading into battle. He strode toward me on the tarmac, his pear-shaped body clad in a gray three-piece suit. He was perfectly erect, his eyes, in this strange, new land, directed straight ahead. At his approach I felt a coldness in my belly. I tried to shake the feeling off, because I knew things would be different now.

He drew near and held out his leather satchel. "Put this in the bank for me," he said. "I need it in Japan."

"What is it?"

"It's cash, stupid."

I TOOK HIM to meet Beck. Mrs. Larsson smiled brightly on introduction but then, receiving my father's mirthless nod, glanced at me and went back to filing papers into her desk drawer.

"Nice to meet you, Mr. Tong," Beck said. "Please come in."

The three of us stood awkwardly in Beck's office. It was late Friday afternoon. Beck wore his fishing hat and I saw his reel leaning against the wall behind his desk.

"We're lucky to have your son with us," Beck said. He spoke slowly, clearly. I had told him my father's English was limited, and I was grateful that he remembered.

"Hm," my father grunted. His face was smooth and inscrutably somber as a temple statue's, his ever-present bow tie perfectly symmetrical.

"He's not afraid to take risks. Been teaching a different course every semester to prepare for his PhD qualifier. Most people just want to stick to the same course. Laziness, I guess." Beck tilted his head slightly, watching my father. He started speaking less deliberately. "He's doing cutting-edge work at Michigan, too, on the upper atmosphere. Exciting stuff."

"Hm," my father said again.

Beck looked at me uncertainly.

I took my father out into the hall and waited for him while he lit his cigarette.

He let out a puff of smoke. "Why was he wearing such a stupid hat?" he said. "I expected someone important, not a small-town hick."

"HE DIDN'T EVEN go to college," Yoshiko whispered to me at night. "He has to cut you down to size."

Even in my own home, bought with my own money, my father was king. He sat in my black vinyl chair, turned the TV to shows he liked, and ordered food from my wife. At times I couldn't bear to see it, and I took him out. This seemed to be what he wanted as well. I thought he would be impressed by the beautiful countryside of South Dakota, so we took him for long drives. He was especially fascinated by American cows; in Taiwan, the cows were black from head to toe.

"Wait, wait!" he exclaimed as we drove by a farm, and I had to stop the car so he could take a picture of a Guernsey calf staring back at us through a segment of wire fence.

Kai-ming stifled a giggle, and Yoshiko shushed him harshly. "You must not laugh at your *akong*," she said.

My father was equally impressed by the mountain goats chewing grass by the side of the road at Custer State Park. At the Badlands, he noted the similarity to the undulating rock formations at Yehliu, on the northern coast of Taiwan.

He took pictures of Mount Rushmore and peered at dripping stalactites in the dark coolness of Jewel Cave National Monument. "There is a lot to see in this country," he said. "I want to see more."

But Yoshiko could not drive, so during the week, while I taught, my father stayed at the little house in Rapid City with Yoshiko and Kai-ming.

"All he does is watch TV," Yoshiko whispered to me at night. "He can't even understand what they're saying. Doesn't he have anything better to do? I'm working like a dog to take care of him and he just sits there like a king. I can't stand on my feet all day when I'm pregnant."

"We'll go out to dinner. We owe him," I said. "He helped both of us get over here."

When summer came, we rented out our house in Rapid City and moved to a Northwood duplex on the University of Michigan campus. It was time to take the gamble of my life, to give up my professorship for a year in the hopes that at the end of the summer I might pass Michigan's fabled qualifying exam and then use the year to write my thesis.

I needed to study even more. Hunching over my books in the library with the other Taiwanese was, however, out of the question. Since my little dinner with Wei-ta, they had stopped being friendly to me, and it seemed unlikely that studying the way they did would be effective in any case. Beck's method of questioning had been the key to my quick mastery of the material in South Dakota. To replace him, I joined a study group of American students who took turns fielding questions. I still needed to work in Gleason's lab, and I often returned home very late.

We invited Wen-chong over for dinner to meet my father. "Professor Hong is safe!" he said excitedly as I welcomed him into the house. "And his wife has been cleared to come to the US! I am so grateful to your father!"

"Ah!"

Wen-chong was in a good mood, and he conversed easily with my father, who was clearly impressed with Wen-chong's tidy appearance and sophisticated Chinese.

Wen-chong sucked delicately on spare ribs in black bean sauce, wiped his mouth elegantly with his paper napkin, and told my father about our first trip to Fort Churchill. "Your son is a bold young man and quite an excellent engineer. It is so wonderful that you could help with his family's immigration, and of course I so much appreciate your part in clearing Professor Hong's name in San Francisco——"

"Who? What? Professor who?" My father chewed and waved his hand, wrinkling his forehead in annoyance. He swallowed a mouthful of lotus blossom tea. "I didn't do anything. No one listens to me anymore. It was that American senator who called the Taiwanese embassy. Scared the daylights out of the Nationalists. That pig-faced friend of Kazuo's got into big trouble with the party. Making up accusations, wasting people's time and resources. Because of Kazuo! Kazuo should have been the one in trouble, but he's so sly he managed to get himself out of it.

"As for Saburo," he added irritably, "I don't know why he has to take this PhD thing so seriously."

That night in our bedroom, Yoshiko sat fuming as my father's footsteps lumbered overhead on the second floor of our duplex. She panted a little; her belly protruded so much now that it brushed against the bureau as she leaned toward her mirror. She untied her scarf and threw it down on the bureau. "He takes every opportunity to shoot you down! And see, he didn't help you or me or Professor Hong, after all! Senator Dickey did everything."

I folded my tie and tucked it into a drawer. "He's frustrated," I said. "I'm too busy to take him around. It's a long time to wait until after summer session."

"Then he should hire a tour guide. You can't just drop everything because he's here!"

But sometimes I would stop studying early and go sit with my father in our little living room to keep him company. Time was passing, passing. Our study group's meetings had accelerated in frequency from once a week to twice a week to daily. The qualifying exam was fast approaching. And then, come what may, there would be one month, and my father would be gone. The time to forge our connection was now. Perhaps that was why he was upset. He wanted to talk.

"Look at this!" He struck his brother's airmail letter with the back of his hand. "What a democracy! They simply take the opposition leader and blackmail him. Thomas Liao's sister-in-law is in prison and they've sentenced his nephew to death. It's all because of the elections. They're afraid Chiang's son will look bad. What does it matter, when all the elections are fixed, anyway? It's simply needless brutality."

Was it still that way? "We don't hear of those things here," I said.

"Don't be stupid. Chiang knows how to pander to the Americans and squeeze the Taiwanese at the same time. The Americans are so terrified of Communism they'll see what they want to see and send Chiang all the money and guns he wants. For all they care, the Taiwanese people can go to hell." He looked to the side, puffing his lips indignantly.

I changed the subject. "And how is Taikong?"

"Taikong!" He waved his hand dismissively. "Going to hell. Everything going to hell. Some kind of fishy business. What business is it of yours, anyway?"

Shocked and stung, I fell silent.

He drank his tea, the once-feared hands curled softly around the melamine cup. "Ah, Li-hsiang," he called to the kitchen, "is this that oolong tea from Chicago?"

"Yes," she answered. "It's almost gone. We'll need to buy more when we go this time." She paused, then added pointedly: "If we can."

My father ate a lot and contributed nothing. Yoshiko kept a weekly account of all our expenses, budgeting down to the nickel.

But this was my father. I couldn't ask my own father to pay for his living expenses.

He took his tea to the couch and sat with a vinyl squeak, unfolding the *San Min Chen Bao*. I felt invisible in my own house, ever the errant child with my silly projects—the noisy toys, the radios, the PhD. When would I ever stop?

41

Tom Reynolds burst out of the Horace Rackham Amphitheatre, his face and neck flushed deep red.

I sprung up from my chair as the double doors closed behind him. I hadn't seen him for weeks; he'd holed up in the library by himself, rereading one textbook after another.

"What happened?" I said. My voice caught. I had thought I was feeling calm.

He put his hand out vaguely, then rubbed his forehead. "Goddamn! I didn't even know what they were asking me! Goddamn! I needed this degree. How am I going to repay all those loans?"

I watched him, horrified, speechless, my pulse quickening.

The doors opened again. "Chia-lin."

Tom looked down, still rubbing his forehead, and shook his head. "Good luck."

I stepped through the door. My heart was pounding, and as I turned down the aisle to the stage, I stumbled. It took me a moment to recover my gait.

I stepped up onto the stage. In the bright lights I floated, blind. My recent study sessions came together in a jumble of frantic thoughts, and the only thing that rose up clearly was that I could never face Yoshiko or my father if I failed. It was not only that we had already signed a year's lease on the apartment and that the School of Mines had already hired someone to replace me for the year. Yoshiko would finally realize that she had misplaced her faith in me, and my father would be proved right. That I had wasted my time. That I should not have bothered.

I walked to the chalkboard slowly, as though I were on the deck of a rolling boat. I picked up a piece of chalk, and it slipped in the moistness of my fingertips, like the pencil slipping in my fingers the day of my entrance exam for Chien Kuo. My mother had sewn me my very first new pair of shorts when I passed. What would she do if I passed this?

"Mr. Tong. First question: How does a fuel cell work?"

My heart lurched against the front wall of my chest. In the three years of Beck's grilling, in all the sessions with my study group explicating the most sophisticated theories in the electrical engineering world, fuel cells had never come up. I hadn't thought about them since junior college.

I cleared my throat. I looked into the bright lights of the amphitheatre, seeing in the front row the five members of the jury, none of whom I knew. This was intentional, to avoid bias. Gleason's imposing figure and Ni Wen-chong's slight one entered through the rear exit and settled quickly into seats near the back, but they were here merely to watch and had no input into the jury's decision.

"Fuel cell," I said. And as the words left my tongue, I was twenty again, rattling around in a cattle car with my classmates, following Yi-yang as he walked his motorcycle down the sidewalk on Chung-cheng Road, catching glimpses through a window of a girl I had met in an air raid.

"Fuel cell." My voice quavered. All had been lost. I would be an electrician for my family's company. I was a failure, rooted to the ground, to the practical world, my ear burning against the cool floorboards of my parents' house.

Gleason shifted silently in his chair.

"Mr. Tong? Shall we proceed to the next question?"

"No." I shook my head and turned to the chalkboard. "In a fuel cell, you have hydrogen, and you have oxygen, in separate compartments." I drew an actuator. I was a child, drawing my fingertip through the wet concrete on February 28. I would be expelled.

But as I continued my diagram, my memories shrank back like shadows at dawn, leaving only the clear lines of white chalk against black as my hand moved across the board. The floor solidified under my feet, and my breathing loosened.

"Why so complicated? Could you put them in the same compartment?"

"No." I paused. My confidence suddenly welled up into an impishness I had suppressed since middle school. "Well, you could," I said, "but then something may happen." I indicated an explosion with my arms.

The little audience laughed and I saw Gleason and Wen-chong whisper to each other. Gleason nodded.

I smiled. This was America.

We celebrated at the Candlelight Restaurant on Route 14. Yoshiko and I had mountain trout, while my father ordered the most expensive item on the menu — New York steak, at $3.25.

"Hm." He popped a piece of meat into his mouth. "We'll see if it is the same in New York."

Yoshiko glanced at me.

Kai-ming looked up from his malted milk. "When are we going?"

"Tomorrow," I said. "In the afternoon."

"Why in the afternoon?" my father said through his steak. "You should always start a trip in the early morning. We should leave as soon as possible."

"I have some things to take care of," I said.

My father stopped chewing and looked up at me.

There had been an edge to my voice. I knew the main reason he was happy I'd passed the qualifying exam: He was sick of being at home. He wanted to go on tour.

"FOUR WEEKS' VACATION?" Gleason sat behind his desk, Wen-chong in the other chair, legs neatly crossed. Between them, on the desk, was a large stack of ionosonde data held together with a rubber band. Gleason frowned, rolling the rubber band off the stack. "It'll be a stretch if you want your model used on the next launch, Saburo."

Wen-chong looked sharply at me. "You could have told me earlier."

"I have promised my father," I said.

Gleason's eyebrows wrinkled together. "Didn't you say you could only afford a year at Michigan? Why would your own father want to jeopardize your PhD?"

I was silent. Wen-chong looked at the floor uncomfortably.

I don't know why he has to take this PhD thing so seriously.

"Anyway," said Gleason, waving his hand, "it probably won't make any difference at the end of the year. No one has ever done their thesis here in a year. Even Linus Pauling spent three years on his at Caltech."

WE BARRELED 450 miles east to Manhattan, where we took a ferry to the Statue of Liberty, shopped at Macy's, and ate sukiyaki. We drove five hours to Buffalo to float in the mist of Niagara Falls, and then to Chicago to eat Cantonese, Japanese, and Szechuan food. Then, Chevy trunk stuffed with dried mushrooms, pickled cucumber, preserved tofu, two gallons of Kikkoman soy sauce, and fifty pounds of Japanese rice from the Chicago Chinatown, we crossed 750 miles back over the Great Plains, taking in enough dairy cows to satisfy fifty Taiwanese politicians, so that my father could enjoy Yellowstone National Park and the Grand Tetons.

My father stood, gazing anxiously at Old Faithful's vent, camera poised. I watched him, reminded somehow of how we watched launches at Fort Churchill. I needed to get my new telemetry unit on that rocket in December. I'd been thinking it over while I drove, while I lay in bed at night. I would have to hit the ground at a sprint when we returned.

Yoshiko was sitting on a bench with Kai-ming a few yards behind me, and I went to join her, my back on fire with pain from the many hours sitting in the car.

"My doctor said I should take it easy," Yoshiko said. Kai-ming lay curled up on the bench with his head on Yoshiko's knee — the only part of her lap not occupied by her pregnant belly. He wore a Detroit Tigers baseball cap, and she took it off his head to fan him with it. "This is not easy. And the smell . . ." She shook open a lace-edged handkerchief with one hand and held it over her nose.

"It smells like rotten eggs," Kai-ming said. "When's the eruption? I'm tired."

"ALL THESE HOTELS!" Yoshiko exclaimed, throwing our keys onto the bed that night. "We can't even afford *one* room at these places, much less an extra one for your father, too."

"Don't worry," I said.

"Don't worry, what? We don't have any more money, and he has a big fat bank account! Why do you think he's bringing the money to Japan? You think your little brother will be footing the bill like us? Why doesn't he contribute here, too?"

The same thoughts had occurred to me. But hadn't my father gotten me the money to come here in the first place? And wasn't it a sign of my father's high regard for me that he thought I could afford to board him? Asking for money would be an admission that I was still a child, not my father's equal at all.

AT NIGHT, IN a motel on the Lincolnway, Yoshiko lay down on the bed and tucked the pillows around her belly. "My back is killing me. Let's take a rest tomorrow. Kai-ming needs a rest, too. He felt warm to me tonight."

"*Hou*," I said. I sat beside her and lay my hand on the taut side of her belly. "Mama and baby will rest." The baby kicked under my hand, and even through my fatigue and frustration and in the blandness of our motel bed, I smiled, thinking that this child of mine would grow up speaking English, eating hamburgers, and arguing about what was fair. And I would love this child no less than I loved his number one brother. No matter what.

THE REST OF the night was long and miserable. Kai-ming's temperature shot up and he spent much of the night vomiting in the tiny bathroom. Yoshiko and I took turns washing his face and pajamas and giving him sips of water until finally he slept. When the sun peeked through the holes in the curtains, we stayed in our beds.

A knock at the thin plywood door roused me from dreams of an air raid. "Saburo! Saburo!"

Yoshiko opened her eyes. We looked at each other for a moment, listening to my father's gruff voice.

"Saburo! Get up!"

She glanced at the door, frowning. "He'll wake Kai-ming."

"I'll take care of it," I said.

Yoshiko turned her face to me and touched my cheek with the soft tips of her fingers. Her hair was squished flat over her forehead, and she looked as young as a girl, her eyes as radiant, frank, and full of compassion as when I had first told her that no one cared whether I came home. I closed my eyes, breathing in deeply, taking in her flowery warmth. And then she gave me a pat and closed her eyes, turning her swollen belly over onto her other side.

"Saburo! Saburo!" The thin door rattled in its frame, the chain swinging in its little arc.

I glanced at Kai-ming. He slept with a child's abandon, arms flung wide, legs on top of the covers, feet hanging over the side of the bed. He wore a Superman T-shirt and a swimsuit in place of his soiled pajamas, and he looked as though he were doing a swan dive against gravity.

The knocking stopped.

I got up and dressed quickly. My father did not give up that easily.

I slid open the chain and stepped out the door. My father sat, fully dressed, on a peeling green bench between his room and ours. In his bow tie and bowler hat he looked incongruously formal against the exterior of the motel, which was painted brick red with white trim to make the rooms look like homey little cottages. He had a dark expression on his face that I knew all too well. I hastily closed the door behind me.

He jumped up, surprisingly nimble for all his corpulence, his bowler hat like an immovable fixture on his head. "Why do you sleep so late!" he said angrily. "I'm hungry, and I can't go anywhere to eat without you! Are you so lazy that you can't wake before nine? I want to see places. I don't want to spend my mornings in lousy motels! Did you forget who made it possible for you to come here?"

A good son should bow in front of his father, should swallow his pride. The trip was almost over; an apology might bring me the approval that I had always craved.

But I was no longer that boy in the rice paddies.

I stepped forward, through the American air that hung, cool and crystalline and smelling of newly cut grass, between us. As I moved, the molecules of oxygen, nitrogen, and carbon dioxide tumbled over my skin, spinning off and crashing into more molecules that in turn careened into others. The waves of invisible molecules rippled across the parking lot, bouncing off the red cottage facades of the motel rooms and, warmed by the sun, up into the layers of the atmosphere. I stepped toward my father, towering over his ample figure, over the round face that never smiled, over the tongue that never spoke a tender word, over the bow tie that was knotted even now, in Wyoming, around his neck.

"Yoshiko is pregnant," I said. My tongue stuck to the sides of my mouth and made clicking noises. My whole body shook. The air molecules vibrated around me, cushioning me. "She is tired, and Kai-ming is sick. They needed to rest."

He waved his hand and turned away. "Don't give me any excuses."

My ears burned at the memory of the blows that had followed these words. But as the gust of air from his hand reached me, the air molecules parted and tumbled off, tumbled away.

I took another step forward, shifting the air around me, air now mixed with the leftover essence of filial piety and the aftertaste of disappointment. My voice was rough in my throat. "I'm driving five hours a day to entertain you," I said. "I've fed you and hosted you and housed you for four months."

He barked at me over his shoulder. "Complaining about hosting your father? How many years do you think I——"

"That's worth at least as much money as you got for me from your brothers," I continued, "and the least a decent father could do is let us sleep in for one day."

He whipped back to face me. "Such disrespect! You speak to your father this way?"

"I do," I said. "I should have a long time ago."

I met his glare. The eyes were fearsome—black, unwavering. I had never stared back at them before. I had been too afraid. I realized now how completely at his mercy I had felt my whole life. At any time he could have saved me at will or let me die. He had meted out fates to his children as he saw fit. He had played his cards shrewdly, and we had all survived. As far as survival was concerned, he was the undisputed master.

"Personal freedom," I said.

"What?" His eyebrows scrunched together.

"Personal freedom," I said again. "In America, it's valued higher than life."

"Stupid," he said. "You're a fool."

And then he stormed into his motel room and slammed its plywood door shut. The air molecules burst into the air and bounced off my body, dispersing into the atmosphere.

In the remaining days, he spoke little.

The morning of his departure, I went to withdraw the money he had asked me to put in the bank for him. For his visit to my brother.

When I returned home, he was buckling up his suitcase. I walked up to him with the bundle of cash.

"We ran out of money," I said. "We had to tap into your account, a couple hundred. This is the rest."

My father looked up incredulously. "You took my money?"

"Here's a check for the difference," I said. "By the time you cash it in Japan, I'll have gotten my next paycheck."

He snatched the cash and the check out of my hands. "Unbelievable," he said.

I did not apologize.

And then my father's imitation-leather suitcases were stuffed full of presents for my sisters and brothers. And then he was onboard, the jet roaring down the runway and lifting into the air.

The plane's nose rose into the stratosphere, blasting through my little-boy dreams of parental love. They streamed in shreds over the birdlike body of the plane and swirled in the eddies of its steel wings, which glinted, smaller and smaller, farther and farther away, in the clear South Dakota sky.

42

THE MONITOR BEEPED.

"Can't they stop it? Make them stop it!"

"They can't. It's too late."

Tears spilled out of Yoshiko's eyes. "I felt the waters coming. I shouldn't have reached up for the clothesline—" She wiped her eyes. The intravenous line in her arm got caught on the siderail of her stretcher, and I reached over her to untangle it, smelling iodine and rubbing alcohol. The blood on the hem of her hospital gown caught my eye and I turned away.

"It has nothing to do with that," I said. "You heard the doctor."

"Ah, what do they know? They aren't doing anything. I thought medical care was so good in America! Tell them to stop it, because I can't because of my English . . ."

"Yoshiko. They can't stop it." I put my hand on her belly. Our American baby was still.

I felt her contracting. She closed her eyes, bracing.

Her belly relaxed. Her eyes opened again and tears fell out. "It's only twenty-eight weeks," she whispered. "Do you think if we were in a big city—"

The doctor came bustling in, wearing a scrub suit.

I stood. "Do you think maybe it's ready early?" I asked him. "Maybe the dates were wrong. Maybe—"

He gave a shake of his head.

"No," Yoshiko said in English. "I know why. Because I have to get in and out of a car, all over everyplace."

Her words hit me in the chest.

" . . . not a primary cause of preterm labor," the doctor said.

"I'm mother, I know," Yoshiko said bitterly. "Backseat all the time. Squeeze a bag, it break."

"It's not your fault," he told her. He released the stretcher's brake.

As he wheeled her away, Yoshiko turned her face to me, her eyes spilling tears. "I miss Toru," she whispered.

43

I LOOKED OUT THE waiting room window, watching clouds blow in over the Huron River. The maple trees on the riverbank, just beginning their autumn transformation, blew in the wind, their golden tips ruffling.

It began to rain.

A thin stream of water poured down from the roof over the window, dripping onto the low roof below. It dripped, dripped, in regular rhythm like a temple *muyu*, like the clacking of a steam engine on its tracks, like the syllabic chant of a childhood schoolroom:

Bo po mo fo
De te le ne

Ge ke he
Zhi chi shi ri

The rhythm calmed me, imposed external order on the desperate chaos in my mind. This was the way of the Old World — thoughtless repetition, relieving a person of the burden of reflection, self-examination, and free will.

Bo po mo fo
De te le ne

Breaking my rhythm, the doctor's voice: *It's not your fault.*
No, it was not her fault; it was mine.
I had stood up to my father. But it was too late.

44

WE TOLD EVERYONE THAT Yoshiko had had a miscarriage. It wasn't true. Our baby boy lived for a day, tiny and gasping, a ghastly translucent pink, the size of a trembling kitten. We didn't have the heart, or the money, for a funeral.

THE SNOWS SWEPT in over Ann Arbor, blanketing the town with white cold, weighing down the roof of our duplex. I shoveled a path from the front door, heaving aside the drifts of snow that trapped us in our little house of grief and devastation.

I had heard nothing from my father. From my sister I received news of the recent death of my fourth uncle's eldest son, who had been left in charge of Taikong while my father vacationed in America.

My fourth uncle's family blamed my father for their loss. "He was too harsh and critical, and this is what caused our brother to die." Why else would someone so young have a brain hemorrhage?

"So," Yoshiko said, "now your father will blame it on us." She sat on our green flowered couch, putting neat stitches into a hole in Kai-ming's winter jacket.

I ran my fingers along the parallel razor marks in the armchair. "It had nothing to do with us," I said. Though I wondered if she was right. My father's silence greatly distressed me. I did not know whether he would ever talk to me again.

"Of course. He would have died, anyway. That's what doctors always say. Isn't that what you told me?"

She repositioned the little jacket. She had been terribly moody since losing the baby, and I hadn't known how to help her except to realize that I would never understand how it could feel to carry a child for so many months and then lose him.

DESPITE EVERYTHING, I worked on my thesis and prepared for the December launch. There was no possibility of my taking time to mourn. My father's little tour of America had completely depleted our finances, and I would have to have some kind of income at the end of the academic year, whether or not I received my PhD. If I did not receive my PhD by the end of the year, I would have to abandon it, as Tom Reynolds had, and retreat to the School of Mines, having wasted years of my life and thousands of dollars. All that studying and last-minute driving for naught — the conflicts with my father, the baby's death, completely, utterly gratuitous.

I could not let it happen. Yoshiko, too, despite her sorrow and physical weakness from losing the baby, felt the same urgency. She did not complain about my long nights in the lab. As December neared, Yoshiko insisted that she and Kai-ming come along to Fort Churchill.

"It's not safe for you there," I said. "It's no environment for a child and you're not strong enough yet."

"People live there," she said. "And I've had enough of sitting around thinking about death. It's not good for Kai-ming, either. He wants to see a launch."

"People don't bring their wives and children."

"You told me someone's wife watched from the bunkhouse."

She did not want to be alone, and there was nothing I could do, once she had come to a decision. At the very least, I managed to persuade her to fly in a week later with Gleason. There was no need for her to ride in the Chevy and then the train all the way from Winnipeg.

THE NIGHT BEFORE I left, after Kai-ming had gone to bed, Yoshiko received word that her oldest uncle had died of a stroke.

I left her on the phone with her parents while I finished packing my papers. By the time I finished, she had hung up.

I was surprised to find the lights turned off in the bedroom. I had not heard Yoshiko wash up or bathe.

I stood in the doorway. It was raining outside, the raindrops splattering on ice. In a moment my eyes adjusted to the dark, and I saw her lying faceup on the bed, her face white as the moon.

"What a terrible year," she said. "I can't wait for it to be over."

"Are you very sad about your uncle?"

It took her a minute to reply. "I suppose," she said slowly. "We all lived together when I was a child. He was always nice to me, in a very patronizing and insincere way."

I sat down on the bed, surprised that she would speak this way about an elder who had just died.

"You're upset that he shut your family out of the lumberyard," I said.

"He ruined my family. He let us starve to death."

I thought of her brother on his bicycle, laughing, handsome, waving his farmer's hat.

"But then he let your father back in."

"Yes, by selling my father his own land."

"What do you mean?"

"My father found out."

"Found out what?"

"His name. Lo, not Cheng. He's always wondered why, remember? Well, it turns out there was a contract between my grandfather and a man named Lo who had no sons. My father would bear his name in return for land. Guess what land? The land around the lumberyard."

"But that was all your uncle's land."

"He took it when Lo died."

"Did he know it was supposed to be your father's?"

"Oh, he knew. He must have laughed when my father bought the land from him."

I lay on the bed next to her and took her hand.

"All these years he drove by in his rickshaw," she said. "My brother died, my sister's living in a shack . . ." She sobbed, the tears falling on the pillowcase by my ear. "He always got the place of honor at our table."

"Is your father going to do something about it?" I said. "Is there any evidence?"

Yoshiko blew her nose. "Evidence? Of course. There's a signed contract. The Taoyuan magistrate signed it, that famous one who was killed right after February twenty-eighth."

"He was a friend of my father's," I said.

"Yes, well, it's a big, fancy contract, all in calligraphy and signed and in a bottle."

"Well, it's yours, then," I said. "It's legally your family's land."

"You're like my mother. 'Sue! Sue! Get the land back!' "

I pictured Chiu-yeh jumping from her chair, her hair coming lose from its bun as she shouted.

"Well," I said, "why not?"

Yoshiko tossed her tissue into the trash and lay back again, sighing. "It's all my cousins living there on that land now. My father doesn't want to kick them all out. He says they're family and that's that." She rubbed her eyes. "Family. They made a fool of him all his life."

We held hands, listening to the rain pouring down in spurts. In a few minutes she turned her head and went to sleep.

The wind picked up. The rain turned to snow, and the wind, whistling and shuddering, threw sodden flakes against the windows. This home was sturdier than my parents', and the wind did not penetrate, did not hiss through the doorframes and rattle the paneling on the walls.

Family.

A wound that never healed. A promise never to be fulfilled.

That was family.

I rose from bed and stood at the window. The dawn was coming, and the pine branches swayed, dark and heavy with snow, against the lightening gray of the horizon.

The sweet sound of a child's sneeze sounded down the hall. Kai-ming was awake. Such a good boy, he didn't cry when he awoke, and he never had. He didn't need to check if his mother was there for him. He already knew it.

Yoshiko stirred and turned her head to look back at me. "Huh?" she said sleepily. "What are you doing? Why are you still up?"

"I'm thinking."

"Don't think. Go to sleep." She turned away and closed her eyes.

I climbed into bed and lay on my back. In the waning darkness, the shadows of the trees danced back and forth on the ceiling like bamboo whips. I put my hand on my chest. The bruises and scrapes were gone, but the nerve endings were still raw. They would never heal.

Yoshiko reached back and touched my arm, her hand so soft it still surprised me, her touch the balm I had sought all my life. Even when she was at her most depleted, she had healing and love to give. "Sleep. You have a long drive."

Her breathing deepened. Her hand slipped away and curled under her chin.

The wind howled and shook the building at its very core, and then it whirled up into the dark night, fleeing the onslaught of day.

I AWOKE TO see pools of light rippling across the ceiling. The storm had passed, and Yoshiko had already gotten out of bed, leaving a warm nest of pillows and sheets beside me. Sounds came from the kitchen — the plunking down of glasses, the rush of the water faucet, the sizzle of eggs frying in oil as Yoshiko prepared breakfast for Kai-ming. The smell wafted through the bedroom.

I rose and entered the kitchen, and Yoshiko handed me a plate with a perfect fried egg on it, sunny-side up. Kai-ming had finished and was getting down from his chair.

"Say good morning to your papa," Yoshiko said.

"*Gau tsa*, Papa," Kai-ming said.

I awkwardly reached out to pat his shoulder, but he ran by me to turn on *The Jetsons*. I watched helplessly as he turned the tuner and hopped onto the couch. Would we ever be like father and son? I wondered.

"Who has the contract?" I asked.

"What?"

"The contract between your grandfather and that Lo person," I said. "Who has it?"

"Oh." She waved dismissively, scraping the egg off the pan. "My aunt gave it to my father, but my father gave it back."

"Gave it back?"

"Yes. He said he has no use for it and life goes on. He's such a fool," Yoshiko said bitterly.

"Actually," I said, "he is the wise one this time."

Yoshiko met me on the tundra at Fort Churchill, she and Kai-ming wrapped in so many layers of clothes they barely looked human. They watched as the rocket zoomed off into the ionosphere, sending signals back with my new, compact telemetry unit.

When we returned to Ann Arbor, the weather had taken another warm turn, the icicles on the eaves of our little apartment building dripping, splashing onto the snow, which melted into slushy puddles. On our doorstep, a telegram in a windowed envelope was waiting. It was from my father:

IT ALL WORKED OUT.

"What is that supposed to mean?" Yoshiko said.

"He got his money, I guess."

"He sent you a telegram just to tell you that?"

"Maybe he feels bad," I said.

Yoshiko took Kai-ming inside. I stayed on our doorstep, staring at the frugal line, the closest to an apology I would ever get from my father. Water from an icicle dripped onto the yellow paper and washed the words into an inky blob.

IN THE SPRING, to our joy, Toru visited us on his way back from a medical conference in Chicago.

He sat in our living room, taking neat packages out of his suitcase and smiling as he handed an aboriginal drum to Kai-ming. His hair looked grayer than I remembered, his face more drawn. He had stayed with Chen, and I wondered whether Chen had told him of our conversation that rainy night.

Toru took out a canister of very fine tea, dried shiitake mush-rooms, spicy beef jerky, a package of rice crackers for Kai-ming, and a small package for me, in red wrapping paper and twine. He smiled a little, handing it to me.

"What's this?" I said.

"For your graduation. Open it."

"I haven't graduated yet."

"You've finished your thesis."

"I have to defend it still."

"You think you won't pass?"

I smiled and untied the twine.

I pulled aside the wrapping paper to reveal a blue book. "But this was burned."

I flipped it over. There was the gold kanji. *The Earth.*

He laughed. "You think they printed only one book? Professor Chen gave me the one I gave you before. He had another copy. It's a later edition."

I flipped through to the illustration of the aurora borealis. It had seemed so magnificent to me as a child.

"How does it compare?" Toru said.

"To what?"

"To the real thing."

"Ah," I said. "Nothing compares."

Toru smiled. "It's a bit elementary now, but perhaps you can keep it for Kai-ming one day." He got up and swiftly retrieved the long package he'd leaned against the wall. "Now, also for your graduation. From Li-hsiang's father."

I put *The Earth* aside so Yoshiko and I could open her father's package together. It was a large scroll with a very fine, heavy handle, and for a split second I thought it might be the contract with her father's namesake. But then I recalled that the contract was sealed in a bottle and had to be small and that there would be no reason to send it to me.

We pulled out the heavy scroll and moved the coffee table out of the way. Toru took Kai-ming onto the couch beside him, and we unrolled the silk scroll across the carpet.

A pair of birds in spectacular hues of blue, red, and gold flew over a peach forest in bloom.

I couldn't speak, and I saw Yoshiko's eyes fill with tears.

AFTER DINNER, I took Toru for a walk through North Campus. We passed the new music building, its expansive grounds overtaking the field where I had first met Gleason, at the model-rocket launch. Yoshiko and I had been to concerts there and she had met friends for picnics on the lawn. Since Wei-ta's group had shut us out, Yoshiko had found a group of international students' wives who traded recipes for dumplings, samosas, and *pastilla* and shared plans for getting their own American education someday.

"What will you do after you graduate?" Toru asked.

"I have two job offers, one on each coast," I said. "I'll probably take the one in Boston."

"Does it pay more?"

"No," I said. "It will be more fun."

He laughed and patted my arm.

He told me that he had seen my father at a banquet in Taoyuan. "He was complaining about all your brothers and sisters, your little brother in Japan, your little sister who's always asking for more money. I mentioned I was coming here to visit and said I wasn't staying long because you were finishing up your thesis and I didn't want to distract you.

"He looked a little embarrassed. And then he said, 'They were the only ones I never worried about.'"

45

A FTER I GRADUATED, ALL that was left was to pack up and
move again, to Boston.

I dipped my paddle into the Huron River, breaking the sky into
slivers of floating blue. A heron rose beyond, wings flapping slowly,
powerfully, a silver fish wriggling and sparkling in its beak. Off it
soared, into the mysterious blue above, through the layers of life-
giving gases that shifted in the wind. I would have believed it could
fly into space.

It all worked out.

They were the ones I never worried about.

So be it. That was all I would ever get.

"I see a fish!" Kai-ming said excitedly. He sat facing me, dutifully strapped into his life jacket. He craned his neck to look over
the edge of the canoe, his cheek still curved in the plump way of a
child's. It pained me every day to think I had missed the whole of his
babyhood; his round cheek and the light fuzz on the nape of his neck
reassured me, in some small way, that I had not missed everything.
And if a lifetime of love would never fill the empty space of those
four years, what else could I do but try?

Yoshiko, sitting in front of him, turned around and smiled so
that her dimples showed, her eyes, tired for so long, glinting

golden in the light. She carefully put down her paddle and buttoned the sleeve of her white seersucker shirt. Toru had urged her not to exert herself; she needed to fully recover before we could try for another baby.

One cannot truly start anew. Our little canoe was full with the memories of those who had died and those we had left behind — of our brothers, Aki and Kun-tai, of our premature son, of Yoshiko's parents, loving through all their faultiness, of my own family even, with its betrayals and disappointments. They were, together with the sights and sounds, the smells and tastes, the joy and the bitterness of our lives in Taiwan, grown into the very core of our nervous systems. They formed the reference points of all that we were now and all that we would ever experience. We felt their loss every day. But still I pushed my paddle through the New World water, sparkling and cold, and somehow we went along.

"A fish! Where?" I matched my son's excited tone.

"There! There!" He pointed.

"Ah," I said. "Then we'll go there."

I paddled to an area by the leafy shore and dropped anchor. There were tiny splashes near our boat, and in a patch of water lit by a shaft of sun poking through the trees, silvery bodies glinted, dancing.

I showed Kai-ming how to cast. Yoshiko ducked.

I handed him the reel, and the line drew taut within a minute.

"I got one! I got one!" His rod bent.

"Turn the reel! Turn the reel!"

He turned the reel.

"No, no! The other way!"

"Oh!"

I shifted carefully to help him. Miraculously he still had the fish, and we pulled it into the boat, settling it, flip-flopping, onto the ice in our fishing cooler.

Kai-ming picked up the reel excitedly. "Let's get another one!"

Yoshiko and I laughed.

"It's not usually so easy," Yoshiko said.

"You were just lucky." I fixed his reel for him. "You have to be patient."

"Why? It's so quick!"

I recast his line and handed it to him. "It won't be so quick all the time."

But so it was. A child expects nothing outside the realm of his own experience. Kai-ming had never tried to catch a fish with his bare hands. He had never chopped a hole in ice to fish for trout. He did not worry about being bitten by a poisonous snake or careening off a frozen mountainside.

"Mama," he said, "I'm hungry. I don't want to fish anymore."

"Give the fishing rod to your father, then."

I took the reel and pulled up the anchor. I paddled, looking for a good spot to land. A train crossed over the river on a bridge up ahead, windows flashing, and Kai-ming whipped his head around to watch, the bill of his cap obscuring my view.

"Where does the train go?" he asked.

"To other cities," I said. "Nowhere better than here."

I found a break in the reeds and we pulled ashore. We walked through a stand of silver maples into a field of tall grass. I set the food cooler down by Yoshiko, and she opened it, taking out neat containers.

After a moment, I said, "I received a telegram from Professor Beck."

"What did it say?"

"He said, 'I told you so.'"

She laughed, eyes sparkling, that rich laugh that I loved. Her hair shone in waves.

"Ooh!" Kai-ming threw off his hat and jumped up and down at the sight of the food, his sneakers flattening the tall grass. He expected sushi. He expected hard-boiled eggs. He expected to be loved.

I laughed and bent down to my little boy, my chest aching with love. His hair stuck up in tufts, and I put my hand lightly on his head, feeling the silky warmth. He looked up at me, his eyes wide in surprise. And then he smiled.

"Let's get ready to eat," Yoshiko called. "We're all hungry."

I shook out a blanket and the three of us spread it on the grass. And I sang, because my heart was free.

The sky clears after the rain; fish fill the harbor.
We are the happiest couple in the world.
Today's reunion warms our hearts.
We need never repair the broken net again.

Acknowledgments

The Third Son exists only because I learned to listen to my parents, Pei-Rin and Susan Wu, who contributed so much time, knowledge, and patience to this book over the years. They translated many texts for me, including the lyrics for *Repairing the Fisherman's Net,* and read many of my drafts. My parents are the inspiration for all that is strong, wise, and loving in Saburo and Yoshiko. Thank you, Mom and Dad.

I am ever grateful to Stephanie Abou for believing in this book, helping to shape it, and championing it. I have been fortunate, as well, to have had two fantastic editors at Algonquin, Kathy Pories and Jane Rosenman, each of whom helped make the story the very best it could be. Many thanks to Rachel Careau, my copyeditor, for her thorough, thoughtful work.

What a wonderful thing it is that I live near Boston, the home of Grub Street Writers! Many thanks to the following Grubbies for their help with my book: Stuart Horwitz, Nichole Bernier, Henriette Power, Amin Ahmad, Andrew Goldstein, Miriam Sidanius, Pat Gillen, Liz Michalski, and John Sedgwick. Thanks also to my ongoing writing group for their terrific feedback and support along the home stretch: Diana Renn, Eileen Donovan Kranz, Steven Lee Beeber, Patrick Gabridge, Vincent Gregory, Edward Rooney, and Deborah Vlock.

Thanks, as well, to reader/writer Amy Sue Nathan, of the Backspace Writers Forum and Book Pregnant, two wonderful groups that have been a great resource of advice, camaraderie, and humor. Through Backspace I also met Randy Susan Meyers, who has shepherded me through the writing scene and pulled me into to the lively and lovely group of bloggers at Beyond the Margins.

Perhaps even more thanks are due to my very early readers, most of them family and friends who have supported me in other, no less important, ways: Linna and Gil Ettinger, Michael and Cheryl Patton Wu, Jussi and Leah Saukkonen, Martina Barash, Deborah Strod, Laura Heijn, Nancy Barron, and Kathy Finucane.

Many thanks to Elinor Lipman and William Martin for giving me advice and encouragement at crucial junctures; to the Pirate's Alley Faulkner Society for their much appreciated recognition; to Rebecca Karl at NYU and Caroline Light at Harvard University for their historical expertise; to Philip Erickson at MIT's Haystack Observatory for letting me pepper him with odd questions about atmospheric science.

To my children, Amy and David, thank you for your patience and for teaching me what is important in life. And to the many wonderful women and men who have cared for, played with, and taught my children, in and out of school: I would not have been able to write this book without you.

Finally, to my husband, Kai Saukkonen, who has supported me through all the heartbreak and joy of this journey to publication: I love you and am so grateful to have you at my side for this — the high adventure of life.